THE DRAGON'S TONGUE

Also by C. J. Brightley

A Long-Forgotten Song:
Things Unseen

Erdemen Honor:
The King's Sword
A Cold Wind
Honor's Heir

THE DRAGON'S TONGUE

A LONG-FORGOTTEN SONG
BOOK II

C. J. BRIGHTLEY

Egia, LLC

ISBN 978-1511648097

Published in the United Sates of America by Egia, LLC.

www.cjbrightley.com

Cover art by Vuk Kostic

For my parents

ACKNOWLEDGEMENTS

Many thanks go to my husband Stephen, who continues to be awesometastic.

Special thanks also goes to my father. One of my favorite things about this series is how he and I have brainstormed together. We've spent hours thinking about the characters, their decisions, and the theological implications. It's been incredibly fun to spend that time with him, and I'm proud to share the results with you, my readers.

CHAPTER 1

NIAMH'S VOICE WOVE like a silver thread through the dark, clear and perfect as snow beneath a full moon. *Why did I envision a full moon on snow, so bright the trees cast shadows? I've never been in a forest at night, and I've never seen snow under starlight.* Ardghal's voice was lower, stronger. *Wind through oak branches.* Cillian's voice was so like Owen's that Aria's eyes filled with tears. *He can't sing now. Not the way he wants to.*

The song brightened the darkness of the train station, at least for a time, and dispelled the ever-present chill. When their voices faded, Aria shivered.

Owen still lay motionless on the concrete, the Fae around him murmuring in low voices that did not quite reach her ears.

Aria chewed her lip and tried to imagine what Cillian might have meant when he said Owen seemed more human. The difference was subtle enough that Cillian hadn't noticed at first, but now all the Fae seemed captivated by it. One, a Fae girl who appeared to be a little younger than Aria, even bent so close to Owen's face Aria thought she meant to kiss him, but she merely sniffed him carefully, then drew back, her face perplexed.

Several of the Fae looked up, startled and wary. One of them stalked off into the darkness. *What did they hear?*

Eventually Aria rose and walked toward the lights in the human encampment near the other end of the platform. The shadows pressed upon her, dank and threatening.

There's nothing to fear. She repeated the words to herself, knowing they weren't true but needing the reassurance. She glanced over her shoulder; the Fae seemed like a distant island of safety in the echoing, inky blackness. Her steps quickened along with her pulse. By the time she reached the lights, she was running.

"What's wrong?" Bartok caught her arm as she nearly collided with him, his pistol half-drawn.

She shuddered. "Nothing. I'm just jumpy."

He held her eyes for a moment, then gave her a wry smile and slid the pistol back into its holster. "I can understand why. Do you have a minute?"

She followed him to where Gabriel sat with a few others, looking at books spread out before them. Electric lamps in the center of the circle cast harsh shadows.

Gabriel looked up at them and gestured toward the books. "Dandra sold history books. No wonder she's missing." He picked up one book and flipped through it slowly.

Levi added, "Plus two books on Jewish history and three Bible commentaries."

Aria leaned across to pick up *Memories Kept*. She ran her fingers over the cover, a blurred picture behind crisp, slightly retro lettering. *If I hadn't questioned, where would I be now?* Her bookmark was still between the pages, and she held one finger on it as she opened the book.

"Did you move my bookmark?" she asked.

"No. That's the page where we found it," Jennison said.

Aria frowned. "That's not where I was reading." A faint blue pencil line caught her eye on the right-hand page, underlining the words *beside the wall.*

She flipped through the rest of the book, skimming pages. The pages were devoid of other markings; there were no highlights, no notes. Aria never wrote in books, and Dandra was strict about her patrons not defacing the volumes. Few people were inclined to do so anyway, and fewer still had ever noticed this book. She remembered her conversation with Dandra about the colored pencil markings used in editing. *Back in the old days, when they printed with big metal plates, editors would use blue pencil on the art boards because it wouldn't reproduce photographically, and so it wouldn't get transferred to the final layout.* She ran one finger over the line again. *Blue pencil was used for communication within the production team, not for everyone.*

"I think Dandra did this." Aria turned the book around and showed them. "As a message."

GABRIEL SENT BARTOK, Evrial, and Clint, a former police detective, back to Dandra's that evening. Bartok, tall and lanky, with his kind eyes, was a comforting presence. Clint was an intimidating character, shorter than Bartok but broader, the sleeves of his jacket stretched tight around the muscles of his arms. His face had a hard edge to it.

Evrial murmured in her ear, "Don't worry. He doesn't bite."

Niall accompanied them; he'd volunteered for the duty by showing up at Aria's side as they were leaving. He gestured at her.

"You want to go?"

He nodded.

"All right." Perhaps he would see something they couldn't. Bartok nodded to Niall, so Aria knew that he'd made himself visible, at least for a while.

Everyone was silent during the long walk underground. Aria shivered in the cool, still air of the tunnels, and even more once they reached the surface. They emerged from the tunnels through an access hatch hidden beneath a small overpass. Deep in the shadows, they waited for a car to pass on the lower street before darting out and around, up the embankment to the upper road. Dodging the cold lights of halogen street lamps, the group walked another two blocks before Niall stopped at a back door in an alley. White stenciled letters marked it as the rear entrance to Dandra's Books and Maps.

Clint tried to pull the door open, but the lock held. He rummaged in his pocket. "Wait a minute. I can probably get it open."

Niall reached across him to touch the door handle, and it unlatched with a soft click. He pulled it open and gestured for them to enter.

"That's a handy trick," Clint murmured.

Niall inclined his head, the gesture reminiscent of Owen's courtesy.

Inside, they risked using tiny penlights in the storage room, though it would be too dangerous in the main shop. With the wide glass windows, any light from the sales floor would be visible to passersby.

"'Beside the wall.' Which wall?" Clint spoke in a whisper.

"I don't know." Aria stared around, biting her lip. "I've never been in the back before."

Two walls were lined with shelves filled with labeled boxes. Self Help. Science and Technology. Children's.

"History books aren't labeled," Aria said.

Bartok shone his flashlight along the rows of boxes and made a thoughtful sound. "Or travel or religion or classics." His frown deepened.

Niall turned away from the light, motioning that he was going into the front. They turned the lights off while he slipped through the door, then flicked the flashlights back on and played them around the walls, shadows dancing in their wake. They covered the whole room, then began again.

"There." Bartok pointed. "What's that?"

A shallow desk, barely more than a foot deep, stood in one corner against the wall. A gooseneck lamp was clipped to the right edge, the head pointing down toward the empty desk top. Beneath the desk lay a blue pencil.

C. J. BRIGHTLEY

They moved forward and studied it, not touching anything.

"I don't see anything," said Aria. "But that's the blue pencil. It must be around here somewhere."

"I don't see anything either." Clint sounded confused. He shifted and considered the pencil and desk from a different angle, playing his light around crack between the desk and the wall.

"There." Aria and Bartok spoke at the same time. Bartok reached down to brush one finger against a blue mark on the floorboard near the wall, then pushed it firmly.

The other end of the board twelve inches away rocked upward, revealing a dark hole. Bartok moved forward to shine his flashlight into the space. The gap was barely wide enough for his hand, and he had to twist and turn pull out a thick, leather-bound book with papers folded into the front cover. He played the light around again and pushed the board back into place.

"How did you notice that?" Clint asked.

"The pencil tip pointed at the mark." Bartok stared down at the book in his hands.

"What is it?" Aria asked.

Bartok was silent, and Aria moved closer.

Finally Bartok murmured, "It's a Bible."

He flipped open the front cover and removed the papers. Everyone huddled closer to read in the glare of the flashlights.

If you've found this, I was forced to flee. You were searching for answers. This book has answers. You were searching for the truth. This book has the truth that will set you free.

14

I regret that I cannot explain it to you myself. I knew my time here was limited and dangerous, but I had hoped to have longer.

This may seem cryptic, and for that I apologize. I cannot put much in writing; it risks others. I can say only this: many outside the North and East Quadrants are appalled at what has happened here. The Empire has committed crimes of a magnitude we could not have imagined.

But you are not alone. We cannot, and will not, risk an open war. Not now. Perhaps not ever. But there is more to be won than physical victory. My party is concerned with souls. The Bible will be of use to you. Study it, but keep it hidden. The Empire does not look on it kindly, and you would do well to stay unnoticed.

Stay away from the man who frightened me that night. I do not know what he spoke of, but he knew too much about me. He may be an agent of the Empire.

Aria frowned. "This last part might be about Owen. That doesn't make sense."

The group looked around again, but found nothing else. Clint led the way back to the tunnels, and Niall shadowed them, invisible and silent in the dark.

BARTOK SAT ALONE at the end of the platform, an electric lantern sitting on a box behind his shoulder. He had a book open in his lap, dark eyes intent on the page. Bartok wasn't as beautiful as Owen was, but there was comfort in his presence. *This isn't a crush; I don't feel that sort of interest. Just… interest. He is alive in his own skin, like Owen is. Content, even when there isn't any reason to be content.*

Aria made her way toward him through the maze of sleeping bags.

"Do you mind if I sit with you for a while?"

He looked up, his expression momentarily puzzled, as if he were coming back from distant thoughts. "Not at all." He gestured toward the concrete floor, and she sat beside him.

"What are you reading?" Aria kept her voice low and quiet, not wanting to wake anyone else. It was 3:30 in the morning, but her body was so confused that she only knew it was night by the fact that nearly everyone was sleeping.

"The Bible. Clint said he was done with it." He looked down. "It's been a long time. Mine was lost. I'd forgotten how much I missed it." He smoothed the page and ran his finger under one line.

"What's the Bible?" She leaned closer, looking at the pages, so thin the paper was almost translucent. Not like the thick academic texts she'd studied, nor like the cheap paper of the popular fiction she sometimes enjoyed. The faded gold leaf on the edges made it seem important, or at least as if the printer had wanted it to look important.

"You don't remember?"

Aria shook her head. "I don't think I ever knew much about it. It was the book of the Christians. That's about it."

Bartok took a deep breath and stretched his legs. "The revelation of God given to men."

She raised an eyebrow, and he smiled.

"It's a long story."

"We have time. Dandra said it was important." She glanced over her shoulder at Owen and the Fae gathered around him, indistinct shadows in the faint light of the dimmed lamps.

Bartok nodded. "In the beginning, there was nothing. God created the universe and everything in it, including our world and people. We were perfect and sinless, but we had free will—the ability to choose to love and obey Him, and the ability to rebel against Him. We did. In doing so, we separated ourselves from God and ensured our own deaths, both physical and spiritual. But God had a plan. He chose the Jews to work through for this plan."

"Who are they? And why them? Are they better than we are?"

"No, they're representative. The Jews made plenty of mistakes, but they were chosen. God gave them laws about how to worship Him and how to live through prophets. But the Jews kept failing. Even when God performed miracles like rescuing them from Egyptian slavery, they would turn away, lose faith, forget or disregard what He'd done for them. We're the same as they are. No matter how hard we try, we always mess up, because that's just how people are. God gave the Jews laws so they would know and understand the sin that already existed within human hearts."

"Why? Why are we so bad? You're a good man. I'm good. I've never done anything terrible. Not like Grenidor or anything."

Bartok raised his eyebrows. "Good? How good is good enough? The standard is perfection. Perfect love. Perfect obedience to God's will. At all times, in all circumstances. You've never lied or cheated or stolen anything? Never thought an unkind thought? Never taken some petty little vengeance on someone after they hurt your feelings? Never even wanted to? Never been jealous of someone for having something you didn't have? It's not just a standard of behavior; it's a standard for your heart. If you avoid doing something bad because you don't want to get caught, but you *want* to do it... that's still sin. God cares about your heart more than your behavior or your situation. I like to think I'm a decent man. But I'm not perfect. No one is. No one is good enough on their own."

Aria didn't want to meet his eyes anymore. Her insides gave an uncomfortable twinge at the litany of sins. *Well, no, I'm not perfect. I'm not bad, but I'm not* perfect. *No one can be that good.*

"God knew that. He knew no one could meet the standard of perfection. But he cannot tolerate sin. He is holy, and we are not. The wages of sin is death. Physical death and spiritual death. Justice demands that we die for our sins."

"Even the little ones?" Aria's voice cracked.

"Even those." His lips quirked up in a tiny, melancholy smile. "We only think they're little because we're so sinful. If we were holy, like God, we would see how bad they really are. So things seem hopeless, right? Except God gave us a way out. He sent his son Jesus to the Jews. In accordance with a bunch of prophecies God had given the Jews over generations, Jesus was born to a young, Jewish virgin in a little town in Israel. He lived a righteous life, completely obedient to God. Sinless and perfect.

"God sent Jesus to die for us. The Jews demanded that the Romans crucify him... it's a long political story, but basically everyone was looking out for themselves and their power and status. Jesus lived a perfect life. Truly perfect, both in his actions and his heart. He didn't deserve to die."

"But they killed him." Aria's eyes were wide.

"Yes. Justice was served, and mercy won. Because then he rose from the dead."

"What?" *Did I really hear him say that?*

"Jesus was completely God and completely man. Divine and human. He defeated death. After he rose, he stayed around for a while and talked with his friends and followers, then went to heaven. We're all guilty of sin, Aria. All of us. We should all die for it. We all *will* die for it, physically and spiritually, unless we ask for God's mercy. But that's the most amazing thing; if we ask for God to forgive us, trusting in Christ's death on the cross and his resurrection, God will look at Jesus's death and forgive our sins. Jesus paid the penalty for our sins. This is grace—undeserved mercy."

Bartok's gentle voice made the absurd story sound believable. Sin. Death. Resurrection. Forgiveness. Grace. *That is inconceivable. Why would an all-powerful god pay the price for the sin his own creation committed against him?*

Aria drew back, her expression incredulous. "You *believe* that? That he rose from the dead? And now we just ask for forgiveness, and it's given to us? That's what Christians believe? That's... bizarre."

Bartok's soft brown eyes held hers. "Yes. I do. I had walked away for a time, when I was angry and disappointed in God. But my anger and disappointment do not change who God is. I may not understand, but I trust that he is good."

Aria swallowed, shaken. *He sounds like Niall talking about Owen. Or El.* "How do you know he's good?"

19

Bartok smiled. "I trust. I have evidence in my life, but everyone has to make their own decision. But what I believe doesn't change the truth. It's only a matter of recognizing truth."

She couldn't hold his gaze and looked back down at the Bible. "What does the book say?"

"The story I told you, the laws given to the Jews, the revelation of God through Jesus, creation, forgiveness, how to live. It's a rich history. Some people think it's a book of laws about how to live, but there's so much more. It's not about us at all; the story is about God and what he did because of his love."

Aria leaned in to read the words. "Who wrote it?"

Bartok moved his hand out of her way. "Many people. The Bible was inspired by God, but written by men. There's poetry, cries of anguish, songs of joy, even a love song. History. Genealogies. Prophecies. Encouragement. No one truly understands all of it, in all its richness."

Aria read aloud, "As a father has compassion on his children, so the Lord has compassion on those who fear him; for he knows how we are formed, he remembers that we are dust. The life of mortals is like grass, they flourish like the flower of the field; the wind blows over it and it is gone, and its place remembers it no more." She sat back with a heavy sigh. "That's depressing."

Bartok smiled easily. "You stopped too soon." He continued, "But from everlasting to everlasting the Lord's love is with those who fear him, and his righteousness with their children's children—with those who keep his covenant and remember to obey his precepts. The Lord has established his throne in heaven, and his kingdom rules over all." He stopped and looked toward the Fae circled around Owen's motionless form.

"What?" Aria glanced toward them too.

He blinked and ran one hand over his face before focusing on her. "I'm just thinking." He glanced toward the silent circle again, his lips flattening. "Didn't you say that Owen couldn't lie? Or didn't lie?"

"Something like that. He said it was difficult, sometimes impossible. Ardghal said deceiving humans was a right they didn't often have and seldom used. I don't know if that means they don't deceive humans even when they can, or..." She frowned. "What are you thinking?"

Bartok shook his head slightly. "I'd like to talk to him when he's recovered a little more." His gaze was drawn back to them again, and she watched his eyes flick across the platform and back toward Owen. "Do you see them?"

"Yes. Why?"

He glanced at her. "Hm." At her prompting motion, he lowered his voice even more, nearly inaudible now. "I think I can only see them when they deliberately show themselves. The rest of the time, there are only hints of motion that I wouldn't really notice, except that I know Fae are here. When they're all together, it's just enough to look a little odd. When they intentionally let me see them, they're clear, but that's only one or two at a time. I assume it's intentional, anyway. I think you're the only one who can see them all the time... assuming you do. If you didn't see them sometimes, how would you know?"

"How can you not see them over there? What do you see?" she whispered.

"Mostly flickers, sometimes a little more. Like a heat shimmer. Maybe they want us to know where they are, else we might trip over them or something. I saw several of them during the rescue, but not often after that."

He rubbed his neck with a tired sigh, then asked, "Were any of them close enough to hear what I said?"

"I don't think so. They can hear farther than you'd expect, but none of them are close now, and they don't look like they overheard. They aren't good at hiding anything other than themselves. Their expressions may be subtle, but they're visible. I think I'd be able to tell if they were paying attention." She watched them for a minute, then frowned at Bartok again. "You really don't see them? They look just like people. Except I feel disgusting without a shower, and they never stink."

He quirked a half-smile. "If I believed in ghosts, I'd say that's what they look like. A flash of a human form or a face. Not ghostly white... well, the faces are all pale, but the hair is dark, and clothes have color. Then it's gone. I've seen Owen there a few times, just a glimpse. He hasn't moved."

Aria swallowed. "No. I don't believe he can."

Bartok flipped to a new page in his notebook and wrote hurriedly, letting her look over his shoulder. *The others don't realize you can see them all the time, or at least much more than the rest of us. If they did, they'd be talking about it. Why can you see them? How can you see them? If you can do it, is it something they can learn too? Etc. Some would wonder about the legends.* She made a questioning gesture with her hand. *Some of the legends about fairies talk about summoning them by spells and making deals with them, exchanging magic services for a price, generally a dangerous price the human wouldn't fully understand. A farmer might promise the next creature born on his land, and then it turns out to be the farmer's own child. Witches are also associated with fairies. No one nowadays really believes in witches, but no one believed in fairies either. They would wonder whether you were a witch, and whether you really supported the Resistance. Maybe you promised the Fae something to gain power. They'd wonder what you'd cost them, either through ignorance or treachery.*

Aria swallowed and shook her head. "But I haven't…"

He shook his head too, making a silencing motion. *Legends are often false. Iron is supposed to burn fairies, but the Fae handle iron and steel like anyone else. Either the legends are wrong or Fae aren't fairies, or… whatever. It doesn't matter. I won't mention it to the others until we understand them and they understand us a little better. If I did, everyone would talk about it, the Fae would hear, and I doubt the conversations would encourage mutual trust. The last thing we need is to earn their hostility. I think you understand them best. You decide when and how to mention it.* He looked up and held her eyes. "Agreed?"

Aria licked her lips. "Yes. That's wise."

Bartok studied her expression. He motioned at the Bible. "Did you want to talk about anything?"

"No. Not right now." She rested her head against the concrete behind her. "Everything is confusing."

"Not everything."

23

"Not for you." She sighed, then froze, her heart in her throat. Not ten feet away, Niamh crouched, icy blue eyes flickering over their faces. Aria swallowed, then looked down, unsure whether to invite her over or not. Niamh didn't seem to realize that Aria could see her, had already seen her. *How long was she listening to us?*

Evrial rose from her bedroll nearby and came over to sit beside Aria, half-turned so she faced them both. "Bartok's going on about his God, again?" She gave him an affectionate punch on the shoulder. "I can't agree with everything he says, but I can't argue with his sincerity. That's enough for me."

Bartok sighed. "Evrial, you know what I'll say to that."

She rolled her eyes. "Sure."

"What?" Aria asked. She didn't look at Niamh, who was still listening. *She doesn't realize I can see her. Bartok and Evrial can't.*

"That sincerity doesn't matter. If you believe you can fly, it doesn't mean you can. You're just sincerely deluded."

Evrial grinned. "Yeah, yeah. But that's nature. Natural laws are obvious. Good and evil aren't so easy to define. I'm not sure I even believe in good and evil. I like to think we're on the right side of things, but maybe that's all just bias. Grenidor thinks he's doing the right thing, I bet. Maybe there's really only expediency." She shrugged, looking down at her fingers laced together in her lap. Her voice softened as if she were struggling with the questions and not merely baiting Bartok. "What if the only valid concepts are effective versus ineffective? Optimal and sub-optimal. Pleasant and unpleasant. Even if the concepts of good and evil are useful, you could define them so many ways. How can you say the Bible has the best definition?"

Aria nodded, then stopped. *Before, I would have agreed. I find myself wanting to, even now. No one is truly good, and how can we know what good is? We're all so limited. But...* she carefully avoided looking up at Niamh. *Owen's sacrifice for the other Fae was good. It wasn't expedient, but I know it was good. Love like that is better than being pleasant or nice or optimal. It has value I don't even know how to define.*

Bartok's voice broke into her thoughts. "... too vague a concept. 'Good' can mean high-quality, beneficial, virtuous, effective... lots of things. The word isn't specific enough. Of course there can be many different 'good' and 'bad' things. But I'm talking about a specific nature—Godly, or righteous, versus ungodly, or unrighteous, which is everything else. This 'everything else' isn't necessarily evil. Imagine a shark."

Evrial snorted.

"As sharks go, it's fine. But its nature isn't Godly, or righteous, as exemplified by Jesus. Humans are not sharks; we are supposed to be righteous. We don't have the option of simply 'being'. We all sin, or fall short of the standard of righteousness."

Aria frowned. "You said that before. But why would God make us sinful and then punish us for it? That's not fair. And it doesn't sound like love."

"God didn't make us sinful. He made us with the ability to choose. A genuine ability to choose inevitably means the ability to choose wrongly."

"But *why* do we choose sin?" Aria scowled.

Now Bartok snorted. "Because that's how we are. Once Adam, the first man, sinned, it was born into us. We're drawn to sin, even though God didn't make us that way. God has a perfectly righteous nature. Sinful things, things that are not of God's nature, can't be in His presence. We aren't God and we can't attain that kind of righteousness, but we don't have to. God's mercy to us is that all we have to do is *choose*. We have to choose God's nature over our own sinful nature, even though we aren't capable of living up to that choice on our own. God will supply the righteousness that we lack. But we have to choose it freely, of our own volition."

"Why? Couldn't God have made us so we would always choose correctly? Maybe he should have." Aria's voice betrayed her frustration.

Bartok gave a minute shrug. "Well, if we always *must* choose a certain way, is that really a choice? If you're asking why it's important that we have a choice... I don't know. I do know that we're described as being made in God's image, distinct from everything else in creation."

Aria swallowed, feeling Niamh's intense gaze burning into her. "We're made in God's image?"

"Yes. I'm not sure exactly what that entails, but choice is part of it. I'm studying the concept now, actually. I think it's important."

Aria glanced at Niamh, catching her eye for one heart-stopping instant. She looked away, her heart thudding raggedly. *She's angry. Or frightened. Jealous? Can Fae be jealous?* From the corner of her eye, Aria saw Niamh shift cautiously, staring back at Aria. *She knows I saw her, doesn't she?*

Evrial scowled. "So we need forgiveness to enter heaven. I still don't see why God would have to kill his own son to forgive us. It seems unnecessarily cruel, and it doesn't make sense. If God is so great, why wouldn't he just forgive us? Assuming sin exists, for the sake of discussion."

Levi meandered over and joined their little huddle. "Your whispering isn't as quiet as you think it is. Anything interesting?"

Niamh opened her mouth, as if she wanted to answer, but kept silent. Siofra, a younger Fae woman, and a male about Aria's age whose name Aria couldn't remember, crouched beside her. Awareness of them kept Aria's face heated. The Fae seemed to grow more beautiful every time she looked at them; it was almost painful to look at them for more than a moment.

Bartok said, "I was telling them about grace. I'm not a theologian, and I'm not sure we've been given the full explanation anyway. So this is my opinion. This isn't God's explanation, it's just my extrapolation from what he did tell us in the Bible.

"As humans, we have two problems, neither of which we can overcome by ourselves. One is the weight of the sins we have committed. The other is the very nature that continually leads us to more unrighteous thoughts and actions.

"We bear the guilt of our sins, crimes against God and against other people. If God were to just forgive the sins in the sense of saying 'oh, let's just forget those', he would be accepting them as if they didn't matter. They *do* matter. The law has been broken. It's God's law… think 'law of nature', not a traffic violation. There is a consequence, a penalty. That consequence is death.

"God will neither break nor devalue his law by ignoring this penalty, but he is willing to pay our penalty, for our crimes, himself. He became incarnate as a man and suffered and died a horrible death in our place, as fulfillment of the judgment against us. *That* is what sounds like love.

"The catch, if you want to think of it that way, is that we have to choose. Atonement has been made, but to claim it we have to reject our sinful nature and choose God's nature rather than our own."

The silence lengthened, heavy upon each of them. The little group of Fae listening to Bartok had grown, though Aria didn't know all their names. *I think they understand this better than I do.* She almost mentioned them to Bartok, to let him know that they were listening, but something held her back. Perhaps they did not want to be included in the conversation.

Levi frowned. "Are you saying Christians don't sin anymore?"

"No, we still sin, at least in what remains of this life. We don't want to, or at least we shouldn't want to. But we're human, and we do. Christ's one atonement is sufficient for all the sins of this life."

Levi didn't look entirely satisfied. "So you just try to not screw up again? And that's good enough?"

Bartok smiled. "Well, no, it's *not* good enough. But God looks on us and sees the redemption we receive through Christ. We're covered by his righteousness, not our own. So we live out the rest of our lives in reliance on God's grace, and in awareness of the times we fail, and in humility and gratitude for what God has done for us. We have the

Bible as instruction on what is right, just, beautiful, and good in life, and we aspire to emulate Christ in our lives. We fail, but we keep trying. We know the direction we're headed."

Aria sighed. *And then we die. Is all that trying and struggling worth it?* She glanced at Bartok.

He met her gaze with a kind smile, and there was peace in his eyes.

CHAPTER 2

THAT AFTERNOON ARIA sat by Owen, unable to offer him any comfort but unwilling to leave him. He was still lying on his back; it had been three full days since the rescue, and he had made no attempt to sit up, much less stand. Even with the Fae singing. Aria tried not to imagine how much pain he was suffering.

The Fae had scattered through the station, scouting the tunnels and doing who knew what else. Only a few remained with Owen, and those few had withdrawn a little. Niall sat beside her, watching Owen's chest move with each slow breath. He flipped through Owen's notebook thoughtfully, and once he reached out one narrow hand to touch his uncle's shoulder. Owen didn't move, either asleep or unconscious.

Niall sighed and bowed his head.

"What are you thinking?" Aria finally whispered.

Niall looked up with shadowed, unreadable eyes. He studied her, pressing the palm of one pale hand against his chest, as if to soothe his aching heart. Aria wondered whether he meant to answer at all. Finally he wrote *I am considering the nature of my anger*. He stopped, the pen poised over the paper, then added *I am also evaluating the danger Cillian mentioned to you before*. He looked up to hold her gaze. *Please stay close to Cillian, my mother, or me.*

"What is the danger?" she murmured, not wanting her voice to carry.

He shook his head. *It... may never come. But it is best that you be wary.*

Owen made a small, pained sound and turned his head a little. Their attention snapped to him, but he did not wake. Aria wondered if he suffered even in his dreams. *That wouldn't be fair. At least he should dream of beauty. I wish I remembered the forest, the freedom, golden light streaming through the leaves. Maybe he's there, in his dreams.*

"Is he hurting now?" she asked, her voice still low.

Niall twitched one shoulder in a shrug.

Cillian knelt beside them, a swift, soundless motion that startled Aria. "Ardghal and Lorcan have brought food. We judged it less dangerous for us to procure provisions."

Aria frowned. "Really?"

"The nearest shop was half a mile from here. Humans would have been seen. We were less obvious," Ardghal answered as he sat beside Cillian.

Owen's eyes fluttered open. "What?" His voice rasped a little.

Ardghal frowned. "I didn't mean to wake you, Lord Owen. We have brought food."

"Thank you, Ardghal."

Even when he can barely talk, he sounds like a king. The authority in his voice is unmistakable. Aria swallowed and ducked her head to hide her sudden blush. She felt Owen's eyes on her, the quiet regard and contemplation in his gaze.

"What would you like, Owen?" Cillian asked.

Owen twitched an indifferent finger. "It matters not."

Cillian glanced around the packages and selected one. "Liver?"

Owen grunted assent, and Cillian opened the package and cut the meat swiftly. He glanced at his brother. "Shall I feed you?"

"I can do it."

Cillian slid the paper containing liver pieces close to Owen's hand.

Aria said, "I thought you ate pig hearts."

Cillian swallowed, then answered. "Often, yes. They are nutritious and cheap. But we can eat most meats. Organ meat is rich in nutrients."

Aria grimaced involuntarily, then blushed when she realized Owen had seen it. He smiled faintly and groped for the pile of liver pieces.

"I can feed you."

Owen arched one eyebrow at her. "You find it... revolting."

Aria bit her lip. Was that a joke? That was her word, from the first time she'd seen him eat. "It's fine. I'm not eating that." *It* would have been more appropriate than *that*, but she was quoting him

32

back. His smile and the sparkle in his eye showed he understood.

The liver had been refrigerated, and the cold meat didn't feel as disgusting as she'd feared. More like something she'd cook than pieces of an animal recently killed. She fed Owen pieces one at a time, only touching the meat with the tips of her fingers. Though he didn't seem hurried, he chewed only once or twice per bite, not as much as a human would. She wondered abruptly whether his teeth were different; his incisors looked human, but perhaps his molars were not. Or perhaps he didn't mind the large chunks going down his throat.

"What?" he asked.

Aria realized she'd paused, one hand holding a liver piece while she stared at him thoughtfully. "Nothing." She blushed and gave him the next bite. At his steady look, she said, "I was just wondering if your teeth were like a cat's in the back, with sharp molars. You don't chew very much. It's very... predator-like."

Owen smiled again. "Our teeth are much like yours. We just—" He closed his eyes, jaw tight for a moment, then continued more softly, "We just don't like to swallow mush."

Aria frowned at him. "Are you feeling any better at all?"

Another faint smile. "Very much."

Oh. She wanted to cry. Scream. Emotion tightened her throat and she looked down so he wouldn't see her eyes filling with tears. *What right do I have to be upset when he isn't? But shouldn't I weep for him? He deserves that, I think.*

33

She forced herself to take a deep breath, look up to meet his gaze. The bruise around his left eye had turned a mottled purple and brown, the right still black and swollen, though much better than before. At least he could open it a little now. Against the dark bruises, his eyes were eerily bright. He opened his lips slightly, as if he meant to say something, but then he merely closed them again.

"How do you buy all this food if you're cut off from everything?"

Cillian answered for Owen. "We've stashed money around the city. Owen and I worked some odd jobs a few years ago when they were easier to come by. Dock men for a few weeks, that sort of thing. It's not a lot of money, but we don't buy much."

Niamh frowned. "It wasn't fitting. I wish you had let others do it."

Owen twitched one hand. "I thought it was interesting."

Cillian narrowed his eyes. "That's where you met that troublemaker, isn't it? That's when it started."

Owen licked his lips. "Yes." His voice was fading, and his eyes drifted closed.

Aria glanced between them. "What do you mean?"

Cillian stiffened. "I should not have spoken of such matters while you were present. It does not concern you."

She opened her mouth to protest, but he was right. "I'm sorry. I just meant... I was just curious."

Niamh said quietly, "You ask many questions about matters that do not concern you. You take advantage of the... rules of engagement under which we must interact. It is unkind to pry into private family disagreements."

Owen opened his eyes again and let his gaze rest on Aria, but his words were for Cillian. He murmured, "He was not a troublemaker, and to describe him as such is willfully inaccurate. You resent him because he changed my views and caused trouble between us." He stopped to take a slow breath and continued, "But he had no such intent. He spoke of love. Peace. Truth. Tell her, Cillian."

Cillian's nostrils flared. "The man was a Christian. I have no quarrel with Christians. I know little of their beliefs and have met few, but those few have been acceptable. He caused trouble for the authorities and was arrested as a religious fanatic some weeks after we had moved on from the job. I do not know what happened to him." He looked down at his hands, then added, "Evangelism, proselytizing, is against Imperial law. Many Christians, along with people of other religions, fled when the Empire came to power. Christians have been coming back. When they are discovered, they are arrested. Generally they are deported. Sometimes they are not allowed to work, which necessitates immigration out of the Empire, since they cannot afford food and other necessities. They cannot receive financial support from Christians outside the Empire; all money sent is confiscated. A few have been executed, but the Empire is more concerned with political spies than quiet evangelism."

Owen's lips tightened. "That is not what I meant." His gaze on Cillian was cool. "I had never heard what he called the gospel. He said it was a story of grace. Dr. Bartok said... I did not know..." he closed his eyes for several heartbeats, his jaw tight. "Humans have a way back. Fae, when we..." Another pause, this one longer. "*Please*, Cillian," he breathed.

Cillian's dark head dropped. He stared at his hands, pressed his long, thin fingers together and studied them. Only Owen's soft, ragged breaths broke the silence.

Finally Cillian said, "Humans are born into rebellion, tainted with sin from their very conception. Whom you call God, we call El; our understanding of him is not as yours is, but it is similar enough that we believe our El and the Christian God are the same. The differences are more the result of our mortal inability to understand him than of inconsistencies in his character.

"Humans! You are frail creatures, weak in body, mind, and heart. Born into sin, you choose it from the moment you are able to choose. Rebellion is woven into your souls. You were not always this way. El created you in his own image, and he is not sinful. Your choice condemned you. These things we know from our own history, and they are confirmed by your human writings."

Owen twitched his hand, and Cillian frowned at him.

"Lord Owen listened to this Christian, and he believes humans have been given a way back into grace. Your Bible tells how El paid the penalty for human sin against himself. Humans may accept this gift and return to fellowship with El. Lord Owen and I, and perhaps a few of the others, heard Dr. Bartok's conversation with you this morning. It was a more complete telling than even Lord Owen had heard before

"Lord Ailill spoke of something similar he heard in his youth, but Fae have had little contact with humans until recently. Most of us are not informed enough on human religious beliefs to know how El relates to you and addresses your sin. We are not human, and even if this grace is extended to you..." he hesitated, then took a deep breath. "We choose not to become informed on it. If it is true, we might become resentful, and the consequences of that would be terrible. If it is not true, we might question the character of El, who would allow children to be born, doomed to eternal death by their very nature. That is El's right, for he created you to be more than you are, but we are not without compassion on human weakness. This questioning also would have negative consequences for us. We choose not to explore these matters of human souls, trusting that El's decisions are beyond our fathoming."

Aria frowned. "I don't understand. How can questioning be so bad?"

"Wondering is not in itself 'bad', as you say. But wondering can lead to doubting El, and that is the beginning of rebellion. For us, there is no way back from rebellion. A Fae who turns away from El becomes dangerous, violent, and hopeless. The kindest thing to do is to kill him. Rebellion is rare, which is El's mercy on both Fae and humans." Cillian looked back at Owen's white face as if wondering whether his recitation had satisfied his brother's command.

Owen murmured, "And yet, do we not doubt El's character by persisting in the belief that he offers grace to humans and not to us?"

Cillian stiffened. "This is the question that provoked trouble between us. Lord Owen, please do not force me to take a position on whether humans are offered greater grace than we are. I do not wish to become angry with them because they appear to be more greatly loved." He breathed quickly, struggling to keep his voice even. "I submit myself to El, and I choose not to address questions with answers I am not mature enough to accept." He shot to his feet and lurched away, stumbling as he brushed by Niamh on his way into the darkness.

Niamh stared at Owen. "Why did you provoke him so? You know this question troubles him."

Owen sighed softly. "I trust him, Niamh. He will not turn on this question." His lips tightened as he fought pain, and he breathed, "Please find him. I wish to… speak with him again."

Niall rose silently and disappeared in the direction Cillian had gone. Aria looked after him. Niall had been so unobtrusive she'd barely realized he was there, a wordless, protective shadow at Owen's side. But he listened. He looked like a child, and he *was* a child among the Fae. But he was also older than she was, and he listened with fierce intensity.

A long, silent hour passed before Cillian and Niall slipped back into the lantern light. Both were covered in cobwebs, and Cillian's face was streaked with dust, eyes reddened and pale cheeks damp and flushed. *Had he been weeping?*

Cillian knelt by Owen's side and bowed his face to the concrete. With exquisite care, he took

38

Owen's bruised hand and put it on top of his own head. Face still pressed to the floor and hair falling over his eyes, he said, "Lord Owen, my heart questioned your election and your wisdom in asking such questions. But I do not defy you. I ask that you take pity on my lesser faith." His thin body shuddered.

Owen murmured in Fae, and Cillian raised his head, tears glistening on his cheeks. A startled smile flashed across his face, and he bowed his head again, breathing slowing, more peaceful.

What just happened?

The Fae had seldom spoken in their own language while Aria was present, making a deliberate effort not to conceal anything from her. This was private, and she wondered whether it would be wrong to ask Niall to explain it later.

She watched the boy's narrow, pale face on the other side of Owen. Niall's eyes flicked into the darkness beyond her shoulder, to her face, to Cillian, to Owen, and then back to the darkness. *He's still afraid of something out there.* Now that she thought about, the others glanced into the shadows sometimes too. Their emotions were harder to read, but they could not entirely hide their tension.

ARIA WANDERED BACK over to the human encampment. *I am so confused. What day is it? Or is it night? I haven't seen the sun in a long time.*

Bartok waved to her and she picked her way through the bedrolls toward him. He was sitting with Jonah, Gabriel, and Eli around an old laptop.

She dropped to sit next to Bartok, and he murmured, "These are the pictures from the second floor. We looked at the third floor already but didn't see too much. A few name plates on desks that might be useful."

Jonah flicked through the photographs. A closed door with an electronic key-card entry designated "Sector Records." A view from a doorway of a cubicle-filled room. A piece of paper tacked to a bulletin board. Jonah zoomed in to reveal a shift schedule.

Another closed door, this one designated "Support."

"That's vague," Jonah murmured as he moved to the next photograph. "Ah." A small dark room with server towers. "Hm. I wonder if he could get us back in?"

"What do you want to do?"

"Nothing yet. But there must be some way to use this." Jonah zoomed in and examined the photograph carefully. There were several more pictures from different angles. Jonah grunted thoughtfully and moved on.

"This is the first floor." Generic office cubicles, with old phones and thick LCD monitors.

"They must not spend a lot of money on this place. Maybe it's not that important after all." Aria voiced her disappointment.

"No. This is good." Jonah smiled, still clicking through. "Secure rooms usually lag a bit technologically. Field officers get the best gear. Desk jockeys on secure work have the old stuff. It's expensive to keep upgrading classified tech every time some new innovation comes out, so they're generally a little behind the open market. Maybe they're doing something interesting here."

Aria frowned. "Ok. But what?"

Another picture, this time of a file folder flipped open and pages laid out inside.

Gabriel leaned forward. "An org chart. That's useful."

"What's that?"

"An organization chart. See, it shows who's in charge."

Aria didn't recognize any of the names, but Gabriel and Jonah studied the penciled lines drawn between different layers.

Gabriel pointed. "Look. Grenidor's still under General Harrison."

Jonah nodded. "Yeah. That's weird, isn't it?"

"About six years longer than he should have been. Harrison's been protecting that program as long as it's been around."

Next was a photo of a jumble of computer parts piled on the floor, mostly removable hard drives but also a few laptops labeled TOP SECRET with various caveats and code words in smaller print.

"Huh. I wonder what this is?"

"We can ask him later."

The door to the basement was labeled "Secure Area. Authorized personnel only." One of the videos began at the door. Owen moved through quickly, lifting the camera over the cubicle walls to give a quick view over the warren of desks and then heading directly for the door to the stairs below. The next few pictures were of the insides of refrigerators, the shelves filled with neatly labeled vials of what appeared to be blood and other liquids of various colors. Jonah zoomed in briefly, noted that the labels were legible, and zoomed back out.

Another floor down. Owen caught the sign with his camera. "Secure Area. Authorized personnel only. Biohazard. Personal protective equipment required. Sidearms required. Team admittance only; no unaccompanied admittance." The door opened, and he stepped through, closing it behind himself to reveal a secondary door of heavy steel, also plastered with warning signs. It, too, opened without a sound.

Owen raised the camera and panned around a huge room filled with cages. Each was perhaps eight feet wide by ten feet long, with thick metal grate on all sides. The floors were reinforced steel, and each cell was topped by a similar metal grate some eighteen inches from the ceiling.

Inside the cages paced vertril.

Aria heard Jonah gasp beside her. "How many are there?" he murmured.

As if in response, Owen panned the camera around again, then held up his fingers in front of the camera. Thirty cells by nineteen cells. Assuming they all held a vertril, that was five hundred seventy monsters, waiting to be released onto the streets.

Owen moved quickly down one aisle, noting a few empty cages. Each was numbered. One cage was labeled 641, with a small, angry vertril that flung itself against the cage bars as Owen passed. Above the handwritten 641 was a crossed-out 235. Aria swallowed. "Owen killed that one earlier. When I met him."

The video continued. Owen found an observation area near a large, empty cage at the end. The metal floor inside was clean, though scored with long, faint scratches. He set the camera atop the edge of the cage, looking out over the room full of cells.

Gabriel murmured, "God help him. That's a room full of nightmares."

Jonah grunted in agreement. The vertril were frothing at the mouth, slamming their bodies into the bars nearest the camera, their eyes fixed on Owen, just out of sight. He stepped into view and moved smoothly toward the first cage. The creature strained to bite him through the mesh as he placed his hand on the lock. It slammed the door open, and he sidestepped, sword raised. A moment later it was dead, and he'd moved on to the next cage.

Several minutes later, he reappeared in front of the camera. Blood streaked his face, but he looked otherwise normal, barely ruffled. He gestured briefly, then shrugged apologetically. He turned off the camera.

"That's the last video. I guess he thought we didn't need to see the carnage," Gabriel said.

Aria remembered how he'd looked when he returned. Blood-spattered, and unfazed by it.

Dangerous.

But he's good. He can be trusted.

COLD SEEPED THROUGH her shirt and stiffened her muscles, but Aria barely noticed. She'd been entranced by the history book for nearly two hours, leaning back against a concrete pillar with her legs pulled up in front of her. But now her shoulders were aching and her eyes were burning. She rubbed one hand across her face and rolled her head around. A movement caught her eye.

Bartok was a little way to her left, alternately scribbling notes and reading from the Bible. Like her, he'd been at it for hours. Now he shifted, put the Bible carefully to one side, and got to his knees to bend forward into a fetal position, forehead resting on his hands on the floor.

He didn't move.

Aria watched him, eyes wide. *What is he doing?* For long moments he stayed in the same position. Finally Aria got to her feet, grimacing at her tingling legs and feet. She had to steady herself against the concrete pillar for a moment.

She glanced across the platform toward Owen. The dim lantern light caught his motionless form, exactly where he'd been for over five days. The other Fae were shadows in the darkness beyond. Bartok remained on his knees, head down, and she went to kneel beside him.

"Are you all right?" she whispered.

A quiet sigh. "Yes. Thank you." His voice was muffled, and she frowned at his shoulders. He rose to his knees and smiled at her, a pensive, quiet smile. "I'm praying. Do you need something?"

She swallowed. "No. I just thought you looked… lonely."

A quick flash in his eyes, and another smile. "Thank you. But I'm less lonely than I've been in a long time."

"Oh." She tried to pretend his answer didn't sting. *Never mind then. I was just trying to be nice.*

His gaze flicked past her and she looked over her shoulder. Ardghal waved to them and she rose. "I think he wants us."

Bartok nodded and stood, his movements stiff. He followed her toward Owen.

Ardghal, Niamh, Cillian, and Niall sat to one side of Owen, and Niamh motioned for them to sit on his other side.

Owen studied them in silence for several moments. The black around his left eye had faded to an ugly green; the right was still swollen, black and purple, but he could open it enough to reveal a sliver of blue, oddly bright in the dim lantern light. The bruises covering his body were concealed by the blanket that Aria had draped over him days earlier. He generated no warmth, so it served little purpose, but the gesture had made him smile. Aria was glad she'd done it.

Ardghal broke the silence. "Lord Owen wishes to speak with you."

Bartok nodded. His eyes flicked up from Owen and around the platform, then he looked back. His smile looked a little forced.

"What were you reading?"

"The Bible."

Owen continued looking at Bartok. "I felt something when you had your head bowed. What were you doing?"

"I was praying. Do you pray?"

"I… yes. Did you feel it, Cillian?"

Cillian shifted slightly. "Perhaps a little." He sounded uncertain.

"What did it feel like?" Bartok asked.

"Like listening to Lord Ailill sing."

CHAPTER 3

SOME TIME LATER, a Fae girl who appeared about Aria's age approached her. "I have been instructed to ask if you need to see sunlight. I will conceal you if you wish to go outside."

Aria smiled, surprised and pleased. "Yes, I would. Thank you."

The girl nodded and turned away, clearly expecting Aria to follow her. Aria glanced behind her as she walked; no one noticed her leave.

"Lord Owen asked you to take me?"

"Yes." There was no inflection in her voice.

"What is your name again? Sorry I don't remember."

"Sorcha." The girl glanced back at her as if surprised to be asked.

Aria pushed down a pang of loneliness. *I should be used to it by now. I know they're cautious about me, and I mostly understand why. I just wish… I wish I understood more.* The loneliness was familiar, a feeling of loss and homesickness for something she'd never experienced. *Maybe everyone feels like this. I miss my parents, but it's more than that. Something deeper.* Even if Niamh were warmer, if Lord Owen returned her feelings, it wouldn't entirely fill that emptiness. It had been easier to ignore back before she'd been drawn into this conflict, before she met Owen. She'd filled up her time with schoolwork, acquaintances, books, research, dates, a string of part time jobs. Trivial things made to feel important.

Sorcha led her up a disused set of stairs, echoing and cast in shades of grey by the winter light and dingy paint. She put her hand on the handle of a large, frosted plexiglass door and slid it open just wide enough for the two of them to slip through. Discarded bits of paper and damp leaves had formed drifts in the corners of the landing and at the edges of the concrete steps before them. Sorcha led her up the steps to emerge at one corner of a small square surrounded by concrete buildings.

Yellow sunlight fought through a layer of dark grey clouds scudding across the sky, their shadows dancing over the ground. Sorcha raised her face to the sky and closed her eyes, drawing a deep breath. The Metro entrance had been long abandoned, though it was not as old as some of the others Aria had seen. The area around them had been neglected, though not entirely forgotten. A row of stunted decorative trees had grown tilted in their sidewalk cutouts, their branches bare. Sorcha walked to one and ran her fingers along a narrow branch. She sighed.

"What's wrong?" Aria asked.

Sorcha glanced at her. "If Lord Owen could move without pain, I would help these grow. They are brave, these trees, living here without a clean wind to breathe. But I must not risk drawing attention."

"You can do that? Help them grow?"

Sorcha nodded, then closed her eyes, resting her forehead against the bark. Aria looked around. People walked past but no one approached them. The buildings around them, all tall and slightly worn, were retail shops on the bottom and apartments above. "Is no one going to see us here?"

"Not unless you want to be seen."

Aria shook her head hurriedly. She turned around in a circle, looking at the sky.

"Are there any more vertril?" she asked.

"Yes."

"Close by?"

"No. Lord Owen killed many of them, and those that remain have withdrawn for a time to the dark places."

"What do you mean?" Aria studied Sorcha's face. "Dark places?"

Sorcha's lips twitched, as if she were considering words and then discarding them. "It is a translation of a phrase we use sometimes, but I think the meaning in English is not the same. Fae who have turned fear the light of El, so we say they live in the dark places. Wherever they live is dark, because they make it so. So when I said the vertril have withdrawn to the dark places, I meant that they have focused their hunting on the turned Fae, who are easier hunting for them now. The turned ones do not cooperate well or often, and they do not protect each other as we do. When there are more vertril to hunt together, they will turn again to us."

Aria's stomach gave an unpleasant lurch. "What would happen then?"

Sorcha glanced at her face, then away, her gaze flicking over the square. *She's always alert. All of them are. I guess you get that way when you're hunted.* "You have nothing to worry about. You are human, and the vertril have no interest in you."

She didn't answer my question. I wonder if she doesn't want to imagine it either.

The clouds slipped across the sky with silent speed, and to Aria's surprise the sky cleared. Winter sunlight brightened the square, gilding the worn concrete with a short-lived glow.

Sorcha glanced at her and Aria pretended not to notice, watching the light fade in a subdued sunset mostly hidden behind the buildings. Between the towers, a narrow strip of sky showed the brightest colors, violent crimson, orange, and indigo touched with gold.

"We should go," Sorcha murmured.

The beauty of the moment faded with the light. A cold wind gusted into Aria's face, stirring the leaves and whipping her hair into her eyes. She followed Sorcha into the darkness of the stairwell.

ARIA MADE HER way toward Gabriel and the others gathered around a computer. She felt their eyes on her as she approached, and she forced a smile. Their serious expressions made the gesture seem pointless.

"What is it?" She sat down and took the bowl of soup Levi pushed toward her.

49

"You knew you were adopted, didn't you?"

She frowned at Gabriel. "I wasn't adopted."

Gabriel looked back at the computer screen. "Where did you live? With your parents?"

"Near the old Union Station. Historic area."

"What was the address?"

Everyone was watching her. *I'm not adopted! They would have told me!* "412 H Street."

There was silence for a moment, and then Gabriel said, "You were adopted. They kept track of you."

Aria shook her head. "No. I..." She moved over to look at the screen.

Project Redemption

Summary: On September 1, 2061, following a tip from Informant 1, a clan of vampires was flushed out of Monongahela National Forest on the border of what was then called West Virginia and Virginia. Six vampires were killed by getlaril bullets: two adult males, three adult females, one juvenile female. One juvenile male may have escaped. The vampires were surprised and offered little resistance; there were no injuries in the strike team.

Two human infants were recovered. Due to the dangerous nature of the vampires and the superficial similarities, extensive testing was required; it confirmed that the babies were human. See linked test results.

Despite exhaustive searches, the department was unable to match the babies with any families reporting missing infants. Consequently, the babies were adopted.

Infant 1 was named James Franklin Martin, adopted by Jonathan and Eleanor Martin. Address at time of adoption was 221 Parker Street. Tracking information is linked.

Infant 2 was named Aria Marie Forsyth, adopted by Bertram and Linda Forsyth. Address at time of adoption was 412 H Street. Tracking information is linked.

This is the second recorded incident of vampires having stolen human children. See linked record from 2016. Human children do not appear to be maltreated. Recovered children have been in good health and well-nourished, with no physical or mental problems resulting from their captivity. However, the question remains... if we believe vampires are intelligent, what do they do with the children?

No adult humans have been associated with vampires. Beyond the obvious assumption that the stolen children are eaten, is there another possibility? Can they (would they?) breed with humans? For what purpose? Would a vampire wish to infiltrate human society? Such a danger has not been previously considered, but should be a part of defense planning.

The project notes ended abruptly, and Gabriel clicked over to another screen.

Colonel Robert Hart passed this project to his successor, Lieutenant Colonel Paul Grenidor, as part of the consolidation of vampire research efforts in 2072. Additional notes are linked.

Gabriel clicked again and leaned forward, scanning the screen.

James Franklin Martin records links: medical, academic, family investigation, death certificate

Aria Marie Forsyth records links: medical, academic, family investigation

"Is he dead?" Aria asked. Who was this boy, who had been captured with her? How had he died? What was he like?

Gabriel pulled up the records. James Martin had excellent grades in school and few illnesses.

He'd been admitted to a prestigious math program at one of the top schools, but only a month before school began, he and his father were killed in a car accident. His mother had moved, but the address was on G Street only a few blocks from where the Martin family had lived for years. A series of pictures made Aria catch her breath. He'd been a beautiful child, with medium brown curly hair and bright blue-green eyes that were laughing in every picture. At age six, he'd broken his leg falling from the drainpipe on the third floor; even in a cast, he had a mischievous grin. At eleven, he'd been an adorable little athlete, with a soccer ball under one arm. In high school, he'd been commended as a scholar-athlete, and several pictures showed him beside his mother and father with his various certificates and awards, half-embarrassed, half-proud.

Gabriel clicked over to Aria's record before she was ready to see it. Her transcripts were all there, showing in embarrassing detail how she'd nearly failed eighth grade introduction to physics and how she'd excelled in history and literature. Copies of scholarship letters from different universities followed, and at the end, the pictures of her family. She bit her lip as Gabriel brought them up.

The first picture brought tears to her eyes. Her father was in his late twenties, proudly holding a baby, the little blanket draped around its body. *That's me.* Her mother, a year younger, stood beside him, one hand on his arm and the other holding up the adoption certificate.

"They never told me," she whispered.

They looked tired, a little worn despite their youth. She wondered why; it wasn't as if her mother had just delivered her. She studied their faces, familiar, younger than she remembered. Her mother's blue eyes, her father's brown. Her mother's delicate but square jaw, her father's face longer, more oval. Another picture, this time of Aria at about six years old, sitting on a bicycle with her father standing beside her.

"I need some space," she muttered. She fled to her bedroll. *They never told me I was adopted! Why didn't they tell me?*

"YOU SHOULD HEAR THIS."

Aria rose and followed Evrial to the little group sitting around the laptop. Cords ran from it to several different hard drives, and messy stacks of papers were arranged in arcs around Gabriel and Bartok.

Bartok spoke as soon as she sat down. "Aria, remember when Owen said you had something in your brain? When you first joined us?"

She blinked. Somehow, with everything else that had happened, she'd nearly forgotten about it. "Do you know what it is?"

"It's a device called a neurostimulator. Back in the early part of the century, deep brain stimulation using neurostimulators was pioneered for use as a treatment for the tremors related to Parkinson's disease as well as some symptoms of depression. For those purposes it's established as a successful, minimally invasive treatment. It sounds serious to go digging around in someone's brain, but it's actually out-patient surgery. The device is minuscule, only about three times thicker than a human hair, and it can be calibrated, inserted, and tested in minutes. There are no side effects and there's no recovery time. It just works."

He paused and took a deep breath. "We found details of how the Revolution and then the Empire used deep brain stimulation to modify subjects' behavior. You must have been one of the subjects they selected. Although it's not expensive, I doubt they did it to everyone. Yours may have malfunctioned. Perhaps they weren't used for very long.

"I think, based on the records we found, their dates, and the chemicals, that forty to fifty percent of the North Quadrant population was chemically brainwashed. This would have been the top half or so, the people the Revolution leaders expected to be most influential. You may have been selected because of your grades and admission into a prestigious academic program. The intelligentsia has always been a target in revolutions, and I expect this is the same.

"Why wouldn't they brainwash everyone?"

Gabriel answered, "Why would they? If everyone with power agrees, what could the others do? Especially if talking about history and arguing with the official account is forbidden."

Bartok continued, "A smaller percentage also received neurotransmitters. Maybe you weren't as malleable as they'd hoped, but they didn't want to kill you for some reason. Or maybe they had plans for you and needed finer control of your actions than they believed the chemical brainwashing could provide."

Aria's breath came fast with outrage and belated terror. "So they stuck a wire in my brain? So I could be a puppet?" Her voice cracked.

"I don't think it worked." Evrial gave her a re-assuring smile. "You're stronger than you think."

"So how many more puppets are out there?"

Bartok gave a slight shrug. "I can't be sure. We've found records for about six thousand. Not many students... you're one of the lucky few, one of the top students in one of the best programs. Most of the others seem to be in mid- to high-level government positions, or directly involved in the brainwashing themselves. I imagine they needed doctors and couldn't get enough qualified people to agree to what they wanted. They had to be... conditioned to do so."

Aria saw the bleakness in his expression and sympathy twisted inside her. "I'm sorry," she whispered.

He shrugged again. "It's not your fault." He forced a smile. "The good news is, if we ever figure out where they're transmitting from, turning off the neurostimulators is easy. It's just a matter of stopping the signal. The device can be left inside with no ill effects."

Gabriel murmured, "So everyone got the propaganda and trackers. The people with power or influence were brainwashed. And a few lucky ones got brain wires. What do we do about that?"

Bartok rubbed his hands over his face. "It's not simple, but if it's just giving people a reason not to question authority, we can probably achieve most of what we want by stopping the constant rein-forcement of that message." He gave a wry smile. "Easy, see?"

ARIA EXCUSED HERSELF to visit the restroom. She didn't really need to go, but she needed a few minutes to herself.

She set a lantern on the counter and splashed icy water into her hands, then onto her face. The electric light played across her chin and jaw from beneath, casting deep, eerie shadows over her eyes.

I'm not a puppet.

Am I?

If I'm not now... was I before?

Her hands were shaking, and she rubbed them together fiercely. The shaking didn't stop.

Everything is cold. My hands, my heart, the little fire of hope I'd held inside. Hope that maybe things would be better. Now it only feels like ashes inside me.

Get over yourself, Aria. Stop being melodramatic. Owen and Niall and Gabriel have a lot more to complain about than you do, and they're not crying about it.

She brushed the tears from her eyes with trembling fingers. She forced a smile and examined her expression in the mirror. It looked less artificial than it felt.

I've been underground for days. The signal would be blocked by the ground, so my thoughts are probably my own. Maybe the Fae singing would keep my thoughts free too; it seems like that would help. Bartok said it wasn't fine control, just a push that would make conditioning easier. So if I know to be careful of it, it probably can't have as much effect on me, unless they captured me and reconditioned me, with drugs and everything.

I can't let that happen. I'd rather die.

After long minutes she was ready to face everyone again. Levi had raised the laptop onto a box and everyone had rearranged themselves so they could see it as much as possible. He'd pulled up a video, and his finger hovered over the button to start it.

Gabriel spoke without preamble. "You know more about the Fae now than I do, Aria. We have questions. We need to know what we're dealing with."

She nodded hesitantly. "I don't know much, though."

Levi sat back. The video could wait.

"How strong are they?"

"Owen, I mean Lord Owen, screwed some eyebolts into concrete with his bare hands. The holes weren't pre-drilled or anything... he just forced them in. And they can hear and see much better than we can."

Everyone nodded. "They eat meat, right? Do they eat people?"

Aria smiled. "I asked Lord Owen that and he laughed at me. No, they don't."

"Can they eat other food?"

Aria shrugged. "I don't know."

"Are they aliens?" Jennison asked.

Aria and Gabriel turned to look at him at the same time.

"What? It's a real question! They look like us, but they're *not* like us in pretty important ways," he persisted.

"Um... no. They believe they're an offshoot of early humans," Aria said.

"Then why don't they die when they're shot? Can they be killed at all?"

"Getlaril is poisonous to them. I think they can be beheaded. Maybe other ways... fire, perhaps?"

"How do they heal so fast?"

Aria tried to explain, using Cillian's analogy. "Think of the universe as a bubble. Everything we know, all of science and physical rules like gravity, is all the film of the bubble. They live partly outside the film, so when their bodies are injured, it's like only part of them is hurt. But they live mostly in the bubbles like we do, so even though it's harder to kill them, it's still possible."

Gabriel leaned back. "That makes some sense, but it doesn't explain everything."

Everyone looked a little confused though. *Probably because I'm confused; I can't explain it when I don't understand it myself.*

Bartok spoke suddenly. "Yes. It's a good analogy. Imagine God is inside the bubble, and everything else, NotGod, is outside the bubble. We live in the film of the bubble. We have to choose whether we want to go inside, to God, or outside."

Someone in the back muttered something unintelligible, but Evrial waved at Bartok to go on. At least one person was interested.

"Going inside requires that we have God's nature. If we don't want to discard the part of ourselves that is sinful, we can't go in. We must go out. God doesn't want us to go out; He died so that we could go in. But we have to choose. The choice is ours only because God offers His grace both to pay for our sins now, then overcome our shortcomings that lead us to keep sinning and take us in. Once inside the bubble, our natures are clean and will no longer lead us to sin."

Aria frowned. "But what if we don't want to choose God? What if we just want to be independent? Left alone?"

"You can't. When you die, you either go in the bubble or out of the bubble. Toward God, or not toward God. Not choosing God is choosing Not-God. You always choose."

Levi frowned. "Bartok, this is interesting and all, but I'm really more concerned about our invisible allies. Or whatever they are."

Bartok opened his mouth, then closed it again. He nodded. "Right." He sighed quietly and rubbed his hands over his face. *He's frustrated, and trying not to be. I wonder how many times he's told them about God.*

"Do they steal children? There are all those legends about changelings..." Evrial let her voice trail away. "I always thought that was more horrifying than the other stuff."

"What other stuff?" Aria frowned. "I don't know much about mythology."

Evrial shook her head. "There are a lot of contradictory myths about fairies. But they," she nodded toward the Fae encampment, "don't seem that much like fairies, anyway. There are myths like 'don't eat Fae food or you'll get trapped in fairyland'... you know, stuff like that. 'Never make a bargain with a fairy because you'll forfeit your soul.' Fairies are dangerous, and not only in obvious ways."

There's so much I don't know. "No. Owen said they don't steal human children. But..." her voice trailed away as she remembered his words. *'No human children.' Were Fae children stolen? Yes; Niall is a child by their counting, even if he's older than I am.* "No. And he never said anything about bargains."

He said he owed me a blood debt. Cillian and Niall took it seriously. He never demanded anything from me, though.

Levi asked, "What other kinds of magic creatures are there? How dangerous are they? Griffins? Dragons? Pegasuses or whatever? What are the limits of their magic? How does it work?"

Aria raised both hands helplessly. "I don't know! And it's pegasi." She fidgeted with the hem of her shirt, not looking up at them. "I met Petro, sort of. He's... he might be a dragon." Her voice trailed away at their astonished, skeptical expressions. "He looked mostly human, but he's not. Cillian said that he's far older than anything else and he doesn't interact with time the way we do. Or the Fae, for that matter. He manipulated time somehow when we rescued Owen... he changed the building, I think. Or something. I'm not sure we can understand what he did. The Fae are terrified of him. He interacts with them differently than he does with me; when I met him, he had one appearance and at the same time, he showed Cillian and Niall a different appearance. He was Owen to them; Cillian said even the taste of his blood was like Owen's. And no, he didn't taste Petro's blood... maybe he meant he could smell it, or they can taste from a distance. I don't understand everything they say.

"Petro is dangerous. The Fae think he's interacted with humans before in the form of a dragon, and in other forms too. Or it might be something else like Petro. They aren't sure. He might be able to be on Earth, physically I mean, in more than one place at the same time. Or maybe it's other creatures like Petro."

Bartok gave Gabriel a long look. "I have a guess about what he is. Why did he change the building?"

Aria explained what Petro had said about how his telling her where Owen was may have been interpreted as an offer of help, and how the Fae thought he'd been terrified of some unforeseen result of that action. How Petro did not care if they died, but had acted to save them anyway, for reasons of his own.

Bartok nodded, his gaze distant.

"But he looked human?" Evrial asked.

"Yes. Except for when he didn't. He looked like... a dragon... for a split second, like an after-image when you look at a really bright light. He looked like a really dangerous, beautiful woman, too, and like Owen, and then like just a young man. Then later when he came again, he looked like a huge metallic statue, like a living sculpture out of bronze. Beautiful, but definitely not human."

Evrial raised her eyebrows but didn't say anything.

Aria shrugged. "That's all I know. You know as much as I do. Maybe more." She glanced up to see Niamh approaching.

Gabriel followed her glance, then looked back at the group. *He didn't see her.*

He frowned. "Their magic is lessened over distance but they can still do some things. I think Lord Owen is the only one with more than a passing familiarity with human technology though. He's been running interference for them for years. When I met him four years ago, he said most of the others didn't speak English at all. They may speak other languages, but they haven't been around humans much."

Levi scowled. "Except for captivity, then. No wonder they're a bit hostile."

Gabriel gave a faint nod. "Yes." He brushed his hand over the pistol on his hip as if to reassure himself it was there.

Levi watched him with a knowing look. "So they're dangerous, then."

Gabriel glanced over his shoulder toward the Fae encampment and licked his lips. "They could be. But they'll do what Lord Owen says. He's friendly enough." He turned back toward Aria without noticing Niamh, who now stood only ten feet away.

Should I pretend I don't see her? If I do, I'm deliberately misleading Gabriel and the others. Do I want to do that? Aria caught Niamh's eye and smiled tentatively. "Come on. Maybe you can help us."

Niamh froze, her eyes wide and locked onto Aria's face. She glanced behind herself, and then back to Aria.

Aria nodded. *Yes, you. Who do you think I'm talking to?* She tried to keep her smile friendly, although nervous tension twisted inside her. *Should we not be asking these questions? But how are we to know if they don't tell us? And if we're going to be allies, we need to know what they are.*

Niamh's eyes widened even more and for a moment she did not even breathe. Then she slipped backward, away from the lights and human voices.

Gabriel gave her a curious look.

"Who are you talking to?" Evrial asked.

Aria opened her mouth, then closed it again and shook her head. From the corner of her eye, she saw Bartok study the darkness. His gaze slid past Niamh without a hesitation. *He still didn't see her, and he knew she was there.* He knew that she'd decided to let the Fae know she could see them, but she hadn't made it obvious to the humans yet, so he didn't either.

Niamh hurried back toward the circle of Fae gathered around Owen, glancing over her shoulder every few steps. She seemed thoroughly unnerved by Aria's curious gaze.

I'm not that scary.

Aria blinked the thought away and watched as Niamh knelt to speak to Cillian, who turned to stare at Aria. She raised one hand in a brief wave, making eye contact across the distance. Cillian twitched, eyes widening. After a few words, Niamh took his place beside Owen while Cillian stood, striding silently toward them. By the time he arrived, every Fae around Owen was watching, tense and silent.

No one else noticed his approach.

Jonah pressed the button and the video began to play.

From just behind Levi's shoulder, Cillian asked, "What are you watching?"

Levi jerked in surprise. "Don't creep up on people like that!"

Cillian blinked at him. "My apologies. I did not mean to frighten you." He glanced at Aria, and she imagined she saw wariness in his eyes.

But not of me. There's no reason to be afraid of me. She sighed and focused on the laptop as Gabriel explained to Cillian how Owen had acquired the video and other materials.

The video was clear and well-lit. A man sat shackled to a metal chair bolted to the floor in a bare concrete cell. Aria leaned closer, studying his face. His eyes were fixed on something just out of view of the camera. His face was angular and handsome, with a strong, straight jaw and sensitive lips. He was bare chested and wore only a pair of worn trousers belted around his lean waist.

"Is he Fae?" Gabriel asked.

"Yes," Cillian said.

"How can you tell?"

"His name is Feichin. He's a cousin."

Feichin's eyes followed movement, and a man stepped into the field of view, his back to the camera. His hair was sprinkled with grey, and he wore a white lab coat that stretched tight across his broad shoulders.

"Wait, why can I see him?" Jonah asked as he paused the video. "We can't always see you."

Cillian's cold gaze shot to Aria for an instant.

"Does video work differently?"

Cillian growled, "He's bound with getlaril."

Jonah nodded and started the video again. The man wearing the lab coat took another step forward.

Aria twitched as she realized the recording had sound after all. Until now, Feichin had been silent, and the scientist had stepped into the video without speaking.

"What do you use the blood for?" Feichin asked.

"Does it matter?" The scientist wrapped a wide rubber strap around the Fae's hard bicep and prodded at a vein on the inside of his elbow.

"It might. What do you use it for?" Feichin's voice was cold, and Aria could hear his restrained anger. He didn't flinch when the scientist inserted a large needle into his vein and drew a vial of blood.

The scientist didn't answer immediately. He stepped away and squinted at the vial, then set it on a tray and picked up a clipboard. He picked up a wand and pointed it toward Feichin.

"What are you doing?"

"Measuring your body temperature and pulse. Why does it matter what we use the blood for?" The scientist turned toward the camera and Aria finally read the name tag sewn on his jacket. Davis.

"If it is a justifiable use, I might give it without need of restraints. They chafe." He jerked one arm, and Davis jumped.

He peered at Feichin's arm from a safe distance. "I have been told your kind are dangerous. I bear you no ill will, but I have not been given authority to remove the shackles. I do not have access to the keys." He kept his eyes on Feichin's wrist. Aria couldn't see anything amiss, but Davis seemed more nervous.

"You have keys in your right jacket pocket and in your trouser pockets."

"They are for my apartment and my car."

Feichin tilted his head. "All of them? I count eleven keys on three rings."

Davis took a slight step backward. "Also my desk drawers, my wife's car, and my wife's mother's apartment. And our mailbox."

"Are you afraid of me?" Feichin's voice was low.

"A little." Davis put his clipboard to his knee and wrote something. "Do you wish to harm me?"

Feichin's nostrils flared. "Not at this time. But I do not appreciate being lied to."

Davis looked up at him. After a long moment, he said, "They are studying your blood for disease resistance. If certain tests work, human lives might be saved. But the tests take time and must be repeated many times, to ensure safety and efficacy."

Feichin held his eyes. "For such a purpose you might gain more cooperation if you asked with respect and consideration. If you remove my bonds, I will not harm you."

Davis shook his head. "I'm sorry, I don't have the authority to do that. I'm a lab tech. I only take the blood. I don't set the parameters."

Feichin's nostrils flared, but he said nothing else. His eyes followed Davis as he wrote again on the clipboard, picked up the tray with the vial of blood and rubber strap, and stepped out of the room. This time Aria noticed the quiet click of the door locking.

The camera remained on for some minutes. Feichin stared toward the unseen door for several minutes, then looked straight up toward the camera. The video continued for long seconds, and Feichin's piercing gaze remained steady, bright cold eyes locked on the camera until the screen darkened.

Cillian shifted beside her and let out a soft breath. "He is close. How old is that recording?"

Jonah clicked and the video flipped away, replaced by a spreadsheet. "It was taken about two months ago. There are more recent ones. The subjects are noted by number rather than name; it looks like these three recordings are also of him."

"I advise you not to watch. I will watch and tell you if anything important happens."

Gabriel frowned. "Why not?"

Cillian drew back and seemed to consider his words. "Sometimes when a Fae becomes... angry, it goes beyond righteous anger. You will not wish to see."

"What did you mean when you said 'he is close'?" Aria asked.

"He was... close to choosing rebellion. I hope he did not. But... when the video was taken, he was close."

Gabriel shifted and stared hard at him. "Choosing rebellion? Rebellion against what?"

Cillian stood with quick grace. "I must speak with Lord Owen before answering more of your questions. These are matters for Fae, not humans. You should not wonder that we disappeared from your knowledge for generations. Human prying into the rules that govern our lives has only resulted in pain for Fae. I do not wish to increase it." He disappeared into the darkness before anyone could reply.

Well, he seems to have been distracted from the revelation that I can see them. At least for now.

Gabriel stared after him, then turned to Jonah. "Start the next video."

Jonah nodded, found the video, and began.

Feichin sat in the same chair. His head drooped forward, shoulders slack. He was muscular, but thin; in his stillness, the hollows under his cheekbones and the sharp line of his collarbone caught at her pity.

"When was this one taken?"

"Eight days later."

A click came, and Feichin's head jerked up, eyes on the door. His hands tensed against the restraints and then relaxed with obvious effort. He took a few labored breaths. Davis stepped into view again.

"How do you feel today?"

Feichin didn't answer for a long moment, his eyes following Davis as he moved across the room to set up the folding tray table that held his box of syringes. "I'm hungry," he said finally. "But you should know that."

"Yes, I imagine so."

"Why won't you feed me?"

"They want to see what your blood does. In humans, triglycerides and electrolyte balances change as fasting progresses. I understand that you feel weak, but you should not suffer too much."

"Should not? So you mean to kill me by starvation?" Feichin straightened with a subtle movement.

Davis didn't notice, or didn't fear him. "I don't know what they intend. But in humans, with acute fasting, hunger is moderate for a day or two, extreme for several days, and then disappears or greatly decreases until food is reintroduced. Even allowing for a much slower metabolism, your discomfort should be already gone or should disappear soon."

Feichin's nostrils flared. "That is not what I experience. Do they, or you, not care that your actions are cruel?"

Davis stepped forward to wrap a rubber strap around Feichin's arm and drew a vial of blood. Only Feichin's eyes moved, following the vial as Davis set it on the tray and replaced it with an empty one.

Davis didn't answer, and Feichin's voice lowered. "Are you treating my daughter with such consideration?"

Davis froze, the plastic vial half-way to the tray. "I'm not aware of what they are doing with her," he said finally.

Feichin growled, "You lie, human! You lie again and again. I smell her on your coat! She is afraid."

Only the top of Davis' grey-sprinkled head was visible as he stepped closer to the camera. "I'm sorry. I'm not allowed to say anything else. But I don't believe she has been harmed."

Feichin's chest rose and fell and his hands clenched. He stared coldly at Davis, who remained mostly out of the video, which stopped in a moment.

Without a word, Jonah found the next video and began. As it started, he murmured, "This one is quite long. It begins five days after the last one."

Feichin sat in the same chair, head bowed forward. He might have been asleep, or unconscious. Dampness darkened his trousers in his seat and on the bottom of his thighs, and Aria realized he'd soiled himself. The harsh lights never varied.

After a moment, Jonah skipped the video forward. Nothing had changed. Again. Nothing had changed. Again, then back a few seconds to watch Feichin raise his head and stare at the door. He let it fall forward again. *They're starving him. How long*

69

will it take him to die? Aria felt a rush of anger at the scientist.

Jonah skipped the video forward again. Feichin sat in the same position, head drooping, hands slack. Skipped forward. And again. "The video has been on about four days now."

Feichin's head jerked upward just as a column of water shot across the room to hit him in the chest. He turned his head away and closed his eyes, enduring the hose spray without a sound. The deluge of water stopped abruptly, and Feichin kept his head down, water dripping from his black curls and dribbling down his arms. His eyes were closed, breaths quick and labored, shoulders tense. The water disappeared down a drain just behind Feichin's chair, leaving the floor and walls dark and damp.

Davis stepped into view, his face visible as he closed the door behind himself. He braced a clipboard against his stomach. "How do you feel today?"

Feichin spoke without raising his head or opening his eyes. "I don't think you wish to know how I feel. I would prefer not to explore the depths of my feelings for this experience." His voice had dropped even lower, barely audible.

"It is for the sake of science. I apologize for any discomfort you may be suffering." Davis' voice had regained the clinical detachment he'd lost in their previous meeting.

Feichin raised his head, his expression visible now. He leaned forward a little, his lean face cold and hard. "Do you? Will you release me, then? I wish to find my daughter."

"I can't release you." Davis flicked a hand dismissively, and Feichin stiffened. "The experiment is ongoing."

Feichin's chest heaved. "You... you humans play with pain as if it is a game! You do not have the right. What you do is evil, and you do it deliberately. You lie and you torture and you feel no guilt. What is that but evil?" He jerked at one of the hand restraints.

Davis wrote something on the clipboard, and Feichin jerked ferociously on the hand restraint again. He snarled and yanked again, and a spray of red arced across the room to spatter Davis' white jacket. Again, and Feichin had his right hand free.

Aria and the others watched in horror as Feichin grasped his left fist with his mangled right hand and jerked them both upward together, once, twice, and again. His lean body wrenched, muscles writhing with effort, and the third time the metal shackle broke free. Davis lunged for the door, but Feichin was faster. He launched himself forward to catch Davis by one arm, spun him around, and pinned him to the ground. Feichin, still bound to the chair by his ankles, was awkwardly positioned, but now his power was evident. Three inches shorter and perhaps eighty pounds lighter than Davis, Feichin held him down with his left arm across Davis' throat. His right hand smeared bright blood across Davis' jacket as he caught the scientist's flailing wrist and forced it to the floor.

He bent to speak into Davis' face. "I kill you not because of what you have done to me. Not because of the blood you want. Not because you wish to help your people. But because you are evil.

71

And you deserve it." He buried his teeth in Davis' neck, and the man's terrified shriek was abruptly cut short.

Aria stood abruptly, unable to watch the rest. She stumbled away to vomit over the side of the platform into the darkness of the train tracks. Over and over she retched, tears streaming down her face.

Someone caught her as she fell to her knees, sobbing, empty stomach heaving.

THEY WATCHED THE rest of the video without her. She couldn't bear it, not yet.

Bartok's quiet presence finally came to her attention. He sat beside her, legs crossed and elbows on his knees. She bent forward, head buried in her hands, and shuddered again.

He said quietly, "You don't need to watch the rest."

"Is it worse?"

He shrugged slightly. "He doesn't kill anyone else. But it's... not easy watching." He glanced at her sideways and looked like he might say something else, but then looked back at the concrete floor.

Aria took an unsteady breath and let it out slowly, trying not to imagine... anything. *Don't picture it.*

Bartok said quietly, "The Empire thinks he's a vampire. Actually, the Empire doesn't seem to distinguish between the Fae and vampires at all."

"Owen told me he wasn't a vampire. Owen wasn't, I mean. He wouldn't lie. At least not about something like that..." Her voice trailed away.

"I believe you. And him. But I'm not sure what they are. Any of them." Bartok sighed heavily. "None of my studies acknowledged their existence. We only began hearing of them a few weeks before I... left the practice and joined the resistance. The rumors were hardly informative." He offered her a canteen.

She took a swig, swished the water in her mouth, and spat it over the edge of the platform. Another rinse, and then a drink. Her mouth tasted sour, and her stomach churned. "I should probably watch the rest."

He frowned, but followed without comment. The others had left, and he skipped the video backward to the correct place.

Feichin lay across Davis' body, sucking hungrily at the blood that flowed from the man's mangled neck. The quiet squelching sound made bile rise in Aria's throat. Feichin's ankles were still bound, and he half-rose to pull the body closer, then knelt in a more comfortable position, lean shoulders bowed for another minute. He held his own mutilated hand away from his body, no longer touching Davis, and Bartok paused the video and zoomed in.

He grimaced slightly, and Aria felt her stomach turning again. From the way Feichin held his arm, it was obvious the wound hurt. The thumb was nearly detached, blood streaming down his wrist and dripping from his elbow.

Bartok moved the still image slightly. "He pulled it through the shackle; he couldn't get that one to come open. It took both hands to pop the bolts on the second one."

Feichin's left wrist was darkening with bruises, with a cut from the edge of the metal, but he ignored the wounds in favor of drinking.

At last he raised his head, mouth covered in blood. He studied the door for a moment, then looked back down at Davis. He rose, a little clumsily, and cradled his right hand in his left. The blood flow slowed, and then stopped. He swayed, steadied himself. He looked up at the camera again, the cold, angry, exhausted look of an animal brought to bay.

He knelt again, pushed Davis' body to the extent of his reach behind the door, blood smearing in bright red streaks across the wet floor. He sat back down in the chair and leaned over to grasp the shackle on his right ankle with both hands, took a deep breath, and jerked on it ferociously. Again, and again, twisting, wrenching, jerking with all his might. It came off on the fourth yank, and a clink told her that one of the bolts had flown across the room. He dropped the shackle and put the foot on the floor, twisting to attack the last restraint from a different angle. Muscles stood out beneath his paper-thin skin, white and hard as marble. He dropped that shackle on the floor, and stood.

Despite his strength and power, he swayed again and shook his head as if he was fighting dizziness. He went to the door, just out of the range of the camera, and they heard metallic crashes and clangs. Apparently the door wouldn't open. Feichin paced around the room, stopped to stare at Davis, then paced again. Restless and angry, he reminded Aria of a hungry wolf, or a big cat that hadn't been fed in too long. Feichin knelt beside

Davis again and searched all his pockets, coming up with several key chains. Back to the door.

Back into sight. He threw the keys savagely at the wall and stood in the center of the room beside the chair, chest moving quickly as he took angry, silent breaths. Back to Davis' body, which he searched more thoroughly. He read the notes from the clipboard and tossed it carelessly onto the floor again, right hand smearing it with blood. He raised the mangled limb and licked the blood from his own arm, starting as close to the elbow as he could reach and moving all the way to his reddened fingers and the dangling thumb. His mouth was still smeared with Davis' blood, and Aria put a hand over her own mouth as she stared at him. The lean, handsome face, so beautiful and so horrible, suddenly turned toward the camera.

Feichin smiled, a mirthless, terrible smile, bright eyes clear and cold. "I guess your experiment succeeded, Grenidor. I hope you're pleased."

Aria caught her breath. *What does that mean? What has he done?*

The video continued. Feichin strode around the room again, then knelt to drink from Davis a third time. He wiped his mouth and stared at the blood. He rose to resume pacing, not looking at the camera. Out of sight at the door, he pulled and yanked again, then threw himself against it with thunderous crashes.

Feichin staggered back into view. He sank to his knees near Davis' body and rocked, holding his injured hand and moaning softly, then bent to bang his forehead against the floor with stunning force. Once, then again, and he slumped to the side, face pressed awkwardly into the concrete.

The video continued, but Feichin simply lay there, an ugly knot rising above his left eye.

"Isn't anyone going to search for Davis?" she asked.

"Keep watching," Bartok replied.

Minutes passed. Feichin moaned softly once, but didn't wake for several minutes. The door opened, and he jolted awake, scrambling to his feet with uncharacteristic clumsiness. Suddenly his body jerked and twitched, and he fell back against the far wall, shot in a dozen places, the sound shocking Aria with its roar. The effect was devastating. Feichin's body lay crumpled sideways against the wall, blood streaming from his chest, one leg, stomach, and even his face. One shot had hit him just beside the nose, and the left side of his face was torn away.

Aria heaved again, unable even to rise before her stomach got the best of her. Nothing came up, and Bartok paused the video while she retched. He put one gentle hand on her shoulder, and she slapped it away, suddenly furious at him for showing her the horror. Just as quickly, her eyes filled with tears. It was hardly his fault.

"I'm sorry," she gulped, unwilling to look up at him, but she heard his soft grunt of acceptance.

"He doesn't die. I don't think they can be killed by ordinary means."

The video began again. Six men entered the room, crowding it with their body armor over broad shoulders and automatic guns. They checked Feichin quickly, then two turned their attention to Davis, while the other four kept their weapons trained on Feichin. Davis was hauled out into the hallway.

The two that handled Davis returned to grab Feichin by the wrists and ankles. They slung him up and out into the hallway too, and the video stopped.

"There's another one. It starts up almost immediately after." Bartok flipped the window away and began the next video.

The soldiers carried Feichin's limp, broken body into a larger room with a cell or a cage against one wall. The bars were of a thick metal mesh, reinforced by solid bars closely spaced. Although the cage was against the wall, that wall too had mesh and bars, as if the concrete alone was not secure enough. The floor and roof were composed of solid metal of the same type, presumably getlaril. It was difficult to see into the cage, though the camera was positioned to capture as much as possible. The soldiers dropped Feichin onto the floor into the middle of the cage floor and stepped out, closing the door and locking it with a key the leader carried.

Bartok skipped the video ahead at intervals as Feichin did not move. They tried to zoom in to see whether he was healing, but with the mesh and bars, they couldn't tell much. At long last, they saw Feichin's foot move slightly. They watched, but he didn't move.

"How long has it been?" Aria asked.

Bartok pulled up the video statistics. "About four days from when he killed Davis." He skipped ahead again, and this time Feichin was sitting, bony shoulders slumped. "This is maybe another day later."

Another man finally entered, and Aria twitched as she recognized Colonel Grenidor.

"You killed Brent Davis." Grenidor's anger and grief were obvious.

Feichin did not answer.

"Do you feel regret?"

Silence.

"With your teeth! Like the monster you are." Grenidor paced across the room and then back, standing close to the mesh to peer inside. "I knew your kind were dangerous, but I didn't realize how strong you were. I had to inform his wife of his death, you know. Tell her it was my fault, because you weren't adequately restrained. She deserved to know that."

A low growl came from within the cage, then faded.

Grenidor pointed a wand at Feichin and clicked a button, then recorded something on his tablet. "Did you enjoy it?"

"Yes." The word was another low growl. "But I'd enjoy killing you more. He was only a tool, wasn't he?"

"He was a scientist. He did good work." Grenidor paced away. He put his tablet down on the table and walked back and forth, then slammed his hand savagely into the metal bars of Feichin's cage. "When this experiment is over, I will enjoy killing you, Feichin. As one would put down a rabid dog, I will rid the world of one more of your kind."

Feichin shifted slightly, turning his face away. Aria couldn't read his expression through the mesh.

Grenidor pulled the chair from the table and moved it closer to the cage, where he sat and stared at Feichin in silence. The Fae did not move for some moments. At last, he pushed himself to one knee, then staggered to his feet. He took a step closer to the mesh and swayed, barely remaining upright. He stared at Grenidor for several long minutes, saying nothing, only watching with dulled eyes as Grenidor glanced up at him and then back toward his tablet.

"What do you do with the blood?" he asked finally.

"It is none of your concern." Grenidor's voice was filled with contempt.

"Is it not? It is my blood!" Feichin's voice rose, shaking with anger and pain.

"You said you were Fae, not vampire. I have proven there is no difference. Your behavior and blood have validated my hypothesis. But I'm not happy about it. It only proves the danger to the Empire is greater than previously acknowledged. There are too many of you, and the number is growing. We have much work to do."

Feichin stepped forward, his hands raising toward the mesh.

"Don't touch it," Grenidor warned.

Feichin stopped, hands still raised. His head twitched to the side, as if listening to a distant sound, then he shuddered and said softly, "You know not what you do. Nor what you risk. I have already paid a price worse than death. If you are a merciful man, which I know you are not, you will let the others go. Or you will reap more violence than you can contain."

Grenidor rose in quick anger. "You dare threaten me?"

Feichin placed his hands against the metal mesh separating them. A brilliant flash whitened the screen as a boom sounded through the small speakers. When the figures were distinguishable again, Grenidor stood in the same place, hands over his ears, peering into the cage.

Feichin's gaunt, white figure lay face down in the center of the cage, motionless. Dark dots and blood smears on his back showed where he'd been shot. His dark curls, dried and previously limp after days in the cage, now stood out around his head like a large, dark mop of dandelion fuzz. A few seconds later, Aria heard a low groan and Feichin curled onto his side, hands cupped over his ears. He dug his fingers into his scalp, moaning softly.

"I told you not to touch it. We're going to see if your kind can be trained. I don't need you for long, but the short time you have left will be less unpleasant if you do as I say." Grenidor stopped and watched, his hands clenched into fists by his side.

Feichin quieted, but he did not shift positions or answer.

CHAPTER 4

COLONEL PAUL GRENIDOR leaned back in his chair and rubbed his hands over his face. He had gone over the security videos twice, but it still wasn't entirely clear what had happened. The videos showed no figures entering the facility at all and did not appear to have been tampered with. The front door had logged an entry at 9:03 PM, but the video feed had blinked out for a period of three seconds and had not recorded who, or what, had entered. The glitch remained unexplained. The front door opening had not triggered an alarm, though it should have, since an after-hours entry should have been followed by the security code at the guard desk within thirty seconds. That also had been unexplained.

Internal surveillance video showed no intruders until the camera running in the interrogation room had caught the confrontation over Owen. He clicked back and watched that one again.

The camera was positioned over the door, intended to capture what happened in the room rather than function as a security camera. The footage caught the top edge of the door as it opened and the vampire's dark hair in a blur as the creature lunged forward and attacked Grenidor. He raised a hand to his bruised throat absently as he slowed the video. The speed was startling, though he'd seen it before. Vampires were faster than humans, even when wounded or ill, and considerably stronger. This one had thrown him ten feet across the room with one arm, so hard his feet had been several inches from the floor when he slammed into the wall. He'd been lucky to escape with only a concussion. It might have killed him easily. It had wanted to.

The one who called himself Owen had let him live, and that puzzled him. He didn't trust Owen; he knew too much about their species for that. But what had Owen hoped to gain?

He watched himself crouch against the left wall, gasping, and grimaced. He looked frightened in the video, and wished he'd made a bolder stand. But what could one do, when faced with a monster? He was lucky to be alive.

He looked closer. Aria Forsyth and the one who called himself Cillian, Owen's brother. That was surprising too; Cillian had been unable to walk only two days before, and now he was strong. Not at his full strength, most likely, but dangerously strong. The data on their healing capabilities was still sadly incomplete. They dragged Owen out of view.

Grenidor switched to another video, this one from the lobby cameras. Aria and Cillian hauled Owen's limp body through the lobby, through the wide metal detector, and out the front door. This time the camera caught it all. Three guards sprinted into the lobby some seconds later, then inexplicably continued up a side stairwell at top speed. Several minutes later, one of the same guards sauntered back into the lobby, fiddled with the door, stepped behind the guard desk, and began pushing buttons. The lights stopped flashing. He picked up the phone and began gesturing as he talked, turning his back to the door as he paced within the short confines of the u-shaped desk. *Just an electronic glitch, sir. No, sir, we don't know what happened. Yes, sir, I'll write up a report.*

Grenidor wasn't due for another painkiller for hours, and his head throbbed. A knock on the door made him wince. "Yes?"

Private Turnata stepped inside. "Sir, the team has returned and will make their report, if you're ready."

"Yes, thank you." Grenidor stood, one hand on the desk to steady himself. The throbbing increased, and he took a deep breath. "I'll be there in a minute. Go ahead."

"Yes, sir." Turnata turned on his heel and strode off down the hall.

Grenidor picked up his clipboard and scowled. Forsyth had stolen his notes on Owen's interrogation. He'd have to rewrite as much as he could remember after the team made their report. He gathered up paper and pens, his electronic tablet, and followed Turnata.

The team was still taking off their armor when he arrived, but they stopped to salute him.

Captain Osborne motioned him to a seat. "Sir. Unfortunately, I don't have much success to report. We followed the trail to a sewer entrance about two blocks from the front gate. The cover was closed, but we assume they entered there and continued. The trail disappeared. There are many tunnels and intersections. We explored them all to at least two hundred meters and found no sign that anyone had passed, either human or otherwise. We left monitors, and we can continue the search, but the trail is lost. We're starting from scratch."

Grenidor rubbed one hand over the bandage on his head. "You found nothing? Not even from Forsyth?"

"A few drops of blood on the street before they entered the tunnels. Nothing underground." Captain Osborne shook his head. "To fully explore the tunnels, we'd need dozens, perhaps hundreds of men. The network is extensive, and if you want us to engage, we need manpower."

"Understood." Grenidor leaned back and sighed. "Did you see them, or just the trail?"

"Just the trail, sir."

"Which was…?"

"Forsyth left two footprints. Six drops of blood on the ground as well as a smear on the edge of the tunnel cover. All the vampire's. It doesn't conclusively prove they entered, but it's a reasonable assumption. Nothing inside the tunnels at all, nor in the surrounding streets. It could be misdirection, though; you know how hard they are to find."

"Anyone injured?"

"No, sir."

The harsh light of the team readiness room made Grenidor's pounding headache worse, and the nausea was rising again. "Write up a complete report, including which tunnels you explored and how deeply. Get the team ready; we'll search again tomorrow."

"Yes, sir."

Grenidor pushed himself to his feet and returned the captain's salute. He walked back to his office, careful to keep his shoulders back and his head high. The doctor had wanted to keep him overnight for observation; he'd insisted he was fine. He had work to do. The light in his office wasn't much better, and he closed his eyes, typing by touch. At least he could get the main points out and fill in the details tomorrow. Or later today, since it was just after midnight.

The vampires and Aria were probably long gone. Grenidor reconsidered his decision to keep the team waiting for him. If they were still close by, he should have had them continue searching. If they pushed hard enough, the vampires might make a mistake, be a little too slow. It was more likely, though, that he'd made the right decision. To search the spreading tunnels would split the men into smaller and smaller groups, and any confrontation would see them likely outnumbered, in the dark, on the vampires' home ground. Any one vampire could take on a team of men; finding a dozen of them in the dark confines of the tunnels was the stuff of nightmares.

He'd send the team into the tunnels tomorrow, with a dozen more teams of fresh men, enough for a fight if they could find the creatures. He'd follow with the forensic team, searching for clues that the soldiers would have missed.

It was another hour before he sighed and leaned forward. There was more, but those thoughts weren't to be entrusted to the electronic system yet. That made them permanent, part of the scientific record accessible by the scientific personnel. He typed a few more questions the team could pursue.

Compare Owen's blood to Feichin's. How close is the genetic connection?

Review the psychotropic drugs that have been tested on vampires. Is the spectrum of reactions comparable to human pathology?

Can their claims of long life be substantiated?

Need a complete graph of the clans as currently understood. Can we access any data from outside the Empire? We need more cultural data; behavioral variations cannot be explained by biological differences.

Increase security at remaining test sites. Add advanced detectors at all entry points. Guards should be armed with getlaril. Vertril are authorized where practical.

He pushed his hands against his closed eyelids, but the insistent throbbing would not lessen. He retched into his trashcan. Not much came up; it had been hours since dinner at the canteen. The attempt only made the pounding worse, and he rested his head on his desk, eyes closed.

He groped for the phone. "Ward, if I don't call you in an hour, send a medic to my office."

"Are you all right, sir?"

"Probably. I'll let you know in an hour." He heard the slur in his own voice and enunciated more clearly. "Yes. I'm fine. I'll call you." He fumbled the phone as he hung it up, cursed, and finally got it into the cradle. Forehead to his desk, he wrapped his arms around his head, the stiff uniform pulling at his shoulders. *Why didn't Owen let Cillian kill me? It doesn't make sense. What does Owen want more than revenge?*

He thought again of his notes. *He said it was impossible. But can I believe that?*

After the intrusion at H Street, it was clear that current security measures were inadequate. Without getlaril and the magically enhanced sensors, it was nearly impossible to oppose the vampires. Time was not on their side.

Where did those sensors come from? I never got a good report. I should probably know how they work.

A knock sounded on the door and Grenidor groaned. "What is it?"

"Ward said you were supposed to call him, sir." The medic clicked his heels together with a crispness that Grenidor found irritating at this desolate hour of the morning. "It's been over an hour. Let me take you to the clinic, sir." He stepped closer.

"Fine." Grenidor struggled to his feet and retched again, the medic supporting his arm with reassuring sturdiness. "We'll make it snappy though. I need to be back by seven." His breath rasped in his bruised throat.

"Yes, sir."

Grenidor knew the response was only a quick acknowledgment of his words, humoring him, but he couldn't muster a scowl.

AFTER MUCH ARGUING, Grenidor managed to check himself out of the infirmary by eight thirty the next morning. It was late, but he wanted the team to wait for him before continuing the search. The trail was cold anyway.

Osborne drove him to the Mayfair Hotel on Fenwick Avenue. It had been cordoned off with yellow and red tape blocking curious passersby from investigating. If the tape wasn't enough, Imperial Police Force personnel stood at each corner, looking appropriately official and stern. *Though no one is as curious as they would have been, back before...* Grenidor cut off the thought. He believed in the Revolution. *Every choice has consequences.* Yet even to his eyes, the few people who glanced toward the hotel looked a little vacuous, as if they had forgotten how to be curious. *Sheep. They're sheep. But they must be protected. Some of us are sheep, and some are sheepdogs. And some are wolves. We must protect the stupid from the dangerous. Even if it means keeping the stupid in the dark. They don't want to know what prowls the streets at night.*

The glass doors reflected his image back at him, and he hesitated, caught by his own haggard expression. *Two nights with no sleep will do that. I'm getting old.*

"Something wrong, sir?" Osborne asked. Just behind him, the young captain was broad-shouldered and robust, M-17 slung across his back and pistol in hand.

"No." Grenidor pulled the door open and stepped inside, then paused, studying the lobby. "You searched it thoroughly?"

"Yes, sir. This lobby area appears to have been mostly unused. We believe they used the underground theater and some of the surrounding rooms while leaving the aboveground floors untouched. Most likely to avoid notice."

Grenidor turned in a slow circle, his eyes taking in everything. There was an air of stillness, of desolation, that brought a pang of sadness. A hotel like this should have been a warm and inviting place, with a fire burning in the cold hearth. He looked back toward the door.

"Did you see this?" He pointed to a chip in the concrete.

"Yes, sir. Looks like a bullet mark. It's consistent with standard issue FMJ with steel penetrator core ammunition. But it's difficult to judge when it was made. Could have been anytime in the past twenty years. Plus, it could have been something else. There wasn't a firefight; we haven't found any other marks."

"I doubt it. Carry on."

Osborne led him through the lobby to a door on the far wall near the reception desk. He stopped and pointed to a balcony on the left wall, where a team of men was examining the railing. "We think they had a sentry posted up there. Fingerprints on the railing are pretty dense, lots of layers. We've identified eighteen different people so far. We may get a few more."

"Anyone important?"

Osborne frowned and spoke into a microphone on his lapel. "Taylor, send Colonel Grenidor a list of the fingerprint IDs."

Grenidor nodded and Osborne opened the door. "Back through here, sir, we have a number of hallways. We've done an initial exploration and are gathering additional data now. Fingerprints, magic residue, that sort of thing. The main area is through here. It looks like it was once a theater." He pushed through another door and held it open. "They probably camped here, with a few in the rooms down that hall."

A young lieutenant jogged up and saluted. "Sir, a report was just sent to your tablet with our initial findings. Do you want a summary now, sir?"

Grenidor pulled out his tablet and tapped the screen. He skimmed the first page. "Who wrote this?"

"Captain Parker and I did, sir."

Grenidor glanced up at him. "Give me the quick version."

"Sir, evidence suggests this encampment was cleaned with the aid of magic. There's very little residue; the scanners are coming up mostly clean. We didn't know they could conceal the use of magic, so that is a point of concern. Or maybe we're just not sensing it correctly. The scanners are still new technology, after all. But the main areas—"

Grenidor interrupted him. "Why do you think it was cleaned, or a sensor problem, rather than nothing to find in the first place?"

"The main areas, where they would likely have spent most of their time, are fairly clean and innocuous. Nothing we could identify or pin to a particular rebel, nor even date accurately. But whoever did the cleaning didn't reach the furthest extents. The sentry post up on the balcony was left untouched, as far as we can tell. They're working on the fingerprints now. It seems unlikely that all the fingerprints, footprints, disturbed dust, and magic use were in the outlying spaces while the central area was unused. The evidence in the out lying areas is because they missed some stuff. They probably left in a hurry."

Grenidor nodded and motioned for him to continue.

"Because of the magic used, we can't get an accurate count of the resistance forces. We can assume vampires are involved, of course, and probably more than a few of them, given the magic required. We also found a room up on the main floor that may have been used as an office for the leader. They left a few scrap papers, pencils, that sort of thing. Nothing especially important, but it's interesting that it wasn't cleaned as the others were. Either they didn't know about it, or they left it for us to find. Which means what little information we get from it may be a trap."

Grenidor sighed. "All right. What information have you gotten so far?"

"If it was the leader, this cell is led by former Colonel Gabriel Peterson. He was a distinguished—"

"Yes, I know him," Grenidor said sharply. He looked back down at the tablet and flicked forward in the report. *Former Colonel Peterson has been at large since the uprising at Takoma Park. It is unknown what his motivation was in joining the resistance; prior to his defection he gave no signs of disloyalty and no grievances are on record. His distinguished career may have given him credibility with resistance fighters. It is believed that his son Michael Peterson, age sixteen, may have been killed early last year. The circumstances are unknown. Peterson's previous assignments have given him experience in guerrilla warfare and, if he chooses to prolong the fight, he could prove to be a difficult enemy to extinguish.*

Grenidor frowned. His head was still pounding. "I'll read the rest. Continue with the search."

A 9mm cartridge, blood smears, and a bloody hand towel were found in the office thought to be used by Peterson. The blood was tested and found to be vampire, but positive identification has not been completed yet. Peterson may be dead or injured. Can vampires turn humans into vampires?

Grenidor frowned more fiercely. This theory had come up many times, and had neither been proven nor disproven. Vampires were rare enough that experiment subjects were difficult to come by. However, that was also changing. Their numbers were growing.

They were dangerous, difficult to control, terrifyingly strong, and unpredictable. And despite the unconventional methods of managing the populace the Empire had already used, Grenidor was not ready to authorize human testing of the vampire conversion theory. His goal was protect humans, not feed them to vampires.

A wave of dizziness washed over him, along with a renewed pounding of his headache.

"Sir, sit down." Captain Osborne pointed to a chair.

He dropped into it and leaned forward to put his elbows on his knees. A nagging, tickling sensation on the back of his neck made him feel like he was being watched. "You've searched the building thoroughly?"

"Yes, sir."

"I want to see a magic sensor."

"Yes, sir." Captain Osborne relayed the request into his microphone.

A moment later, Grenidor's tablet pinged and he pulled up the list of fingerprints he'd requested earlier.

Malachi Bryant.

Fernando de Silva

Lieutenant Colonel Evrial Waterton.

Michael Rogers.

Dr. Tobias Bartok.

Dominic Gray.

Caleb Freeman.

The lieutenant colonel was interesting; he'd look up her history. And Bartok. Grenidor frowned. The name sounded familiar.

Osborne slipped a sensor in front of him.

The sensors were still basic, screens which showed the concentration of certain ions and fluctuations in a form of energy that wasn't really understood. There was so much research to be done, but humans hadn't investigated magic with any sort of systematic, scientific process until now. Progress was being made, certainly, but the vampires understood and manipulated nature in ways of which humans could only dream. *And the more we find out, the more terrified we are.*

The device didn't show much, and Grenidor pushed his throbbing headache aside and meandered around, holding the sensor in front of him. It showed background residue, indicating that something magic had perhaps once been here, or happened here, or perhaps nothing. The field barely deserved to be called a science yet. Grenidor studied the screen again. *We're like children studying the sidewalk in front of our house, hoping that by under-*

standing it, we'll understand the city. Our hubris is astonishing. But what else can we do? The readings stayed low, and he followed Osborne slowly through the theater, glancing up from the screen occasionally to watch the teams scanning the area for fingerprints with electronic readers.

Osborne opened a metal access door and pointed down a short hallway to a battered, heavy wooden door at the end. The floor was scored with long scratches and dark brown stains marred the walls and floor. "Sir, this is interesting. We didn't find any magic residue, but they may have concealed it. Those scratches and blood indicate that a vertril found the door and tried to enter. But there isn't a body. It may have been killed elsewhere. Here's the log, sir." He pulled up a list on his own tablet and passed it over.

"It's that one. Number 289. One of them led it away from the others before killing it." Grenidor rubbed one hand over his face and tried to think. What did that mean? The idea of vampires caring for each other, risking capture, stretched the imagination. Admittedly, they had talked of such emotions before. But Grenidor had discounted that. Vampires were known to lie. Yet what other reason could it have had for leading the vertril on such a long chase? "Can you date these marks before or after the vampires escaped from Eastborn?"

"Not exactly, sir. We suspect before, but we can't be sure."

"Is there anything else here it would want to protect?" To risk capture, perhaps death, for humans was even more unlikely. *Cillian risked himself for Owen. And Owen risked himself for the escaped vampires. I did not expect that.* Grenidor turned in a slow circle, staring around the theatre. His neck prickled again, and he shook his shoulders out. *What's wrong with me?* "You're sure there aren't any still here?"

Osborne stared at him. "We've searched as well as we can, sir. You know they're devilishly hard to detect when they want to be. Would you like a security detail?"

"No." Grenidor glanced down at the screen again. "Take me to Peterson's office."

"Yes, sir."

Up the stairs. Grenidor pushed down the nausea that threatened again. The room was small, with a desk and a chair behind it, with two others pushed against the near wall. A tech was crouched behind the desk and stood to salute.

"What have you found?"

"Sir, we received the results on the blood in here. It belonged to the one that called itself Owen. The one that just escaped."

Grenidor blinked. "Owen?"

"Yes, sir."

"Any sign of human blood?"

"Not yet, sir. We're still scanning."

Grenidor studied the evidence laid out on the desk. A hand towel stiff with dark, dried blood. Two pencils. A cheap pen. A crumpled piece of paper that had been flattened out.

"What are these?"

"We don't know yet, sir. This appears to be some sort of poetry, or prophecy, or… something." The tech's voice trailed away uncertainly.

1 "Return, Israel, to the Lord your God.
   Your sins have been your downfall!
2 Take words with you

and return to the Lord.
Say to him:
   "Forgive all our sins
and receive us graciously,
   that we may offer the fruit of our lips.
3 Assyria cannot save us;
   we will not mount warhorses.
We will never again say 'Our gods'
   to what our own hands have made,
   for in you the fatherless find compassion."
4 "I will heal their waywardness
   and love them freely,
   for my anger has turned away from them.
5 I will be like the dew to Israel;
   he will blossom like a lily.

... *I wish I could remember the rest. And I wish we were Israel, so I could hold on to this promise. Because I am not confident we can put our trust in this. Our sins have been our downfall, certainly, but we are not the Israelites, with an enduring covenant with an almighty God. We were blessed, perhaps, for a time, but we have long since lost any favor in God's eyes.*

Would we, even if we could, repent? People are comfortable. There is nothing to remind them of the abyss into which we are even now leaping.

Grenidor shivered, cold to his bones.

"What's wrong, sir?" Osborne asked sharply.

"This is... chilling. The writings of a madman." Grenidor turned the paper over, fighting the urge to shiver again. More writing greeted him, cramped and familiar. *Then you will know the truth, and the truth will set you free. I fear this truth has left us behind. The truth of God is that he has forsaken us, and there is nothing we can do. My prayers never reach his ears, that's certain. Maybe they never have.*

Grenidor leaned forward to rest his hands on the desk, eyes closed. He could almost hear Colonel Gabriel Peterson saying the words aloud. A hard man. Difficult. They hadn't gotten along. Grenidor was the rock, the steady, relentless force in pursuit of his goal. Peterson was the firebrand, the one who sparked and exploded at every hindrance. The one who rallied the troops and united their disparate passions into an army.

In the words and the cramped, angry writing, Grenidor heard Peterson's despair. That, more than the scientific findings, encouraged him. He didn't hate Peterson, exactly; the feelings weren't personal enough for that. Peterson was human. A deluded criminal traitor, but human.

"This is encouraging," he finally managed. "This is Peterson's handwriting, and he's not hopeful."

Osborne nodded, and the tech stared at him doubtfully. "Sir, you look... perhaps you need to go back to the infirmary."

"I'm fine!" Grenidor snapped. He stalked back into the hallway. "Captain, come with me." He shivered, a quick prickle of premonition that made him turn his head suddenly to stare into a far corner. Nothing was there.

He took a deep breath and let it out, forcing his voice to remain even. "Have them bring vampire M19, Feichin."

Osborne twitched in surprise. "Sir?"

"He can tell us a lot more than the sensors, and we need information. Don't forget he's dangerous."

"Yes, sir." Osborne swallowed and relayed the order into his lapel microphone.

THE TRANSPORT SECURITY measures had been thoroughly discussed and evaluated, and Grenidor watched the transport team arrive with professional admiration. Feichin's wrists and ankles were shackled by getlaril manacles to prevent magic use. The manacles were chained to the floor and barred roof of a transport cage also made of getlaril. His feet were chained at shoulder width, to allow him to keep his balance, and his raised, bound hands would not let him fall when the cage jostled. The cage itself was bolted to an electric transport trolley, which was operated by remote control. Six armed guards accompanied the cage, their weapons trained on the vampire.

Feichin gazed about the hotel lobby with icy calm until his eyes found Grenidor and he smiled coldly. "You. What do you want now?"

Grenidor ignored the vampire's attempt to be intimidating. It was adequately restrained; he would not make the same mistake again. "Some of your kind have been here. Tell me about them."

"I owe you nothing but pain." The vampire held his eyes; the soft answer almost masked his burning fury.

"Vampire, I have no time for your dramatic pronouncements. Answer me, and get a meal. Otherwise, I'll send you back to your hole."

Feichin twisted in his bonds, fingers curled away from the getlaril as much as possible. It still burned his skin, of course; even from a distance, Grenidor could see the raw welts raised on his wrists and ankles. He answered slowly, as if considering his words. "Lord Owen, favored of El, was here. And Niall, his nephew. The others were human, and stank of fear."

"Where have the humans gone?"

"I neither know nor care."

"Who were they?"

"How should I know?" Feichin's cold gaze never wavered.

Grenidor rubbed his hand absently over the bandage on his head again, studying the vampire. Like the others, he looked more or less like an unusually beautiful, pale human. Even weak with hunger, so thin every rib showed, the taut muscles of his torso stood out as he shifted, trying to minimize the pain of the getlaril. His eyes were nearly the same color as Owen's, with the same inhuman iciness. *Monsters. They look like us, but they are* not *like us.* Davis had forgotten. But Grenidor would not.

"What else can you tell me?"

"Can or will?"

"Can. Is there anything else here?"

"Yes." Feichin smiled at him, enjoying Grenidor's irritation.

"What is it? Vampire like you?"

"No."

"Fae, then?"

"No."

"Make yourself useful, vampire, or I'll lose any reason to keep you alive." Grenidor rubbed his hand over his aching head again. The fact that he'd rephrased the question perturbed him. Whether he admitted the difference between Fae and vampires or not, the slip betrayed his previously-unacknowledged realization that at least Fae and vampires believed themselves different from each other. *Maybe they're the same in ways we think are important, but different in ways they think are impor-*

tant. Or perhaps they are different factions. Are they in conflict with each other?

If so, would it be possible to use Fae against vampires? It probably wouldn't help. They are more like each other than like us, and could not be trusted. They would betray us, or we would be forced to take preemptive measures against them. We are still in inevitable conflict with them. Perhaps only some of them, perhaps all of them.

"What use have I of life? You've taken what I most valued already."

Grenidor frowned. He could threaten the vampire, certainly, and hurt it, but he didn't actually want it dead yet. It was the only one that proved his theory so far, and he wanted more information from it first. *What did he most value? What does he think I've taken from him? Liberty?* That didn't make sense. Neither was it the most important question now.

He finally walked over to one of the guards. "Do you have the control with you?"

"Yes, sir."

"Shock it, then. Hard, but only once. I want it coherent."

The guard nodded and pulled the control from his belt. He adjusted the settings. The vampire ignored him, staring off into a far corner with his head slightly raised, as if he almost saw something, or heard something. So he was completely surprised when electricity surged through the manacles. The vampire arched his back, snarling, eyes wide and white as the irises rolled back in his head. He convulsed, jerking violently on the manacles, and the guard held the button for another second before flicking it off.

Feichin slumped, hanging limp from his wrists, dead weight slowly twisting in his bonds. His head flopped forward, eyes closed, not breathing. Grenidor stepped closer and the guard followed him.

The guard kicked the trolley. "Wake up, vampire."

A harsh gasp greeted him. Feichin twisted again, sharp ribs showing his erratic breaths steadying. He straightened with obvious effort and would have fallen but for the manacles that kept his hands above his head. He turned his head, shook it like a dog, and finally found Grenidor. He blinked, and for once his burning gaze looked unfocused. Then he snarled, hatred burning in his eyes again.

"What is here, vampire? If it's not Fae, or vampire, or whatever you want to call yourself, it's certainly not human. What is it?"

"Something else." The answer was an almost inaudible growl. "What happened to your head?"

Grenidor almost snarled his own response, but then stopped. Perhaps answering the vampire might result in valuable clues. "One of your kind threw me against a wall."

Feichin tilted his head to the side, interest sharpening. "Who?"

"Cillian. He would have killed me, but Owen told him not to." Grenidor hadn't meant to say that much, but the question of *why* Owen had spared him was constantly on his mind. *I alternate between calling Feichin an 'it' and a "him". I should be careful of that. Don't want to lose objectivity. But even dogs get gendered pronouns; perhaps that isn't too dangerous.*

"They escaped?" Feichin's eyes were on his face, his expression unreadable. "And didn't kill you?"

"Yes. But that's not your concern. What is here, if it's not Fae or vampire?"

Feichin raised his head again and straightened a little more, eyes roving over the room. Not looking at Grenidor, the hatred in his face faded, leaving weariness and... something else. Fear. He took a short breath, stopped, and finally said, "Lord Owen once spoke to something that called itself Conláed." He stopped and shook his head, as if shaking water from his ears.

"What was it? Is that what's here?"

Feichin blinked slowly. "I never met it. But I think not." He turned abruptly to stare at Grenidor again. "I had the impression that it was like Lord Owen. This thing is more like... me. If you were a wise man, you would run."

Grenidor felt a surge of anger. "I asked you a question, vampire! Answer me."

"My name is Feichin, human." Feichin didn't flinch, even as the guard pulled out the wand again. "I grow tired of your attempts to make me an animal. I have not yet forgotten what I was."

"You were and always will be a monster until you are dead. Which may come sooner than you realize if you don't answer my questions." Grenidor was the one snarling now, stalking around the cage.

Feichin watched and smiled slowly, white teeth showing. "Your choices condemn you. If you wish, it is not hard to contact it. You are an evil, stupid man, and probably think you can control it. You can't."

"Who are you to talk of condemnation?" Grenidor's voice cracked with rage.

The vampire looked away. "One who knows its weight." He said nothing else, and did not look back at Grenidor.

"Shock it again."

The vampire tensed in anticipation, but it didn't help; the arc ripped into his body, convulsing it for a long minute. Off again.

Feichin hung limp and silent. He didn't breathe or twitch, even when the guard kicked the trolley hard again. Thin lines of blood seeped from his ears and nostrils.

Grenidor drew his pistol and clanked it along the bars, and the third time the vampire jerked and twisted against the getlaril that burned his wrists.

"And what were you, vampire? What do you think you were?"

The vampire's thin chest heaved, head still hanging down, hair ragged over his lean, handsome face. He spoke with eyes closed. "I was... beloved. Now I am..." He opened his eyes and forced himself to straighten again, shuddering. His eyes went toward the corner again, and Grenidor looked too.

Nothing was visible, but the vampire kept his eyes there as he said quietly, "I wish to live because my body has reflexes. But I hate what I am, I hate what you have done, and I hate every breath I breathe. I hate the sunlight and the darkness, I hate the getlaril, and I hate Lord Owen for being stronger than I am. I hate Cillian for his obedience and myself for my disobedience. I hate my daughter for her purity and myself for my impurity. I hate the blood I drank, and I hate the hunger that consumes me." He turned to met Grenidor's eyes, and despite himself, Grenidor took a step backward. "Most of all, I hate you, Grenidor."

Grenidor swallowed. *This one must never get free. Never. He will kill me slowly.* "What is out there, and what does it want?"

Feichin blinked slowly, perhaps considering the question or his answer, or perhaps merely dazed. He licked at the blood flowing from his nose. Finally, he muttered, "It wants you."

"For what?"

The vampire let his head hang down again, barely breathing, and Grenidor let him think. Rest. Whatever he was doing.

The answer came quietly. "I hate you, Grenidor, so this kindness is because of what I was, not what I am now. If it is what I think it is... you have no hope of using it. It will consume you. Leave it, and pursue your ends through other means."

Grenidor paced. The vampire could not be trusted. None of them could. They were monsters through and through. But this answer seemed honest. Genuine, despite Feichin's hate.

Yet perhaps Feichin did not understand the thing. Perhaps it wasn't evil like Feichin was; he would be incapable of understanding good. *Do I even believe in good and evil? Isn't there only logic and illogic? Our interests opposing their interests?* Besides, if Fae and vampires were out in the world, and humans had only just discovered them, how many more magical species were there? Grenidor was duty-bound to investigate, particularly species that might pose a threat to the empire.

His name would already be in the history books for proving that Fae and vampires were the same. He'd nearly discovered the species too; before his work, both variants had been unconfirmed rumors. Discovering an additional species would be ground-breaking!

"How do I contact it?" he asked finally.

"I shouldn't tell you." Feichin's head lolled back. The getlaril was sapping his strength, and he hadn't been fed in… Grenidor considered. Aside from Davis, it had been three months. Hunger was impeding his healing, too. His hand and the gunshot wounds had healed without scarring, but it had taken him nearly five days to sit up afterwards. Another, well-fed vampire had been similarly shot for an experimental control; he'd sat up only three days later.

"I'll feed you. A full meal. Whatever you want, aside from human meat and blood."

Again Feichin was silent, and Grenidor wondered whether he was even conscious. The blood from his nose and ears had slowed and darkened, and his head flopped to the side and back, smearing blood from his ear across his bare shoulder. The pulse in his neck was visible, too slow for a human. His throat moved as he swallowed and shuddered.

"Your choices condemn you, human. You are foolish to want this."

"Just answer the question!" Grenidor roared.

"It says it is always listening, you have only to ask it to appear."

Grenidor blinked. *If that's true… I shouldn't speak to it in front of everyone.* "Take him back and feed him. Clear out the teams."

The electric trolley lurched into motion. Feichin swayed as he hung in the center of the cage. He raised his head slightly, and Grenidor felt the vampire's cold gaze on him until the trolley turned the corner into the hallway and he was lost from view.

Grenidor breathed a sigh of relief. He'd been careful to hide it, but the vampire unnerved him. He nodded Osborne out along with the others and waited until everyone had left. The lobby echoed with the sound of the closing door. Osborne and one of the team leaders were visible outside, their backs to the glass doors.

The empty space felt cool and quiet, and Grenidor switched off his tablet. He walked to the far end of the lobby and studied the fireplace, feeling himself tense with anticipation. He turned to face the room, eyes searching each corner. There were shadows, but none dark enough to hide a figure.

He raised his voice. "The vampire said all I had to do was ask you to appear. So I'm asking. What are you?"

A dark figure walked into view from just out of his peripheral vision. "Hello." The man smiled.

Despite himself, Grenidor jumped at his sudden appearance. He held up a hand and the man stopped and inclined his head in polite acknowledgement of Grenidor's... fear. *Yes, call it what it is. I'm afraid. Appearing like that isn't natural. This thing is dangerous.* "What are you?" he repeated.

The man blinked and drew back slightly. "That's not an especially polite question. I'm a creature like yourself. My limitations are different, but I'm fundamentally similar, just doing the best I can given the circumstances. I've been wanting to meet you." His smile was disarming.

Grenidor eyed him warily. He was perhaps fifty or fifty-five, slightly portly with gentle brown eyes showing a quick intelligence, and a thick head of mostly grey hair. He stepped closer and Grenidor raised his hand again, telling him to stop. He smiled and stuck his hand out, waiting for long moments while Grenidor debated with himself.

"What do you want from me?" he asked finally, the man's hand still waiting in the air.

"Just to be friends. Perhaps later we can help each other out. I'm working on a project." He waggled his fingers and added, "You can call me Edwin."

Grenidor reluctantly shook his hand. Edwin's grip was firm and warm, very human. Despite his caution, Grenidor relaxed a little. "The vampire thinks you're like him. In what way?"

Edwin frowned. "The vampire is a liar." He studied Grenidor, then asked, "What do you want from me, then? You wanted to speak with me about something."

"The vampires are getting stronger. More numerous. How do I defeat them?"

Edwin snorted softly. "You ask a lot. Anything else you'd like? The moon?"

Grenidor studied him in turn. The man wasn't disturbed by the request; instead, he seemed faintly amused. "Is that beyond your capabilities?"

Edwin smiled and paced away, head down and hands clasped behind his back. "No." Another step. "No, I can do many things. But I also have... goals. Desires. My price for defeating the vampires may be higher than you wish to pay, at least now, while we barely know each other. Perhaps we should start with something small."

"Such as?"

Edwin glanced over his shoulder. "Your head aches. What would you do if I were to take away the pain?"

Grenidor blinked. "I can take a pain killer in another hour. Don't touch me."

"I won't touch you." Edwin smiled gently. "As a token of friendship then." He flicked his fingers toward Grenidor.

Grenidor blinked at a flash of light, and then shook his head. The pain was gone; indeed, he felt refreshed, despite his sleepless nights. He stared at Edwin. "Thank you. Don't do that again."

Edwin turned away, waving a hand dismissively. "As you wish." He paced away with ponderous grace. Grenidor studied him, knowing that Edwin was aware of his watchful eye. Both face and movements were somehow familiar. The face... something about it reminded him of... someone. Perhaps a professor from the Army Academy? He couldn't place the name. The way his steps rolled as he walked, hands clasped behind him, was like... someone. General St. James, as he'd been when Grenidor met him as an undergraduate. Or his uncle Philip, perhaps. The impression was comforting.

Perhaps that's the point. He wants me to lower my guard. How much does he know about me?

Edwin turned toward him with a smile. "What exactly are your concerns about the vampires? You appear to have the upper hand."

"They prey on humans. They're physically dangerous. Their control of magic is far beyond ours. From what we can tell, their population appears to be growing."

"You wish them exterminated?"

"I wish to understand them, and yes, I wish them exterminated."

Edwin tilted his head as if considering. "Concern for your species? Or for your career?"

Grenidor frowned. "They're a very real danger! My concern about the vampires is not selfish."

Edwin waved a hand again. "There's nothing wrong with advancing your own career by good work. It's only relevant because I want to consider my own methods and how I can best be of use." He strolled further, eyes on the floor as if deep in thought.

Where did he come from? Perhaps it would have been useful if I had seen how he appeared. Grenidor considered Edwin and felt himself relaxing, despite the warning klaxon in his mind. *I specifically, explicitly told him not to touch me. He didn't, but... he knew I did not want him to... meddle. It was a demonstration. He can do with me as he pleases, and he wants me to know it. Perhaps he's friendly, but this negotiation, or whatever it is, should not be continued. I am at his mercy. It would be wiser to have others here. He is unlikely to harm us directly, at least not now.*

Do not be like Davis. Do not forget he is dangerous. Do not risk the others.

Do not negotiate from a position of weakness.

Grenidor walked to the lobby door. He didn't want to appear afraid, but he didn't put his back toward Edwin. "Osborne, bring the security detail in here."

"Yes, sir."

The team jogged in, weapons pointed at the floor.

Edwin glanced up, unconcerned, and continued his slow circle of the lobby, moving toward Grenidor again.

"Come no closer. Do not make any sudden moves," Grenidor ordered.

Edwin paused, met his eyes, and smiled.

Grenidor said, "The guards are armed with getlaril bullets. I don't want any trouble. But I want you to understand that I'm not helpless. We are negotiating; I'm not begging for your help."

"You called me. You know I can give you what you want." Edwin stepped closer, steps slow and steady.

"Stop. Stay where you are." Grenidor's voice was hard. "If he comes any closer, shoot him."

Edwin raised his right hand, fingers cupped as if he were holding something. He took another step closer.

"Stop!" a guard shouted. "Stop or we'll shoot!"

Closer, steps easy and even.

The shots rang out, a deafening roar that echoed in the lobby.

Edwin stopped in front of Grenidor just as the shots ceased. He held out his hand, and Grenidor stared at him, heart in his mouth. Edwin seemed unaffected by the shots, clothing unruffled, no blood or injuries visible. He still held out his hand, eyes on Grenidor's as he waited patiently.

Grenidor finally extended his hand to take what he offered.

A handful of bullets.

He smiled as Grenidor met his eyes. "No offense taken. I just want to make our positions clear. I don't mean you harm. If I did, you would be dead, not healed."

Grenidor's heart thudded in his chest, and he nodded.

This was a bad idea.

GRENIDOR'S HEART WAS still thundering when Edwin turned away and began another unhurried circuit of the lobby. The security detail stared at him with open mouths, then looked back at Osborne and the team leader, and finally to Grenidor.

He forced himself to straighten. "Osborne, you can take your team out."

His eyes followed Edwin as the man paced. He looked like a man, but he wasn't. He wasn't a vampire either. Powerful as they were, they were physical beings and could be neutralized and controlled by physical means. Edwin was something else entirely.

And friendly? He may be willing to let us live for now. But something so powerful cannot be trusted.

"What knowledge do you have of the vampires? Or Fae? They call themselves different things. Why?"

Edwin spoke deliberately, as if considering his words. "Some are open about their hostility to humans. Some are more discreet. But you are correct in your belief that all are dangerous. In the past, they preyed upon humans as their preferred food source. They are predators. Today, some clans scorn such hunting as unsporting or uncivilized; these are the ones who call themselves Fae. They can turn upon humans when threatened or insulted but generally don't choose to kill humans unprovoked. Others have no such compunctions and prefer human blood."

Grenidor considered the explanation. Edwin drew a sharper distinction between Fae and vampires than Grenidor had, and gave the Fae more credit for civilization. Yet his reasoning justified Grenidor's fear. "Are the clans in contact with each other? Do they work together?"

"Sometimes." Edwin continued pacing slowly, and Grenidor stepped away from his path to put his back to the fireplace. Edwin glanced up with a knowing look, but did not veer toward him. "Authority is fragmented and they pursue their own interests."

"What are those interests?"

"Survival, primarily. Territorial fights between clans." Another few steps, then he turned on his heel and walked toward Grenidor again. "You have asked me for information. It's my turn now. What interest do you have in the vampire Owen?"

Don't back away. Never show your fear.

Despite himself, Grenidor could feel his shoulders tensing. "He is one of their leaders, isn't he?"

"Yes." Closer.

Grenidor held his ground. "He had reason to let Cillian kill me when they came to retrieve him. The others would have, and Cillian wanted to. Why did Owen let me live?"

Edwin stopped and his eyes flicked away, then back. "He wanted something else more than your death at that moment. He was testing his authority over Cillian. His brother has, at times, challenged him, and if Cillian had killed you, even out of a protective instinct or revenge for your... work... on Owen, Owen would know that Cillian was a threat. He would kill Cillian at some later point. As it is, Cillian bowed to Owen's authority, and you were allowed to live."

Edwin paused and stared at the ground, distant for a moment. Then he added, "That may not always be the case. For now, I'll leave it at that." He strode away and around a corner, and then was gone.

CHAPTER 5

NIAMH AND CILLIAN sang over Owen again. Afterwards, he seemed a little better, but Niamh was upset with his slow progress. At five days after the rescue, he had not even sat up yet.

"What is wrong, Owen? Why are you not healing?" Her voice cracked.

He murmured, "I am healing, my sister. Do not be afraid." He groped for her hand, and she slipped her hand into his.

"I am not afraid!" She brushed at her eyes. "I'm angry, and... *fherthana gres-thil.*"

Owen answered her in Fae as well, the words even quieter. He switched to English to say, "I don't regret it, Niamh. I can't. Forgive me." He watched her until she nodded, then sighed and let his eyes close again.

Niamh and Cillian might have been carved of marble; they sat like beautiful, gaunt statues as they watched over their brother.

Aria's mind wandered, and every thought brought up more questions. "Will Grenidor be able to find us here?"

Cillian sighed. "Not quickly. Niall and I removed the obvious traces of our presence from the hotel as we left, but it was only a cursory effort. We did not remove all traces of human presence from the main areas, and we did not touch the outer rooms. But Gabriel is intelligent enough to remove anything critical."

Aria licked her lips. "He might have left a sign that Lord Owen was there. Is that bad?"

Cillian's frown deepened, but he shook his head. "Grenidor will know that my brother is at least cooperating with the human resistance by the fact of our rescue."

Owen moaned so softly that Aria barely heard it. Niamh bent to put her ear beside his mouth, but shook her head after a moment.

Owen said he'd lied about the dark ones. Grenidor wanted to contact them. Why?

"What are the 'dark ones' that Owen mentioned? The ones he said humans could not interact with?"

Cillian answered, "We have no contact with them. We have never seen them, nor spoken with them. But we know they exist. Turned Fae, the ones who have chosen rebellion, see them sometimes. It is rare, we think, but then we are rarely in contact with those who have turned, so it is difficult to judge. From what little we have heard, we believe they are beings of spirit.

"Perhaps they are of Petro's... species, if you can call it that. We know that Petro is dangerous and unpredictable by our understanding, though we do not believe he is malicious. We do not know if the dark ones are allowed to interact with our universe beyond rare sightings by the turned Fae. But unlike Petro, we believe they are malicious, and they have power we cannot evaluate."

Niamh added in a low voice, "Or perhaps they are all Petro. We can only guess."

"So you don't really know anything?"

Cillian gave her a hard look. "We do not wish to know. Perhaps that is important."

"Why did he lie about them, then?" she asked.

Niamh answered, "To protect humans. If Grenidor thinks he can manipulate Petro, or something like Petro, the human is deluded at best. It is better to obey El, even in ignorance, than to meddle in things that we cannot hope to understand."

Cillian added, "Perhaps it would be wise of you to ask no more questions about it."

Aria huffed in frustration. Conversations with Cillian seemed to end in confusion more often than not. She wished Owen were healed. He was a better conversationalist, at least. He seemed kinder. Cillian tolerated her because Owen wished it, and Niamh was no warmer. The other Fae had not spoken to her at all, despite her constant presence in their midst. At least Niall sometimes answered her questions.

She glanced around, but didn't see the young Fae.

Owen was asleep, but Aria didn't want to go back to the other end of the train platform. The images of Feichin and Davis kept rising in her mind, despite her attempts to forget. She thought again of Feichin's handsome face, covered in blood and twisted in frustration and anger.

Cillian frowned. "I did not see the video, but I could hear what happened. Feichin turned, did he not?"

She blinked and glanced at him. "Are you reading my mind?"

"No. Your fear is evident. You flinched when I shifted beside you. I assume you had forgotten I was here, and my movement reminded you that Feichin and I are of the same species." His clear blue eyes held hers. Even so, she had difficulty reading his expression. A hint of pity, or perhaps compassion. Anger.

"Why are you angry?" she muttered, glancing down at her lap. Her fingers were twisted together, and she spread them, consciously relaxing her shoulders. She *was* afraid. Surrounded by beings who could do what Feichin had done, who could kill her and every human in the train station before they could draw a gun.

Cillian sighed. "It was unwise to watch the video. I feared that you, and the other humans, would become afraid. As you have. I was afraid Feichin would turn. He was pushed, but that does not excuse him." He rubbed his left hand absently over the scar on his right forearm. It had faded from the livid red she had first seen to a pale, shiny pink.

"What happened?"

"He turned." He looked down at his arm and rubbed the scar again, then flexed his fingers.

"Turned?"

"Turned away from El. He chose hatred over trust. Anger is permitted but judgment is forbidden." Cillian glanced at her face then back at Owen.

"Judgment? I don't understand."

Niamh shifted but said nothing.

Cillian answered. "To pass judgment on a soul is forbidden. Feichin suffered and felt it unjust. He watched others suffer as well, ones he loved. At some point his patience turned to anger. This was not his turning. Perhaps his anger at the suffering became anger at those who caused it. Anger can turn to hate and judgment that the one who causes suffering is evil. Evil is not a thing to be respected or afforded the rights of a soul created by El. This is judgment and it is forbidden. We have neither the right nor the ability to judge evil and good. That is reserved for El."

Aria's voice rose. "But some things *are* evil! Can't you recognize evil and stop it, if you see it?"

"It is permitted to recognize acts as evil. But not souls. Evil is a thing to be hated, but it is not permitted to hate a soul."

Niall slipped into the circle beside Aria, tapped Cillian's arm, and gestured over his shoulder. The motion was discreet, but Aria frowned. He looked shaken, almost frightened. Cillian nodded minutely and murmured, "I know."

"What?" Aria whispered.

Cillian turned his gaze on her. He mouthed silently, "Stay near me. There is danger."

Aria glanced around and looked back at him. "Grenidor?"

He shook his head.

THEY SAT IN silence for some time, merely watching Owen breathe. Aria wondered what the danger was, but she didn't ask again. Cillian's tension faded, and she imagined the danger had passed. Once he leaned down to whisper in Owen's ear. His elder brother didn't respond, but his breathing deepened as if a little of his pain had been soothed.

"Why is Niall Lord Owen's heir? He's Niamh's son, not Owen's, and he's so young," Aria said.

Cillian answered, "That was Lord Owen's decision. The rules of authority do not follow strict blood inheritance. Lord Ailill may choose anyone within his clan, but first right goes to his own sons and their sons. Lord Ailill did not choose Niall, that was Lord Owen's right, but Lord Ailill approved of Lord Owen's choice."

"Never the women? Niamh is oldest."

He frowned at her, head tilted in confusion. "No. Never."

"Why not?"

"Niamh's responsibilities are different. El's authority rests on whom it rests, for His own reasons."

Aria frowned back at him, but didn't know how to question his statement. The statement seemed so self-evident to him that her protests of unfairness sounded juvenile in her own ears. "Do you resent not being chosen?"

"It is not for me to resent. If both Owen and Niall were killed, and Ailill had to choose another, I doubt I would be his next choice."

"Who would be?"

"Before… I would have guessed Feichin. Now, I could not guess."

"Feichin?" Her voice was incredulous.

"You did not know him as he was." His head bowed with grief.

Despite herself, Aria found more questions slipping out. "Does everyone know he's Lord Owen's heir? Would there be problems if leadership was questioned?"

Cillian looked up at her, his brows drawing together as if he were utterly baffled by the question. "How could we not know who held El's authority? Is it not clear to humans?"

"So you always know? How?"

He tilted his head, studying her anew. "I... it is impossible to describe. I know who holds El's authority the same way I know which direction is north."

Aria blinked. "I don't always know which direction is north."

"You don't?" His confusion deepened. "Perhaps it is like how you know which direction is down. Gravity pulls you that way, but the weight of gravity is not a burden; it is a stabilizing force that makes sense of what would otherwise be chaos."

ARIA SAT ON the concrete with her back against a box, her arms around her knees. The low voices of the men and women around her merged with a few snores from the night watch catching up on sleep.

She'd retreated to the human encampment to give the Fae some space. Niamh and Cillian spoke with Ardghal over Owen's motionless body. They weren't speaking English anymore, and while that didn't prove they were talking about her, the way they kept studying her made it clear.

They don't seem capable of much of a facade. They do not say everything, but what they say is true. As their words must be honest, so must their faces.

What must it be like to be excruciatingly honest at all times?

At this distance, their words were inaudible, but she couldn't help being aware of their eyes on her.

Niamh finally nodded and stood, walking directly toward Aria, her gaze never leaving Aria's face.

When she was close, Aria asked, "Is there something I can do for you?"

Niamh's mouth tightened and she knelt before Aria, her piercing blue eyes cautious. "Yes. Tell me how you can see us. You should not be able to see me now. Nor should you be able to see the others, except maybe a flicker now and then across the lantern light. Yet I saw you watching us. I saw you watch me approach."

Aria blinked. It still surprised her that they didn't expect to be seen, because they were so clearly visible to her. Yet Niamh had passed so close to Levi she could have touched him, but he hadn't noticed her at all.

"I don't know. I think I've always been able to see Fae, but how would I know if I couldn't see you?"

Niamh's eyes did not leave her face, though her gaze sharpened further. "I have noticed you watching us; you see us, even when we mean to be hidden." She licked her lips, a gesture that probably meant only that Niamh was thinking, but nonetheless reminded Aria that Niamh could, if she chose, rip out Aria's throat.

Aria shuddered. *No. She hasn't threatened me. She isn't angry, I don't think. She's just curious.* Aria took a deep breath and tried to explain. "Actually, I think I see you Fae better than everyone else. Like you're more... colorful. No, that's not right. More like... you're painted in clear, bright colors, and everyone else is painted in colors that are just a little muddy. Or the light reflects off of you better, so I see you more clearly. Something like that." She blinked at her belated realization. "When I saw Lord Owen on the bridge that night, I wouldn't have noticed a human. It was dark, and the angle was difficult. I wouldn't have seen him if he was human."

They're all so beautiful I can scarcely look at them, and scarcely look away. It's almost painful; something inside twists with jealousy and longing, appreciation of what I'll never be and what I'll never have. They were beautiful to start with, but the more I look at them, the more beautiful they seem.

Are they changing, or do I just see them better?

Niamh cocked her head to the side and stared at her. "You are thinking something about me that makes you frown. What is it?"

Aria swallowed. "It's not important."

Niamh held Aria's gaze, and finally Aria muttered, "You just look so much like your brother. Brothers."

Niamh nodded. "Yes." She seemed oblivious to the heat that suffused Aria's cheeks. After a moment, Niamh leaned close to her and took a deep, slow breath, as if she was inhaling Aria's scent. Her eyes narrowed, and she drew back.

"What?" Aria asked.

"There is something different about you." Niamh cocked her head to the side.

Aria watched her, but she didn't seem inclined to say anything else for long moments. *Like being kidnapped by Fae?* Finally Aria said, "Lord Owen said Fae don't steal human children. But what if that's not true?"

Niamh's eyes blazed with fury. She hissed, "No Fae has *ever* stolen a human child!"

Heart pounding, Aria pressed herself back against the cardboard box, her breath coming in terrified squeaks. "I'm sorry! I didn't... I'm sorry."

Niamh's nostrils flared, and she spoke in a low, rage-filled voice. "You should know that making such an accusation, after a Fae who still lives in the light of El has denied the truth of it, is justifiable grounds for your death. Do not tempt me again."

Aria nodded, trembling. "I'm sorry." The next words came without thought. "Forgive me." *Where did that come from? It sounds like an archaic phrase... something I heard a long time ago in a literature class.*

Niamh, too, was shaking, her thin, graceful body coiled and tense.

She almost killed me. I wonder why she didn't?

Niamh did not answer for long moments, still staring at Aria, her expression now cold and un-readable. Regal. She licked her lips again, revealing perfect white teeth. "Yes. I will." Her expression softened almost imperceptibly. "Turned Fae have committed crimes against humans, but none of us who live in the light of El would commit such an outrage. Humans, however, have committed many crimes against us."

Aria tried to still her trembling, but the combination of fear and cold made her voice a little shaky. "What is different about me, then?"

Niamh frowned. "I do not know." She stared at Aria for long, uncomfortable moments, then finally said, "Cease your shaking. I have already said I will not avenge the insult."

"I'm just cold." Aria smiled weakly. *That was a lie. They're so vulnerable, being lied to and being honest in return.* "Is something wrong with me, then?"

Niamh blinked. "Not to my knowledge."

"Then what is it? Why do you all keep staring at me?"

An uncomfortable silence fell. Aria held Niamh's gaze, willing her to answer. *It worked on Owen, didn't it? Direct questions are harder to deflect.*

"Initially I suspected you might be the result of one of the human studies on captured Fae, a test of some means to allow humans to penetrate our defenses. It might explain your ability to see us.

"But your fear is real; I smelled it coming off you in waves. Your concern for my brother was real, though of a type different than ours. You have ignored several opportunities to betray us and the human resistance. Surely if the humans were testing some means of detecting us, they would have done so using a subject who would report back to them. Also, you could have reported back to the Imperial forces after seeing my brother in the shop, or perhaps following him to his apartment." She stopped, studying Aria's face. "I have also not forgotten that you risked Petro's wrath to save my brother. I doubt an agent of the Empire would have done that, not after Cillian's explanation. I owe you a blood debt for that."

Her eyes blazed a little brighter, and Aria tried not to flinch.

Niamh said softly, "But my debt does not obligate me to allow you to threaten them some other way, intentionally or not. Petro's reaction to you frightens me.

"You have something like the scent of a Fae-human hybrid, but not exactly. Perhaps it is a natural ability that appears in humans occasionally. I have never heard of it, but I have not heard everything, nor read all the records."

Aria's mouth formed a silent *oh*. "Um… well, I don't plan on betraying you."

Niamh gave her a tight smile. "I know. But I don't know what you are. That makes you dangerous."

Aria watched Niamh leave. She walked through the soldiers unnoticed, slim and hard and inhumanly graceful. *If they wanted to, they could kill us all. They wouldn't even have to wait until we were all asleep. No one else can even see them.*

She forced herself to remember Owen's sacrifice. *He's good. He won't let them. Even if he would, I bet they wouldn't do it. Niamh didn't, and she said she had the right.*

Aria looked around, wondering if anyone had seen her conversation with Niamh. No one appeared to have noticed, though Bartok glanced up as she looked at him. He gave her a pensive smile and raised his eyebrows, as if asking if she needed anything. She shook her head.

If they spent much time with humans, they'd be in the habit of showing themselves when they talked to us, even though they know I can see them anyway. Maybe they can make themselves visible only to the person with whom they're talking. But then someone would have noticed me talking to empty air; I'm sure I looked terrified. If I was visible and Niamh wasn't, then I'd look like a crazy woman.

So instead of becoming visible herself, she must have hidden us both.

That explains why the rest of the Fae don't ever talk to me. They didn't know I could see them!

Niall slipped past Aria on his way back from a tunnel on some unknown errand. She called to him, her voice barely above a whisper.

He turned to her, eyebrows raised.

"Can I ask you a question?"

He nodded and came closer, pulling his battered notebook from his pocket.

She lowered her voice further. "What did Lord Owen tell Cillian, after they argued? It seemed to comfort Cillian."

He regarded her with an unreadable expression. *Why do you ask?*

"He seemed pretty upset, and Owen knew exactly what to say." Aria frowned. "I'm glad it helped. I was just curious."

Lord Owen said that he trusted Cillian more than most. Lord Owen is struggling with important decisions that will affect all of us, and he believes Cillian has a greater capacity to understand the questions than Cillian himself believes. He pushes Cillian because he loves him and trusts him.

"Questions about what?"

About El. About our role. About humans. He took a deep breath, then added, *Perhaps it is all one great, complicated question.*

"Oh. Um... good luck."

His blue eyes flashed. *I don't think luck has much to do with it.*

CHAPTER 6

VAMPIRES DID NOT need to breathe. That discovery had taken some time, but Grenidor had realized it after an interrogation session. He'd later tested it in order to prove his theory. Vampires *wanted* to breathe, but they did not *need* to. When submerged underwater for extended periods of time, they behaved much like humans did. They held their breath for as long as they could. They became progressively more panic-stricken and frantic when unable to reach air. At last, when unable to hold their breath any longer, they let out the air and inhaled water, coughing and choking convulsively. After long, agonizing minutes, they reached some sort of equilibrium, inhaling and exhaling water with long, slow breaths.

M27 had been violent, perhaps insane, when they attempted the experiment; he was much the same afterwards and was terminated shortly after the last test. The test had been performed multiple times in increasing duration. The first time, it became apparent that vampires could hold their breath for longer than humans could. It took nearly twelve minutes for him to let loose the first bubbles of air, and another six minutes of struggling with the getlaril cage that held him underwater before he began to breathe the water.

It was odd, studying the creature through the reinforced glass. The vampire's bare chest showed slow breaths, his nostrils flared in anger and lingering fear. His gaze was locked on Grenidor's, hatred burning in his eyes. His lips lifted in a snarl, silent through the water but still full of menace.

Subsequent tests indicated that vampires, while obviously intelligent, did not seem capable of deliberately breathing water. Despite proof that they could survive the experience, they would struggle and fight it every time. The longest test had lasted thirty-six hours, and M27 survived with no apparent physical repercussions.

Removing the caged vampire from the water revealed reactions similar to those that would be expected from humans. The vampire gagged and choked, coughed water, sometimes vomited water, and struggled to re-acclimate to breathing air. The first and fourth tests, the vampire had coughed so hard he expelled some blood, but that result was uncommon, and no lasting damage had been done. Within eight minutes, the vampire was alert and breathing regularly again, though his cortisol levels were still elevated.

The mental results of the tests were difficult to determine. Other questions took precedence. It was clear, however, that the vampires' mental states generally trended downward... more hostile, more irritable, more paranoid, and more prone to speaking to phantoms.

Or are they phantoms? Feichin heard Edwin before Edwin spoke to me. Grenidor pondered that. Were the vampires insane? Were they merely... losing touch with this reality as they paid more attention to another reality? *Is Edwin real?* Of course he was; the bullets proved it, as well as the reactions of the security team members.

What is *Edwin?*

GRENIDOR TYPED HIS notes from the morning's interrogations.

Feichin's daughter was Aithne, who looked to be about eighteen but claimed to be one hundred twenty years old. He hadn't read the full report attempting to evaluate the validity of their claims of long life, but given the consistency in their assertions, it seemed possible. She was disturbingly beautiful, with icy blue eyes and pale, fine-boned features framed by locks of curly black hair. She was lucid and calm, and Grenidor fought the urge to look through the camera at her again. *She's a monster like the others. Even if she's beautiful. Get a grip, Paul.* Feichin had said she was afraid, but Grenidor hadn't seen it. *What do they see that we don't? What do they sense?*

The majority of the vampires had escaped in Owen's attack on Eastborn Imperial Security Facility. Those that remained, Ailill, Feichin, Aithne, and Meallan, had been held elsewhere. Meallan was of no use in interrogations; but Feichin,

Aithne, and the leader Ailill were coherent, if not always helpful.

Perhaps we should end the research and kill them. It might discourage another raid and we could devote our resources to finding the vampires at large. They're the real threat.

Grenidor grimaced, drumming his fingers lightly on the keys. *But there's so much still to learn.*

The thought stayed at the back of his mind as he continued typing. *Subject M41. Age appears to be between 35 and 37. Says his name is Meallan. Claims to have been Fae of the clan of Falling Water, but to have left the clan some years ago (time indeterminate). Subject has repeatedly attempted to attack Dr. Scott and Dr. Martinez. Subject is often confused about how much time has passed since the last interrogation, when he last ate, which staff member is which, etc. Subject is prone to self-harm, repeatedly throwing himself into the concrete wall headfirst until he loses consciousness. He has also scratched his face and arms bloody and broken his fingers and toes intentionally. The sound is appalling. His reactions are erratic and unpredictable. Sometimes he shrieks in pain and curses the scientists by name, but other times he stares at the broken digits in stony silence for hours. He speaks mostly in his own language, but is capable of speaking in accented English when he chooses. He screams and rages, demanding meat and blood; whatever meat is fed to him, he devours with horrible greed until his stomach bulges. On three separate occasions, he has screamed in apparent horror at nothing and cowered in a corner, hands over his head.*

It is unlikely we will get much additional information from M41. Observation will continue but he may be of no further use. Termination to be scheduled.

Grenidor jumped as a shadow fell across his desk.

"Good afternoon." Edwin smiled and sat in a chair across from him. "You seem troubled."

Grenidor scowled. Edwin looked thoroughly unthreatening. He wore a slightly threadbare suit of decent quality over a plain white shirt and a narrow, fashionable tie that didn't flatter his protruding belly. His shoes were slightly too scuffed, and his socks had slithered down to reveal bony, old man ankles. *Don't forget he's not human. It's an illusion.*

"I'm thinking." *The door didn't open. How long was he here before I saw him? I only see him when he wants to be seen.*

"About the vampires?"

"Yes." Grenidor considered his words. "They are difficult to detect at any time. We captured the last group purely by luck. Attacks on humans have increased, and we can't count on luck any more. How can we find them?"

Edwin recrossed his ankles and leaned back in the chair. "They're predators. They like meat."

Grenidor nodded warily.

"Specifically, they like organ meat and blood. Their preferred food is human hearts, but that draws attention. Some of them hunt in the poorest areas, where missing persons are unlikely to be noticed. Most avoid attention by purchasing offal and blood at butcher shops. Perhaps you could find where they spend their time by tracking such purchases."

Grenidor blinked at Edwin, who smiled blandly back at him. *Huh. That makes sense.* Grenidor pulled up the information request form to be sent to Imperial Investigations, part of IPF. He glanced at Edwin as he typed; the other man crossed his arms behind his head and leaned back farther as if lost in contemplation. With the press of a button, the form was sent to IPF; they would act on it immediately. Grenidor had been careful to maintain friendly relations with the IPF mid-level leadership, despite the tension between the military and the civilian IPF. Things got done faster that way.

"Did you know the security guards would shoot at you?" he asked abruptly.

Edwin's eyes rested on him. "Yes."

Grenidor pondered that a moment. "Can you see the future? Or was it a guess?"

Edwin smiled again. "Imagine a chessboard. I see the position of the pieces, and I know all possible moves from that position. I do not know for sure which move will be made, but I can guess that some are more likely than others. From any resulting new position I can also see all possible moves. I see many moves into the future. Humans cannot grasp the probabilities and options involved; to you, the future is a vast, unknowable chaos. Many times there is one action that seems obviously the best choice. To humans, this appears to be seeing the future, but in fact it is more of an educated guess. It is often possible to influence this choice by making a minute change in the information available to the human or the circumstances surrounding the human when the choice is presented."

"I see."

Edwin leaned forward slightly. "Is there anything else I can help you with?"

"No."

"Then I'll leave you to your work. I'm sure you're busy." Edwin smiled, then stepped out the door, closing it softly behind himself.

Grenidor stared at the door for several minutes, too disconcerted to continue his notes. When he'd returned from the hotel, he'd received a notice on his tablet that he was required to report to the medical suite for another observation. He'd grumbled but gone as ordered. Dr. Avery had frowned in confusion at Grenidor's insistence that he felt fine. After another CT and an MRI, the doctor had stared at the computer screen, flicking back and forth between the new scans and the old ones from that morning. Finally, he'd frowned across the desk at Grenidor. "I don't know what happened, but I don't see anything wrong now. Look." He pointed to amorphous blobs on the screen. "You had a lot of swelling. I don't know why it went away, and I don't know if it's going to come back. Get back here pronto if you have any symptoms at all." He frowned at Grenidor again, as if he were some strange puzzle to be worked out.

Grenidor didn't tell him about Edwin.

"Sir, this came from the lab for you." The lieutenant placed a small box on his desk.

"Thank you."

Grenidor waited until the young man closed his door before he opened the box. Bullets, neatly packaged in individual, labeled plastic bags. These were the bullets Edwin had handed him at their first meeting. Grenidor pulled out the card with a delivery code and waved it at his computer. The accompanying report popped up automatically.

This is unprecedented. Where did these come from?

The bullets have been fired: four each from guns 1, 4, and 5, six from gun 3, and five each from guns 2 and 6.

Anomalies: As noted, the bullets have been fired and can be traced to individual guns, which have been identified as belonging to the members of Security Team Delta. However, the bullets exhibit no deformation as would be usual when the bullet strikes.

Explanation: Even when a bullet is fired into a soft surface such as water, tissue, or gelatin, bullets expand and deform in predictable ways. The lab, and our literature searches, have not found any previous instances of fired bullets not exhibiting some sort of distortion resulting from deceleration. Such distortion is one piece of crime scene evidence.

In a lab, it may theoretically be possible to produce fired bullets exhibiting no discernible distortion, but I am unaware of any such experiments. Please explain how you acquired these samples.

Grenidor groaned and dropped his head into his hands. He should have expected something like this.

Conláed. He searched on the web for the name Feichin had mentioned. It took several tries to get a spelling that the computer recognized. Conláed, an old Irish name possibly meaning 'chaste fire' or 'purifying fire.' There were no references to a supernatural being, though there were a few old monks who had borne the name centuries ago. Grenidor frowned at the screen. Edwin didn't seem like that applied to him, but then, Feichin didn't think Edwin was Conláed anyway.

A message arrived while he researched. The comparison between Feichin's blood and Owen's blood had come back, showing a close familial relationship. They shared a relative no more than two generations back. *They're the same, genetically. Not just different tribes of the same species, but the same family.*

Genes aren't everything.

CHAPTER 7

ARIA DIPPED A folded cloth square into the bucket of water and worked gently at the blood still caked into Owen's black hair. Cillian was off somewhere in the darkness with Niall, and Niamh was meeting with Gabriel. Ardghal and Lorcan were nearby; Aria suspected that the danger Cillian had mentioned earlier still lurked. But they had withdrawn a little, leaving Aria alone in the circle of lamplight with Owen.

Even in the unusual privacy, silence drew out between them. His head was turned away from her and she bent down, trying to find a good angle to see the wound. A flashlight propped on a pencil lit it from a different angle than the lantern sitting by her shoulder.

"Why do you love me?"

Aria froze at the question. With some effort, she forced her hand to move again, pushing aside his dripping curls to wipe at the dark blood. Even in the cold air, she felt her cheeks flushing. "Do I need a reason?"

His soft breath might have been a sigh, but she wasn't sure.

Finally she said, "Because I choose to."

He was silent so long she thought he didn't meant to answer, but finally he said, "Thank you."

The simple, quiet words brought sudden tears to her eyes. She scowled and brushed at them with the back of her hand. But he wasn't done.

"Why did you pretend you didn't before?"

"I was embarrassed." She turned away and washed the cloth with unnecessary vigor. *Why is he prying?* "I'm sorry. I was stupid. It doesn't matter."

He turned his head back toward her, and she felt his eyes on her face. She wrung the cloth out, twisting it hard and watching the rust-colored water drip into the bucket. Her cheeks burned.

After a long moment, he moved one hand to touch her knee with the back of his fingers. "You should not have been. Love is never something to be ashamed of." He closed his eyes, mouth tight.

She stared at him. Even with the Fae singing for him as often as they could, pouring their strength into him, he had not healed as much as she had expected. Hoped. His breathing was difficult, though the gurgle had disappeared.

His eyes remained closed, and she pulled papers from her jacket pocket.

Grenidor's notes. She'd nearly forgotten about them. In the rush and emotion of the previous days, they'd been transferred from pants pocket to jacket, to the floor beside her bedroll, and back to her jacket. She wasn't sure if she wanted to know what he'd written.

3:00AM, 3 February 2086: Injuries sustained before and during capture: six broken ribs, broken tibia, eight gunshot wounds to the chest, two to the lower side, numerous contusions, collapsed lung, internal bleeding. Initial questioning has relied upon pressuring subject through existing injuries rather than enhanced methods. Initial questions focused on the location of the escaped test subjects as well as the resistance fighters who helped them. Subject is restrained with getlaril bonds and remains unwilling to provide any information.

7:00AM, 3 February 2086: Enhanced methods are now required. The getlaril bonds have prevented the subject from any healing, so far as can be determined, but he remains conscious. PVTs Thomson and Carlin assisted with the first session beginning at 5:45AM and lasting for 45 minutes. The primary tool was a steel baton; subject remained restrained for the duration.

PFC Carlin became quite disturbed and was relieved of duty. Despite the subject's inhuman nature, his human appearance made it difficult for Carlin to continue. I will write a further report separately, but let it be noted that I am not recommending him for disciplinary action at this time, only for further education on the subject's species.

PFC Thomson has also been relieved. A separate report is forthcoming; let it be noted here that Thomson's enthusiasm for the enhanced methods has alarmed me. I recommend his immediate referral for psychiatric counseling and perhaps therapy. Carlin's reaction was unfortunate and requires a greater understanding of the subject's dangerous nature; in contrast, Thomson's behavior betrays a violent pathology that I fear may erupt on humans in the future. Questioning of subject and others of his species should be aimed at extracting information and useful data, not the mere production of pain. Pain is a tool, not the goal.

Subject has additional broken ribs, possible broken jaw, presumably internal bleeding, and more visible contusions, including a head wound that may impede his ability to answer questions.

9:45AM, 3 February 2086: Subject may have healed somewhat, though it cannot be determined with any certainty. He remains conscious and lucid. I have questioned him further using only existing injuries. However, both sessions have been ineffective in provoking the desired compliance, so I have decided to try an experimental method. I have mixed a solution of dilute getlaril in water; I believe the dosage to be within nonlethal bounds, but am prepared with a stomach pump in case death appears imminent.

10:50AM, 3 February 2086: The getlaril solution may have been stronger than desired. Convulsions made it impossible to use the stomach pump, but subject appears likely to live. Convulsions and seizures continue and make questioning impossible for the moment.

11:45AM, 3 February 2086: Subject has given the location of the human guerilla fighters and possibly the escaped vampires as the Mayfair Hotel on Fenwick Avenue. I have sent teams to capture and/or eliminate them as possible. Interrogation continues.

1:00PM, 3 February 2086: Teams reported that the hotel was recently vacated. Despite the recent use, teams were unable to determine where the humans and/or creatures may have fled. Magic may have hidden any trail they left. Subject either knew or guessed they would flee and waited to give the location. I confess to more than a little frustration and anger.

The Dragon's Tongue

3:15P.M., 3 February 2086: PFC Turnata assisted with a session lasting from 1:15 and ending now, while I compose my notes. Experimental methods used include choking, partial drowning, application of force to pressure points, striking the bottom of the feet, and sound. Sound proved most effective; subject apparently has exceptionally sensitive hearing. I obtained headphones from PFC Turnata. Initially I used harsh music, but around 2:00 I obtained a recording of high-pitched tones used for testing sonar as well as a recording of stereo feedback. Subject showed extreme pain comparable to if not greater than that during the more standard force application.

Little additional information has been gained directly from subject's answers to questions. However, these methods have not been used on vampires before and the physiological and psychological reactions require documentation.

Aria hunched forward, the papers slipping from her grasp. She buried her face in her hands, her hair falling forward as her eyes filled with tears.

A cool hand touched her shoulder and Cillian dropped to sit beside her. "What is it?"

"I was reading..." She couldn't finish, and pushed the papers toward him.

He glanced at them, eyes skimming halfway down the page, and then thrust the papers back at her. "Burn it."

"What? Why?"

Cillian was trembling. "Lord Owen may be able to forgive, but others may turn when they read it. Burn it. For everyone's sake."

She hesitated. He snatched the papers from her hand and wadded them into a ball. Teeth bared in

141

a silent snarl, he blew out a harsh breath, then dropped the paper onto the ground, where it blazed into sudden flame. He watched the paper curl. His jaw was tight, hands clenched into fists.

Owen breathed softly, "Thank you, Cillian." He mustered a faint smile and moved to clasp his brother's hand. He said something in Fae.

Cillian took a deep breath, let it out slowly, and dropped his head. "May I ask you questions, brother? You are in pain, but I am... struggling. I need to understand." Cillian studied Owen's bruised hand, then glanced up at his face. At Owen's nod, he asked, "Why did you pray?"

"Because I had no strength left."

"I don't understand. You could have told him the truth." Cillian stared at Owen, as if the answer was to be found in his brother's face.

"I could not sacrifice you to end the pain! What kind of king would I be? What kind of brother?" Owen's voice cracked, and he tightened his hand on Cillian's. "And them. You know what he asked."

"You lied! Yet there is no stench of rebellion on you. Was it because you prayed?"

Owen didn't answer immediately, and Aria realized Niamh and Niall crouched across from her, waiting and listening.

A soft sigh. "It is possible. El... took mercy on me. I chose to obey love. Perhaps a human could explain it."

Cillian and Niamh looked sharply at Aria, and her eyes widened. She shook her head and shrugged. *How should I know? I don't understand what they're talking about.*

"Not Aria. Bartok, perhaps."

Niamh's eyes narrowed.

Cillian glanced at the human encampment at the other end of the platform and then back at Owen. "He knows little about us. Why Bartok?"

Niall frowned and glanced up at Aria with a knowing look. *He understands what Owen means.* He started to gesture, but stopped when Aria said quietly, "Bartok is a Christian. Is that why?"

"If El is God, then Bartok may have understanding we do not." Owen held Cillian's gaze. "Ask him."

Niamh frowned, but Owen said nothing else, and his eyes closed again.

Cillian met Niamh's eyes. "One of us should stay with him. Do you wish to speak with the humans, or shall I go?"

"Go. I will sing for him."

Cillian rose. Niall hesitated, then rose too, motioning that Aria should come with them.

Aria couldn't help smiling as they drew closer. Bartok was asleep lying on his stomach, his face pressed into the pages of an open notebook and pen still between his fingers. Aria craned her neck to read the half-hidden words. *Rebellion = sin? Are they then sinless? If they were created as a sinless parallel to humanity, shouldn't there be mention of them? And why would they look human? What does that leave? Not angel (too vulnerable). Not demon (too vulnerable and too good). Nephilim? Mighty men of renown... no, they were wiped out, and besides, nephilim would not be concerned with rules, lying, or justice. What if...* The rest was lost in an illegible scrawl.

Aria touched Bartok's shoulder. He groaned and shifted before he jerked awake and his eyes snapped open. "What is it?"

"We just have some questions. Sorry to startle you."

He rubbed his face as he sat up, then ran his hands through his hair. "Sorry. I was thinking. Got tired." His voice was scratchy with sleep.

Cillian spoke before Aria. "Lord Owen believes you may be able to explain some... anomalies to us. May I ask you questions?"

"I'll try to help. What questions?"

"We cannot sense when humans have sinned. We know sin is common to men, but we are not given authority to judge, nor the ability to sense sin in humans. We can sense rebellion in Fae."

Aria swallowed, forcing the image of Feichin's savagery out of her mind.

"Feichin..." Cillian hesitated, then said, "The video of Feichin made it clear to you. You can see by his actions. But rebellion is not an issue of action; it is a choice. Feichin turned when he chose to judge Davis as evil, not when he murdered. We can sense the heart of Fae. When a Fae turns, it is clear to all other Fae, even from a distance. Even through video." He took a deep breath. "Lord Owen lied when Grenidor was torturing him. A lie is one of several ways to turn. It always results in turning, and there is no way back. The choice is irrevocable. The consequences are both cata-strophic and obvious. And yet..." he glanced over his shoulder toward Owen. "And yet, Lord Owen does not have the stench of rebellion on him. If anything, he seems..." Cillian stopped.

Bartok stared at him.

Cillian clenched his hands so tightly they shook, and he took a deep, steadying breath. "Lord Owen *prayed*. Not with words, because he had no strength for words. He asked for forgiveness. We wish to know if you can explain this."

Aria's throat suddenly constricted. *So that's what Niall meant!*

Bartok glanced past her shoulder toward Owen. "You mean Owen... should be like Feichin?"

"He is *not*. But his choice would, normally, have resulted in a similar outcome."

Bartok kept his eyes on Owen's still form. "May I speak with him?"

The reluctance in Cillian's nod was obvious, but Bartok rose anyway. He followed her and Cillian toward the rest of the Fae.

CHAPTER 8

GRENIDOR WATCHED F11, Aithne, over the video feed. Her beauty had been more distracting the last few weeks. He was losing his professional detachment. The thought didn't bother him as much as it should. He didn't intend to act on his attraction, of course; lust and disgust mixed in equal measure. *They're animals.*

Aithne stiffened, and he focused on her. Tears welled up in her blue eyes to streak down her cheeks. She closed her eyes, knelt, and bent her head to the floor. She lifted both hands and put them on top of her head, fingers laced together as if she were forcing her head to the floor. She remained in that position for long minutes, then sat back on her heels. Her face was solemn, tear tracks damp on her face.

Grenidor frowned and zoomed in on her face. She appeared to struggling with some emotion, biting her lower lip fiercely. A few deep breaths and her trembling stopped.

He flipped to M15's feed.

The vampire shook his head as he walked. "No. If Owen is lord now, I'll not bow to him. I won't. Ailill was strong, but Owen is stronger. He'll break me. I won't be broken." He whirled with a savage snarl and began to pace the other direction. "I'll not be told what to do! Not anymore. I'm free! I'm hungry and I'm free." He ran his hands through his shaggy locks and growled. "I do what I want! I won't be ordered around."

Grenidor flipped to the video feed from Feichin's cell. The vampire was struggling to his feet, clumsy with weakness. Aside from Davis' blood and the one meal after their conversation at the Mayfair Hotel, it had been five and a half months since he'd been fed. Despite the bizarrely normal blood test results, it was obvious he was starving. White as paper, his skeletal body swayed in the middle of the cell.

He bared his teeth and snarled, "I won't submit!" Something in the light or shadow seemed to make his white teeth look longer, the black smudges under his eyes darker. The effect was ghastly, and though Feichin wasn't looking at him, Grenidor flinched back from the screen.

The only other vampire in custody was M6, Ailill. Grenidor flipped to his video feed.

There was nothing. The video was rolling, but Ailill was gone. Grenidor panned around the cell again, sick with horror.

It was free.

He punched the alarm into his tablet, then shoved it into his belt as he raced for the door. Pistol in hand, he careened into the hallway as lights flashed and sirens blared.

The alarm was specific and unmistakeable. The teams knew what to do. Vampire loose. Contain and destroy.

Grenidor headed toward the cells. Aithne was the only one who seemed coherent enough to explain; he would question her.

Pounding steps echoed in the halls and he passed troops taking their positions. He had a feeling it was useless, but they had to try. If a vampire was free, it might kill them all before they isolated it. They could become invisible, or close to it, walk and run silently, leap farther and higher than a human. If it meant to kill, it would do so. If it meant only to escape, it would be long gone.

Aithne stood at the bars at the entrance to her cell. "Did you kill him?" she asked as soon as Grenidor came into view.

He skidded to a stop a safe distance away. "What?"

"Did you kill Lord Ailill? Or was he taken by El?" Her eyes were locked on his, and he found himself answering.

"I didn't kill him. What are you talking about?"

Her lips curved in a sudden smile; the first smile he'd seen from a vampire in his years of research. It startled him with its sparkling beauty.

Don't forget she's a monster!

"Thank you." She stepped away from the bars, still smiling.

"For what?" he asked, not sure what had happened. He glanced down the hall, wondering if Ailill was about to kill him from behind.

"I was… angry. I might have chosen bitterness, if you had killed him." She lowered her chin. "You are testing me and my strength is limited. I wish not to fail, but we do not always do the things we mean to do, and sometimes we do things we do not mean to do. Perhaps humans are the same." She offered him a gentle smile.

Grenidor swallowed and backed away. *I do things I do not wish to do. I do not do things I wish to do.*

He turned and ran back to his office to pull up the video feed from Ailill's cell. Back thirty minutes.

Ailill sat on the bench in his cell, broad shoulders bowed. His face was familiar; a straight, strong jaw, clear blue eyes, and a shock of disheveled silver hair that matched his bushy eyebrows. His expression wasn't visible, though; he leaned forward with his elbows on his knees, head drooping. He'd be tired; his most recent regimen had been experiments with sleep deprivation on behavior and moods.

He raised his head and stood. Grenidor zoomed out, but there was nothing visible in the room. Ailill's hands were bound with getlaril, but his chains were long enough to allow him to move around the cell. He continued to gaze at something, and Grenidor paused the video and pulled up the feed from another camera. From this angle he could see the other two corners of the room.

The room was empty except for Ailill. He took a step forward and knelt stiffly. He pressed his face to the floor for a moment, then straightened. His face broke into a radiant smile; through the camera, the joy in it caught at Grenidor's heart.

Then he disappeared.

The shackles that had bound his wrists and ankles clattered to the floor. Grenidor let out a grunt of surprise and skipped the video backward. He zoomed in. He slowed the video to advance one frame at a time. Click. Click. The smile. Click. Click. Click. From one camera, he saw Ailill from behind his left shoulder, the grin crinkling the corner of his left eye. The other camera caught Ailill's face from the front right, white teeth gleaming. He almost laughed, joy so profound Grenidor found himself shaking with anger. *How dare he be so happy when he's in chains?* Grenidor growled under his breath and advanced a few more frames. Click. Click. Between one frame and the next, Ailill was gone. The shackles hung in the air, just beginning their descent. In the next frame they were lower. He watched them clank against the floor.

Ailill was gone. The shackles were clearly empty; he hadn't merely turned invisible. He was *gone*. The door did not open. Grenidor panned the cameras around anyway and studied every inch of the cell, knowing he would find nothing.

What is happening? He pulled up Aithne's video feed again. She sat with her back against the wall, knees pulled up to her chest. Her head rested against the wall and her eyes were closed. A faint smile curved her lips.

Meallan paced in his cell, more agitated than before. "I won't submit to him! I won't be ordered around! I'll die first. Freedom or death. Freedom and death. What's the difference?" Chains trailing behind him, he whirled to punch the getlaril-lined concrete wall. Grenidor winced at the sickening crunch of bone. Meallan stared at his mangled hand, lips lifted in a silent snarl. "He's naive. But I'm not!" He cradled his wounded hand and licked at the blood, growling low in his throat.

Grenidor grimaced and flipped to the feed from Feichin's cell. The vampire crouched in one corner, head turned away from the cameras. He let out a soft, monotonous moan.

Back to Ailill's cell. Nothing. Grenidor went to examine the cell himself, wincing at the alarms still blaring. He knew they would find nothing, but he didn't cancel the alarm yet.

"Osborne. I need a team at the holding cells in the basement."

The team arrived when he did. He keyed in the code to open the door and stepped inside.

Empty.

The team searched the room. There was no magic residue. No invisible Fae hiding in the corner, waiting to slip out. Nothing. The room was devoid of clues. The shackles lay on the floor, still locked but empty.

The team left, replaced by a forensic investigation team.

Grenidor knew they would find nothing.

He walked back to his office, shoulders tense, the alarm still blaring.

CHAPTER 9

BARTOK AND ARIA knelt beside Niamh as the Fae began to sing, the music rising around them like silver threads woven in the darkness.

A white-haired Fae stood on a rock outcropping above a small clearing. His shirt was tattered, torn edges waving in the breeze. Or was his shirt made of leaves? The sky was shot through with scarlet and gold, fantastic colors that made Aria blink in wonder. The sun set behind him, but his face was lit by the glow reflected off the rock. A strong face, sharp-featured, with piercing blue eyes beneath bushy white brows. A shock of untamed curls, a few dark strands remaining among the silver. High, hard cheekbones and a lean, strong figure, despite his age. Shoulders unbowed, back straight. He spoke, but Aria could not understand him.

Owen stepped forward from the crowd. His hair fell to his shoulders, thick black curls any girl would have envied. He knelt solemnly before the old Fae, head bowed, eyes closed. The family resemblance was strong.

The elder Fae spoke again, one hand resting atop Owen's head. His words seemed to glitter in the air, bright as diamonds. His lips curved in a proud smile. He bowed his own head, then turned and walked away.

He was gone.

Owen rose and looked after him, then turned to face the assembled Fae.

Aria caught her breath.

Tears streaked Owen's cheeks, and those of the others.

"What happened?" Bartok whispered. He looked shaken.

"Lord Ailill, our father, has been taken away. Lord Owen is now high king." Niamh's voice was soft.

Niall bowed his head first. He lifted Owen's hand gently and placed it on top of his own head, pressed it down so that his face touched the floor. Then he straightened and smiled through his silent tears.

Niamh did the same, white hands standing out against her black hair. Then Cillian. Ardghal. The others in turn.

"Where is Lachtnal?" Owen whispered.

Niamh's head dropped. "He has been spending time in the tunnels. He is…"

"I know. I can feel it." Owen sighed softly. "If he were here, perhaps…"

"He may come." Ardghal did not sound hopeful.

Owen took a deep breath and winced, let it out slowly. He turned toward Bartok. "We have questions. Many things we do not understand."

Cillian glanced toward him and frowned. "I will speak for you, Lord Owen, if I may. We have always believed—"

Owen interrupted him. "I do not cease to be your brother because our father…" he caught his breath with a grimace. "You wish to call me brother. Do so."

"Yes, my brother." Cillian dropped his head, hiding a smile. "Getlaril is poisonous to us. The touch of it on our skin burns, as you have seen. Getlaril bullets are fatal to us if the metal stays inside. It impedes our healing; indeed, it prevents us from using any megdhonia.

"We believe our power is a gift from El, refined by practice but innate to us. Since getlaril prevents us from using megdhonia, we have always believed it was a barrier." He stopped and frowned, as if a sudden thought had caught his attention.

Niamh spoke, her eyes flicking between their faces. "Do you understand our question?"

Bartok looked confused, and she continued.

"Since this power is from El, and getlaril prevents us from using it, we have always believed that getlaril separates us from El. Use of getlaril is perhaps one of the worst crimes humans have perpetrated against our people."

Owen spoke then, his voice so faint Bartok and Aria leaned forward to hear him. "But we were wrong. Getlaril did not prevent El from hearing my prayer." His eyes turned toward Bartok.

Bartok licked his lips. "If your El is our God, I cannot imagine that getlaril can prevent you from being heard. I know next to nothing about your power, but God can always hear you."

"What then of our power that is gone?" Ardghal asked. "Why is Lord Owen, beloved of El, still suffering?"

Bartok frowned. "You think you should be exempt from suffering because you are beloved? That makes no sense."

Cillian stiffened. "He meant..."

Owen twitched a finger. "El hears us even with getlaril, Cillian. That is enough for me. His forgiveness is proof."

Bartok's eyes met Owen's. "Yes. Humans sin, and can be forgiven, many times. We ask for forgiveness, and we receive it when we come with humble hearts. To receive mercy, we ask in humility. You are different, yes, but God is the same. His character does not change, though his methods of interaction may vary."

Cillian leaned forward, hands steepled together under his chin. "What does this mean, then?"

Their reflection was interrupted by a shout from the other end of the platform.

"Police. We have but moments. Help me, Ardghal." Cillian flipped back the blanket covering Owen. His black bruises had barely begun to turn mottled purple, and Aria clenched her fists in sudden fury at Grenidor.

Ardghal and Niamh slipped their arms under Owen's shoulders and lifted him. He choked back a groan at the movement, and they draped him over Cillian's back. Cillian rose, and Ardghal led the way into darkness.

Bartok turned off the flashlight and stuffed it into his pocket, then blew out the lantern. He found Aria's hand in the blackness. "Where are they going?" he murmured into her ear.

Niall's cool hand slipped into hers and tugged her forward. Niamh brushed by her, pausing to whisper in her ear, "Siofra and I will cause a distraction and cover your trail. Follow Cillian."

Bartok hesitated beside Aria, then followed, his hand warm and strong around hers.

They jogged through the darkness. The Fae made no sound, except for one barely audible gasp of pain from Owen. Only Niall's cool hand led them forward, around corners, down halls and stairways.

A long climb up a pitch-black stairway ended in a metal door, and they exited into a narrow alley that smelled of urine and old grease. The Fae were gone except for Niall, who led Aria a short distance to a fire escape and motioned her upward.

"Where are the others?" She stopped.

He gestured upward again, then made a motion with his hands.

"They're going another way?" Aria guessed.

He nodded, although with an expression that made it clear she'd missed some nuance. Again, he indicated she should go, with a quick glance down the alley.

They climbed only halfway up, then Niall led them inside, carefully closing the door behind them. Aria and Bartok followed him down a long hall to a room at the end with a balcony that faced a sheer brick wall. He motioned toward it, then mimed jumping and rolling.

"What?" Aria frowned in confusion.

Another series of gestures.

"Jump at the wall? Are you kidding?" The question was not entirely serious, but Niall motioned again.

"What? No! That's crazy."

Niall stared at her in frustration for one heartbeat, then turned. With two strides he reached the balcony, then jumped, one foot pushing off the railing. He somersaulted across the alley directly toward the brick.

Aria bit back a shriek as he disappeared.

A moment later, he reappeared, sailing over the railing to land in a crouch just in front of them. He patted his chest and then pointed at her, then pantomimed jumping again.

"I can't jump that far." Aria stared at the wall. Perhaps fifteen feet away, it appeared to be solid brick. But Niall had just passed through it, disappearing as if by magic.

But magic exists. If not magic, at least many things I'd never expected and can't explain. Why don't I believe this?

"What's on the other side?"

Niall nearly threw up his hands in irritation, but took a deep breath instead. He stared at her as if puzzled. Finally he mimed sleeping, putting his head on his hands and closing his eyes.

"A place to rest?"

Bartok patted her shoulder. "I'll go first if you want. How far down does the entrance go? I'm not sure I can jump that far."

Niall smiled. He crouched next to the railing and laced his fingers together, then nodded toward Bartok.

With a deep breath, Bartok ran forward to plant his foot in Niall's hands. Niall launched him up and forward, and he flew across the alley. Natural athleticism turned his flail into the beginning of a credible roll before he disappeared into the brick.

Niall nodded that Aria should do the same.

This is crazy.

She ran forward anyway. It happened too quickly for her to be afraid. She sailed through the air, landing in a clumsy roll that jarred her shoulder and wrenched her neck. Niall crouched beside her only a moment later, failing to hide his amusement at her awkward landing. He touched her shoulder with a small, cool hand, and the pain disappeared.

Only then did she look up.

CHAPTER 10

"I NEED MORE. The vampires are dangerous, and the threat is growing. You haven't given me anything more than logical advice."

"Yes. It is time we discussed these matters. We are in a Conflict."

Grenidor could hear the capital C on conflict, the weight that Edwin gave the word.

"It is beyond your understanding. Beyond time as you comprehend it. We, and my kind, are one side. We believe in freedom. In independence. In choosing your own path. The others do not. They are led by one we call the Slavemaster. They obey him. They *worship* him, and believe we should too."

Grenidor pondered that for a moment. "The Slavemaster must be powerful then, if you haven't already defeated him."

Edwin frowned. "Yes. He is. We shall have the victory, of course. But the other side is powerful, and the Slavemaster is the most powerful of all."

Grenidor said, "Then I see no reason for humanity to become involved. What would we do against power like that?"

"You are *already* involved. You can't help it. The other side is actively helping the vampires."

"What?" Grenidor's voice cracked.

"You are part of what is at stake. One of the primary questions of the Conflict is whether you will be willing servants—willing *slaves*—of the other side, or whether you will remain independent, perhaps even ally with us."

Grenidor stared at him.

"We would prefer for you to ally with us, of course. But even if you don't, we have no objection to you choosing to be nonaligned, as long as you don't ally with the Slavemaster and his servants. We will be friendly with you as long as you don't actively oppose us. However, we won't aid you much until or unless you choose to be our allies. Note that I say allies rather than servants. We don't require that you serve us the way the Slavemaster wants you to serve him."

Grenidor's mind raced. *I believe him. I wish I didn't.* "Can you prove it?"

Edwin nodded. "Yes. One of the Slavemaster's servants aided the vampire Cillian and the human Aria Forsyth in their attack on Forestgate Imperial Security Facility in which they escaped with the vampire Owen." Edwin's voice hardened when he said Owen's name, hatred creeping into his tone.

Edwin gestured toward him, and suddenly Grenidor's mind was flooded with images. A door

160

that slammed across the corridor intersection; it didn't exist that morning. The guards and their bizarre decision to go upstairs rather than look out the front door, when the vampires and Aria would have been clearly visible. The incredible inability of the guards to shoot the intruders. The disappearance of the trail and the guards' inability to track them past the tunnel entrance, though Owen was bleeding and they could not have been moving quickly.

"I don't understand." Grenidor's voice quavered, and he swallowed hard. "Did he... did it... he... was the past changed to include the doors, or were our memories changed? What *happened*?"

"Both and neither. What he did is beyond human understanding. You understand, though, that he was actively aiding the vampires. They are allied with the Slavemaster and his minions." Edwin sat back and watched Grenidor's face.

Even for me, this is too much to understand at once. I thought I had a grasp on the hidden things of the world. But this? What have we gotten into? If the vampires have allies like that... humans, as a species, are doomed. What can we do against power like that?

Was that Conlάed?

"I can offer you more than good advice. I can offer you a weapon that would be effective against vampires and their allies."

Grenidor looked up sharply. "Like what?"

Edwin smiled slowly, showing slightly yellowed teeth. "So eager. I can teach you ceremonies and techniques to manipulate magic more effectively. Your human methods are puerile at best, and the vampires' are not much better. My methods are stronger. They won't make much sense to you at first, but there is power behind them."

Grenidor nodded. "All right. I'm listening."

"First, you must understand a little more. You have been concerned with the human resistance to your newly minted Empire. Yet the vampires represent a greater existential threat, do they not? They have powerful allies, and the Conflict is more important than you understand. You have ignored the Christians infiltrating the Empire."

"Because they cause no trouble. Few of them engage in political activities. They come in and have little meetings with five or ten others and then go home. If they get agitated, we deal with them as with any other troublemakers." Grenidor shifted under the intensity of Edwin's gaze.

"You are correct that they are not usually politically active. This is a choice they make in order to escape notice. It does not mean they pose no threat. On the contrary, they are valuable to the other side and cause great problems for us. The Conflict is a war of choices and decisions. Physical power is important, but only insofar as it affects the decisions that are made. Those Christians are persuading... *misleading*... people to pledge their very souls to the Slavemaster. If you want a more powerful weapon, you must lend our side a little support."

"Like what?"

"Arrest the Christians and execute them as you would any other traitor to the Empire."

Grenidor tapped his pen against his leg, considering. "On what charges?"

"Any charges you wish. It doesn't matter for our purposes."

"I'll consider it. I don't have the power to effect legal changes, you know. I'm an army colonel, not a politician."

Edwin blinked and gave him a slow smile. "I can ensure that your efforts are not opposed, if you choose to work with me. Pretty much anything you order will be done. Obviously this benefits you personally as well. We don't mind you profiting as long as you deliver."

Grenidor gaped at him. "Uh... I'll consider it."

"Of course." Edwin rose and flicked his hands over his trousers, smoothing the wrinkles. "My offer for more powerful techniques awaits. Make an effort to help our side in good faith, and I'll return the favor." He smiled, all warmth and kindness. "We don't expect total commitment all at once. You can work up to it as you feel comfortable."

"Understood." Grenidor watched him leave.

He pulled up the message center for Imperial Security Headquarters and looked through the names.

What difference does it make? If they're traitors, they're traitors. Infiltrating the Empire is a crime, even if they're not causing trouble once they're here.

Finally he found the name he wanted. Mark Fletcher, Head of North Quadrant Intelligence and Investigations. He hesitated. *Do I really want to do this?*

He took a deep breath and let it out, remembering the details of the last report of a vampire attack. The victim had been a nobody, simply a man walking in the shadows. But no one deserved to die like that. He'd sacrifice a few traitors to gain Edwin's help against the monsters.

"Fletcher, this is Grenidor." He nodded and leaned forward over his desk, twirling a pen as he listened to the obligatory pleasantries.

"Yeah. I received some information I thought you should know about. Can you go secure on this phone? Good." He waited while the phones synced and then beeped readiness. "You know when we were prioritizing arrests, and we put those religious freaks near the bottom? The Christians? Yeah, I thought they didn't do anything either. I have some new information. It's a sensitive source, but I have reason to believe the info is good. The Christians are a threat. Yes. I don't know exactly. No, no, just move them up the target list. Arrest and interrogate. … See if they're loyal. You know they're not. Right, exactly."

Grenidor hung up and leaned back in his chair, fingers laced behind his head. *They're traitors anyway.*

GRENIDOR PULLED UP the list of questions for Aithne on his tablet. She and Ailill were the most pleasant of the remaining vampires to interrogate. Ailill was interesting, magnetic, surprisingly soft-spoken for someone who had caused so much trouble. But Aithne was just as compelling, and gorgeous, too. *Keep your eyes to yourself, Paul. Don't be stupid.*

She was already watching the barred door when he came into view; she must have heard his footsteps. But she said nothing.

"I have questions. How is Owen related to Feichin?"

She gave him a cool look, and then deliberately turned her face toward the wall.

"Look, I know you'll have to answer me eventually. The faster you answer, the faster I'll leave you alone to the joys of your concrete box." He growled the words, but he couldn't muster the same visceral hatred that came so naturally when he looked at Feichin. She was too beautiful, too perfect. *She hasn't had an opportunity to kill anyone yet. That's the only difference.*

She did not answer.

"How is Owen related to Feichin?" he repeated.

Her jaw tightened, and she bit her lower lip.

Grenidor couldn't entirely hide his grim satisfaction. "How is Owen related to Feichin? Answer me. It's important."

She turned her blue eyes on him, her anger so intense he could almost feel it as a physical force. "Why do you ask?"

"I need to understand your clans. Meallan," he mangled the pronunciation, but her expression said she understood, "said he was from the clan of Falling Water. What clan are you from?"

She could not help answering. He knew that; even silence was difficult if he asked enough times, with enough intensity. But would she tell the truth?

"What are you going to do with the information?"

"Nothing. I just want to understand." That was true enough. He didn't have any plans for the information yet. But more knowledge of the vampires was always better.

"Lord Ailill is Lord Owen's father." The words sounded as if they were dragged out of her. "Feichin is the son of Lord Ailill's youngest brother. Feichin is my father. Meallan is from my mother's clan, the son of my mother's father's brother."

Grenidor tried to picture the family tree. "Don't you have words for those relationships? Meallan is your cousin, then?"

"He is of my parents' generation. I do not know the word for that in English."

His tablet gave a soft beep and he glanced at it. General Harrison's name showed for a few moments, superimposed over the Empire's symbol, the bison. *Why did we change to the bison again? A new government. A new symbol.* The bison recalled the old times, when the country was open and free, before even the old government had been formed. But the adoption of the new-old symbol had been carefully executed, reminding people of the strength and power and freedom of the bison while omitting any historical context.

He looked back up at Aithne, considering what other questions he might ask. "How old are you?"

"One hundred twenty years." She gave him a curious look. "I have told you that before."

"Why did the Empire choose the bison for its symbol?"

She blinked. "I have no knowledge of the Empire's political or propaganda strategies."

No, she wouldn't. But why did I hope she would remember? Because I don't, and I should.

He glanced at the message from General Harrison. *Rec'd your last report. Good work. Have instructed IPF to continue supporting you as necessary*

166

on capture attempts. Read the attached report re: an attack near the Northern/Eastern Quadrant line and tell me what you think. -H.

Grenidor took a step back to lean against the wall as he pulled up the report. Aithne watched him neutrally, her expression unreadable. A government official had been murdered on his way home from work last night. The details were familiar, and Grenidor barely needed to glance at the photographs to know it was another vampire attack. *Throat ripped open. Body nearly bloodless. No evidence of a human attacker; no hair, fingerprints, or footprints. No evidence of a weapon.*

He scowled at Aithne and pushed away from the wall. "Cursed vampires!"

FLETCHER SENT A courtesy copy of the report on the first six arrests of the Christians. Grenidor scanned it on his tablet. Michael Fishman, age 45. Admitted to previous political activism, but said he was currently interested only in religious affairs. Seeking converts. *Proselytizing.* Grenidor read the word with a scowl.

It was like a slap in the face, a statement that the Christians thought Grenidor and the others were wrong. Wrong about everything that mattered.

Jennifer Bates, age 31. Myra Solomon, age 52. Devin Carlisle, age 27. Angela Carlisle, age 26. Christopher Lewis, age 29.

Bates had been quoted as saying, "The Imperial leaders seem to believe they have a monopoly on truth. Empires fall when leaders begin to believe they're invincible, that they can do no wrong.

Or worse, when they forget that there is such a thing as right and wrong, when they believe what they want is right and whatever opposes them is wrong. Neither we nor the government can define right and wrong. I'm not here to oppose the empire on political grounds. But I must tell people the truth."

Grenidor rubbed his eyes. Surely she'd meant to continue, but the report did not include her words. It didn't matter. "I'm not here to oppose the empire... *but...*" That meant she *did* oppose the Empire. She and Solomon had been arrested together. Between them they had nine illicit books, including five Bibles as well as three books that appeared to be biblical commentaries and one history book. Grenidor tapped in a request to see the confiscated books after they had been examined.

He reread the report of the intrusion at the facility on H Street, where the majority of the adult vertril had been kept. Obviously there had been an intruder, but no evidence had yet been found to indicate how the intruder had entered.

Despite the lack of evidence, Grenidor was sure the intruder had been Owen. Another vampire would have killed the guards if he'd wanted in; Owen, for reasons yet unknown, would not. He wasn't opposed to destruction for his own purposes, though. In addition to killing five hundred twenty-eight vertril, he'd also started a fire that destroyed a significant portion of the computers used by the research teams. Most of the data had been backed up on the secure network, of course, so the loss wasn't as devastating as Owen had probably hoped. Still, it was alarming.

Grenidor assumed Owen had acted alone; perhaps that assumption was false. In the raid only a few hours later, it appeared that Owen had only human allies, with the possible addition of M8, the vampire boy whose tongue had been removed. Now there were dozens of vampires free, operating together. Grenidor felt fear slithering down his back. Owen alone was terrifying, despite his restraint thus far. Assuming he'd been the one to conduct the first raid, he'd killed five hundred twenty-eight vertril in the space of hours, perhaps less, and had been strong enough to lead a mission immediately afterwards. If the Empire was very fortunate, he was the only one capable of such a feat.

Grenidor jiggled his foot and thought, then pulled up the communications portal for the research teams. He typed *Vampires appear to be less vulnerable to vertril than previously believed, yet they also appear to consider them a threat. Increase the vertril breeding program immediately, and bring all young vertril to maturity and full operation as soon as possible. Hormone treatments are approved.* He clicked over to the most recent report and checked the numbers. *Increase aggression and ferocity through any possible means (hormonal, training, hunger, etc.). Prepare for release upon my authorization.*

The intruder had burned a sizable pile of computer parts on one of the secured floors. The forensic analysis indicated that the fire had been incredibly hot; the various computer components had melted into a messy puddle of plastic and metal. They couldn't yet explain why the entire building hadn't gone up in flames; a blaze that hot should have taken down the whole block.

Vampires had little knowledge of human technology, though this incident may have revealed more than Grenidor feared. Without the ability to read the hard drives, the intruder must have simply wanted to destroy the information, not imagining that the information was copied elsewhere. Grenidor allowed himself a faint smile of satisfaction.

"YOU PROMISED ME a weapon. You promised something useful."

"Yes. Tell me about the Christians. Have you pursued them?" Edwin stared across the desk at him.

"Yes. There have been arrests. Executions." Grenidor pushed down a twinge of guilt.

"Good." Edwin regarded him for a long moment.

Grenidor tried not to squirm. *Why am I nervous, like a kid waiting to hear whether he passed the exam? Do we really need this weapon? Maybe it would be better to back out now.*

Edwin leaned forward to lace his hands together on the desk. "Do you know why the vampires feed on organ meat?"

"No."

"Organ meat contains power. You can't measure it; your technology is inadequate. But the vampires feed on it for a reason." He waited until Grenidor nodded. "The vampires' bodies have evolved to utilize this power to fuel their manipulation of magic. It is an interesting evolutionary phenomenon, but it has reached its apex in the current generation. Their abilities will no longer increase.

"Humans cannot manipulate magic with your bodies' natural abilities. However, there are ceremonies and techniques I can teach you that will enable you to manipulate magic as vampires cannot dream."

"How?" Grenidor leaned forward in his eagerness.

"The ceremonies sound dramatic at first, but think of them as routines, or perhaps as simple computer programs. Go through these motions and receive predictable results.

"Begin with this simple, yet effective ceremony: Make a small wooden statue of some kind. A calf or a bull works well. Cover it with gold, if you can. Real gold; it is the expense that matters, not the color. Gold paint is worthless. Put the live subject in front of it, kill the subject with a knife, and put the blood and organs over the statue. You may eat the organs and blood afterward, or burn them if you wish."

Grenidor frowned. "The subject?"

"An animal will suffice, but a human is better. Human organs are much more powerful than those of animals. The organs of Christians are best, because they represent the other side of the Conflict. Those you have executed would be an ideal source."

Grenidor felt his mouth twisting in disgust, but Edwin wasn't finished.

"I hope you aren't too squeamish. Blood also has power beyond that which your science can understand. Harvesting the organs while the subject is still alive is important; death steals the

171

power quickly. The manner of harvest can also concentrate the power. The ceremony I told you about is basic, but effective."

Edwin smiled a little at Grenidor's expression. "Why a bull? It doesn't really matter, but an animal image helps focus the power. Understand, of course, that the image itself has no intrinsic power. You know this and understand it. Just going through the motions is sufficient to gain power through the ceremony. The important thing is that the image replaces any unconscious respect for the Slavemaster, any inner turning that a man's heart might have toward the other side.

"However, if you could find some people who *do* believe that the statue itself has power, the ceremony can be even more valuable. Since you have expertise in creating an impressionable attitude in people, this should not be difficult. I suggest taking a group that is already undergoing re-education and telling them that the statue is, or represents, a spirit that can protect them. They need not be told what the protection is from, although if you wanted to use the specter of the vampires, that would be effective. You can release them afterwards, or execute them, whichever serves you better. If you release them, though, I can guarantee that they will cause no trouble. They won't discuss the ceremony. You could even save them and use them again. The more of them, the better." Edwin's eyes gleamed.

"Anyone who performs this ceremony will receive some power. For your purposes, the most useful result will be that your thoughts will be hidden from the vampires and their supernatural allies. The vampires will not be able to sense you approaching by magic, although you will still be visible and audible. You could also put some bullets in front of the statue and cover them in blood. Those bullets would kill the vampires immediately; even getlaril takes time to kill them, and you won't have time to spare."

Grenidor put his face in his hands, unwilling to look at Edwin any longer. He dug his fingernails into his scalp, mind racing.

Edwin continued, "The ceremony will work merely by going through the motions, following the instructions I have given you. But, the magic can be greatly magnified. If you invite me, I can enter your body and do the ceremony with you, using your voice and hands and my power."

"No!" Grenidor looked up, horrified.

Edwin raised his hands placatingly. "I understand your reluctance. Alternately, you could select a few trusted people to volunteer to do it on your behalf. They could invite me in, and I could perform the magic on your behalf, to your benefit."

"I thought the whole point of cooperating with you was to retain my free will."

"I won't take control of you. I would merely assist you in the ceremony in order to increase its effectiveness. You know the Slavemaster wants willing slaves. My side merely wishes to aid people in rejecting any form of submission. I speak more of a partnership. You would keep all your free will, and could, if you chose, turn away at any time. But I'm confident you won't, after you see the benefits of cooperation, and realize that you are still free."

Grenidor swallowed. "I need to think. Please leave." He had a brief, unsettling memory of Meallan, the vampire, pacing in his cell, reveling in his freedom and cursing with every breath. But the image faded as he looked back at Edwin.

Edwin hesitated, then nodded. "As you wish. Consider it. There is nothing to fear and much to gain."

"Leave. Please."

Edwin stepped out and closed the door with a quiet click.

For the first time in three years, Grenidor left his office early. The cold, steady downpour fit his mood. He stood under the narrow bus shelter outside the front gate with his coat collar flipped up against the damp gusts.

His thoughts whirled, circling back on themselves to begin again. Edwin's physical form had become familiar, and it took effort to remember that he was not human. He was, if not attractive, at least unthreatening. Only what he asked caused Grenidor any unease.

It didn't exactly bother him that Christians were dying. They were a name, a label, nothing more. Humans, but not ones he could identify with. They believed something bizarre about a man who rose from the dead. Obviously it was a foolish superstition.

What, then, was the issue with Edwin's ceremony?

The animal totem was strange; it reminded Grenidor of some long-forgotten superstition. Why would Edwin suggest something so seemingly random? Yet he didn't seem to care what symbol was used. Did it matter?

Sacrifice ceremonies had been used for centuries. Was it possible that those who performed them had an understanding of magic that was unknown to modern science, like folk medicine sometimes showed the way to new cures? Or... had Edwin convinced those people as he was trying to convince Grenidor himself? For what purpose? Vampires probably lived for hundreds of years, and Edwin was more powerful than they were. Had the ceremonies ever been beneficial for those who performed them?

The only civilization Grenidor could remember that had practiced human sacrifice was the Aztecs. It didn't seem to have done them much good. Maybe ancient Mesopotamians and others in the Levant... all those little tribes that fought with each other for generations. Obviously it hadn't been helpful for them either; he couldn't even remember the names of their tribes, much less any of their leaders or accomplishments. Ancient Egyptians? Well, they'd made the pyramids, so that was something, but they weren't exactly a world power anymore. Some of the African tribes had throughout history, and they weren't world powers either. If the practice was Edwin's doing, then the people who did it hadn't been the primary beneficiaries.

What were the costs and benefits of going through with the ceremony? Using an animal would be safest. The Empire wouldn't object to that. *And Edwin's more of a fool than I think if he believes I'll let him use my hands and mouth for a ceremony. He is not coming into my body!* But Grenidor had always prided himself on his leadership. *Can I really ask anyone to volunteer for something I find so terrifying? Even if they're willing, I don't have the right to ask it. Nor would it be wise. How do I know he would leave them after the ceremony is complete? More disturbing... if he's offering, he must be able to enter humans. How do I know he hasn't already? I can't trust him, that's obvious. How devious is he?*

The bus arrived, and Grenidor was so lost in thought that he nearly missed it. The driver shouted at him through the open door. "Colonel! You getting on or not?"

He grumbled an apology as he stepped into the bus over the small river running through the gutter. Water cascaded off his jacket as he remained standing, one hand wrapped around a pole as the bus lurched forward. Already full of early commuters, the bus was humid and stuffy.

What is he, really? How deceptive is the human form?

Grenidor nearly jumped out of his skin when he saw Edwin sitting in an aisle seat a few rows back.

Edwin smiled, showing his teeth. Grenidor felt that it was vaguely reminiscent of Feichin's smile, a predatory gleam in his eyes. "You're wondering if you're in over your head, aren't you?"

Grenidor nodded once, heart thudding.

"The answer is yes. You are. But you always have been. Now you're just aware of the Conflict. The Slavemaster and his minions have always been working."

"You said the other side is powerful. They want us to be their slaves. Why haven't they enslaved us yet?"

Edwin frowned a little. "They... have strange ideas. The Slavemaster wants you to be his *willing* slave. You must decide to be his slave, his servant.

Under compulsion, your service would be meaningless to him. So he and his side will not attack by force. That does not mean they are not dangerous."

Grenidor studied his face. Edwin stared back at him seriously, as if willing him to believe. *If they won't attack by force... what happened at Forestgate then? Was that not an attack? ... Technically speaking, I suppose it wasn't an aggressive maneuver. No one was hurt, despite the power available to them. What of Eastborn? Nine soldiers were shot. Three died. Were they not allied with the other side? Were they independent... like me? ... Or is Edwin lying?*

He realized several people were staring at him. "What?"

"Who are you talking to?" a young man asked.

Grenidor gestured, and then blinked. Edwin's seat was occupied by a middle-aged woman who glared back at him. She held her oversized handbag on her lap protectively.

"I... um... sorry," he murmured and shifted to look forward. Their gazes burned into his back. There were few people of questionable sanity out in public anymore; they'd all been cleaned up in the last three years. None of them had been active duty military, seen talking to non-existent companions while in uniform.

Perhaps the casualties at Eastborn were the result of human actions. The human traitors can obviously kill. Still... what does that mean? If they won't attack by force...

Lost in contemplation, he nearly missed his stop. The steady rain continued as he walked down the block, shoulders hunched against the drizzle.

A flicker at the corner of his vision caught his eye. He whirled, but it was gone. He stared at the empty alley, heart thudding. It might have been a dark flame, or perhaps a flame shaped like a man. He had the impression of scaly reptilian skin. Feathers, perhaps. He rubbed at his face and took a few steps into the alley, searching the ground for a trace of... what?

What do I expect to find? Nothing. And there was nothing unusual. A dark alley, empty but for a discarded candy bar wrapper smashed against the edge of the drain.

He kept his eyes up as he walked the last block to his condominium, but saw nothing out of the ordinary.

He lived in a luxury high rise, but the amenities meant little. He'd never used the heated swimming pool on the rooftop terrace, nor enjoyed the spa on the first floor. There was always work, and the imperial security facilities all had gyms for active duty military personnel.

The doorman, Max, opened the door for him. "You're back early."

"Yeah." Grenidor brushed past him. He felt Max's eyes on him as he strode to the elevator. The inside of the elevator was mirrored, and he stared at himself as he rode up. The bandage from his head was gone, but he looked tired and worn.

A shiver ran down his back, and he had the unpleasant feeling that he was under scrutiny. Yet he was alone in the elevator. He shook his shoulders out and sighed. Maybe he'd feel better with some sleep.

THE DRAGON'S TONGUE

COOL WINTER SUNLIGHT streamed across the blankets. Grenidor woke slowly, swimming upward through tangled threads of dreams. Disjointed images jockeyed for position. Drifting into wakefulness, he remembered Jessica's death again.

He'd been away at the time, studying in the Himalayas as part of his survey of nonstandard biologies. The Cherustin people and their ancestor spirits had been particularly interesting; he'd thought their legends had more truth to them than western researchers had previously believed. Cherustin accounts of mysterious killings bore a striking similarity to a string of murders back home.

The Army flew him home to identify her body.

Some images cannot be forgotten.

His younger sister Jessica had been a sweet girl. Grenidor always thought she was too sweet for the law career she'd chosen; she hated arguing. Much younger than he was, she'd been wide-eyed at his youthful descriptions of bootcamp and various field trainings he'd endured as a young officer. He'd been excited by the travel and opportunities. She preferred to stay home.

The method of killing was not known at the time, though Grenidor was convinced a vampire had killed her. Her throat was bitten as if by an animal, her body nearly drained of blood. Her eyes were wide open in terror. Her fingernails had skin beneath them; the DNA had not been identified. The Pyorski test had been invented only a few years ago, and by that time the evidence had been long destroyed.

The Pyorski test was an incredible breakthrough. It identified vampire DNA by looking at

179

changes at the molecular level. Approximately ten percent of the molecules in a sample taken from a vampire would show a faint glow when subjected to Pyorski radiation. Both tissue and blood samples could be tested with no change in the test's astonishing accuracy. Pyorski radiation itself was a mystery, but the test had proven reliable, even with very small sample sizes.

Federico Pyorski was a researcher on one of Grenidor's teams, and his breakthrough alone had justified many hundreds of thousands of dollars of allocations. When asked about how he'd come up with the idea, or how he'd identified the radiation he'd used, or how he'd devised the testing apparatus, he'd flatly refused to give any information. Grenidor had once wondered whether he'd been taking credit for another researcher's work, but the team had good rapport and he didn't sense any tension or resentment from anyone else.

The test worked, and the only regret Grenidor had about it was that he couldn't prove his suspicions about Jessica's death.

Feichin's murder of Davis was horrific. Imagining Jessica suffering a similar death brought tears to Grenidor's eyes and set his heart thudding.

Her murder was twenty years ago. Fresh grief had solidified into deep, hidden pain and anger.

Not long after Jessica's death, a vampire had assassinated three senators one night. The victims had not been together when they died; two were at their expensive, well-guarded apartments in separate neighborhoods, and another had been in a private room at a posh restaurant. The images of the bodies still appeared sometimes in his dreams. The vampire had used a knife on the victims' throats, then cut out their hearts, taken an enormous bite, and left the heart sitting on the victim's open chest. Dripped blood dried rust-brown and black on the wall near each body where he left a handprint and a phrase.

I am death at one body. *I am hate* at the second. *I am despair.*

The handprint pattern proved the same vampire killed all three. The murders had shocked the old government. Soothing lies were publicized while the vampire research and elimination program was established. How could one creature move so quickly across town? How could it get past motion detectors, heat sensors, and bodyguards?

The program's official name was Hostile Humanoid Identification, Research, and Elimination Program, or HHIREP. In good governmental style, the acronym was pronounced "high-rep". In addition to the vampire research itself, HHIREP also included the vertril breeding program, ongoing research on Pyorski radiation, and various research programs on magic and magic sensors.

Paul Grenidor had been part of the program from the beginning, first as deputy director, then director. Grief and anger had turned to obsession. HHIREP had made significant strides under his leadership.

He'd long known that some vampires called themselves Fae and did not accept the title of vampire, but their factional differences had never mattered to him. He was a biologist, not an anthropologist. The only thing that mattered was that their numbers appeared to be increasing. When he was feeling optimistic, he told himself humans had gotten better at detecting them. More often he believed vampires were increasing in number and aggressiveness. There couldn't be many vampires; there had been few such incidents as the triple murder of the senators. But even one vampire was a threat to the Empire.

He rose and dressed in a crisp uniform. Black coffee and a piece of bread sufficed for breakfast. *A normal person would eat a bagel. I should go to the store and get some after work.* He knew it wouldn't happen. *The menu isn't one of the perks of bachelor life.*

On the bus, he remembered why Bartok's name had been familiar. Three years ago, Grenidor had injured his left knee at the gym, and Bartok had been the resident who triaged him at the hospital. He'd made Grenidor laugh out loud with quiet humor while he examined him; it kept Grenidor's mind off the pain. He'd barely avoided surgery and moved on to recovery and physical therapy. He'd forgotten Bartok's name until now, but he hadn't forgotten the doctor's skill.

At the office, he found a box on his desk.

Col Paul Grenidor, you might find this useful. It came from one of the recently arrested Christians. - Fletcher

The Christians. The word made his stomach twist into knots.

He didn't open the box immediately. Instead, he pulled up the list of fingerprint identifications from the Mayfair Hotel. Bartok had worked at the hospital, last he'd heard. Maybe one of the doctors there knew him.

Finally Grenidor picked up the phone. "Hugh, do you know a Dr. Tobias Bartok?" he asked without preamble.

"Yeah, why? Haven't seen him in a while."

"His name just came up on something I'm working on." Grenidor waved his hand vaguely, as if Hugh could see it over the phone. "What's he like?"

"Straight as an arrow. He's a new doc, went to a pediatrician's office a few years ago. I worked with him while he was in residency."

Grenidor flicked his fingers against the arm of his chair, debating how much he should say. "You like him?" he asked.

"Yeah. Nice guy. Really nice. You know how some people are so fake? He's genuine. Give you the shirt off his back, that kind of guy. He didn't get uppity with some of the support staff the way some doctors do. Smart, too. Even for a doctor, I mean."

"Is he a Christian?"

"Yeah. He didn't shove it in my face though. It kind of made me curious. Weird thing for such a smart guy to believe, you know? Do you know they're being arrested now?"

The knot in Grenidor's stomach tightened. "I heard." He rearranged the pens on his desk to form a square. "You know anyone else who worked with him?"

Silence. Finally, Hugh asked, "Paul, what are you doing? Is he in trouble?"

"I can't answer that. You know anyone else who worked with him? Or friends?"

Hugh sighed. "He's a good man, Paul. I mean it. Don't hassle him. You can ask Phil Marquez if you want."

"Thanks."

He hung up and dialed again. "Phil, how've you been? Paul Grenidor." The answer didn't mean anything to him, and he aligned the pens end to end on his desk. "Yeah. Do you know a Dr. Tobias Bartok?"

"Sure. Why?"

"What's he like?" The pens reached from one of the desk to the other, with a few left over. Grenidor began to stack them crosswise as he listened.

"Brilliant doc. Overworked last I saw. Quiet guy, real nice. We had him over for dinner a few times so he'd get some home cooking. You know how Mona loves to bake. I haven't seen him in a while, actually. I should get back in touch."

"Don't. He's… off the grid." Grenidor looked at the pen tower and began to dismantle it. "What did he think about politics?"

"We didn't talk about it. Why? What do you mean, off the grid?" Marquez's voice rose in curiosity.

"I can't talk about it. We're still investigating. Hugh told me Bartok was a Christian. Is that true?"

"Oh yeah. He talked to me about God a few times. It's not my thing, but I respect him. He isn't a hypocrite. We'd be doing a lot better if there were more people like him."

Grenidor closed his eyes and rubbed one hand over his face. "All right. Thanks. That's all I need."

"Sure. Glad I could help." Marquez sounded quizzical.

Off the phone, Grenidor opened the box with the blade of his scissors. Inside was a book.

The Holy Bible.

Grenidor considered it for a moment before he stood, stepped around his desk, and closed his door. He sat again and stared at the book as if it were some kind of trap.

The Christians read this book.

What sort of madness was inside? Bartok didn't seem like a madman or a traitor, though. The Christians read the whole thing, of course, but it was tremendously long. It would take a team of people weeks to go through it. The Christians said... *Why do I care what they say? They're traitors. ... Aren't they?* The Christians said that it was more complicated than that, and that a man could study the Bible for a lifetime and not understand it all. Whether that was true or not, it was more than Grenidor had time for.

Does Bartok deserve to die?

Grenidor pushed the question down. His stomach was already in knots; pondering the question of Christian executions didn't help. It was easier to think of them as traitors than as people like Bartok. Kind. Intelligent. Funny. Human.

Traitors deserved to die.

Grenidor opened the cover and flipped through the first few pages. A title page. Copyright information for the translation. This was a study bible of some sort; there were explanations of the notes and the qualifications of the commentators. A table of contents.

John. Back before the Empire had any sort of power, someone had once told him that a new reader shouldn't start at Genesis. It was the beginning, true. But if he was curious about the meaning of it all, he should start in John, near the beginning of the New Testament. Even the word "testament" made Grenidor feel that he wasn't meant to understand. Testament, as in legal testimony, sworn to be true?

He found the page number, flipped forward, and began to read.

CLOSING THE BIBLE was like coming up for air. Grenidor's heart thundered, heartbeat slowing raggedly as he stared at the book. He'd never imaged there was so much drama inside. Tragedy and triumph. If it could be believed.

He pulled a notebook from his desk and found a pen. His questions could not be committed to the computer yet; they were too dangerous.

Is it true?

If it is true, what does it mean?

He methodically wrote out sub-bullets. *Edwin believes the Christians are dangerous. Is that true? Or a convincing lie? Is he lying to me, or is he deceived? What archaeological evidence is there for these claims? What historical evidence? Have any miracles been documented?*

He shook his head and crossed out the last question. Of course there were supernatural occurrences; his own research validated that. The question was what power was responsible.

Bartok is a Christian. Can I justify what Edwin suggests? He was reluctant to put the words on paper. Incriminating. Although the laws already forbade proselytizing within the empire, considering pursuing the Christians for Edwin's purposes felt... wrong.

It was all well and good to talk of Christians dying. They meant nothing to him, and were obligated by their faith to break the laws against proselytizing. The laws had not been enforced regularly; the Empire had more pressing concerns. Quiet declarations of faith caused little harm, and the Christians had been careful to keep their meetings small and semi-clandestine. Bibles were not readily available and, since no one asked for them, no one noticed their absence.

Did Bartok deserve to die? Did he deserve to have his blood poured out on a little statue of some animal? Death was fine in the abstract, but imagining a familiar face brought unwelcome emotion.

Grenidor ran his hands through his short hair and closed the notebook.

Edwin slammed open his door and lunged across the room to growl, "What were you doing?"

"What?" Grenidor's heart thudded in his chest, breath coming fast.

Edwin hissed, "Just now. What were you doing?"

Grenidor put the notebook on top of the Bible and pulled them both toward himself. He lined up their edges and placed them out of Edwin's reach on the other side of the desk. "I don't see that it's any of your business." His voice shook, and he cursed himself. He needed to maintain control in this relationship. "Why do you ask?" *That was better.*

Edwin drew back, eyes glinting. Grenidor flinched at the cold fury, but Edwin covered it quickly with a smile. *A smile like a crocodile, all teeth and cold eyes, waiting for me to step a little too close.*

"I lost perception of you," Edwin said finally. He stepped away from the desk and began to pace, hands clasped behind his back.

"What do you mean? I was here." Grenidor watched him.

"I can see many things. But I cannot see where the Slavemaster is working. I cannot see his servants. I deduce where they are by identifying blind spots, but I cannot see them or understand their motivations. Their minds and hearts are a mystery." Edwin's voice had taken on a harsh growl that seemed to reverberate in the small office. He seemed to realize it and softened his tone a little. "I was concerned that something had happened to you."

You asked what I'd been doing. You weren't concerned. You were angry. Grenidor smiled. "I'm fine. Thank you for your concern. I did have a few questions about your offer though."

"Ask." Edwin turned again, his smile more friendly.

"The promise of such power is intriguing, but I am concerned that my superiors will not approve of human sacrifice." Grenidor watched Edwin for his reaction to the phrase. He hadn't put those words to Edwin's suggestion for hours, but now the phrase would not leave his mind.

Edwin smiled and waved a hand dismissively as he dropped into a chair. "That is not a concern. I can assure that you will face no human interference."

"You can." Grenidor's voice was flat. "How?"

"Yes. My ways may not be perceptible to you, but I can assure that your efforts in this matter will not meet with any human interference. The other side will..." He hesitated, and his gaze flicked upward, then settled back on Grenidor. "The other side will not interfere too much. In many ways they have what you would call a 'hands-off' policy. They do not take care of their pawns as we take care of our allies. You would be protected."

That is far too much power in human affairs. Even for a weapon of such power, I can't consent to that. How can I believe he leaves me free will if he offers to prevent anyone from interfering with me?

Grenidor swallowed before he spoke. "Thank you for the offer. I'll consider it."

He didn't argue with the words human sacrifice either.

For a split second, Grenidor saw a golden figure where Edwin had stood, something monstrous and beautiful, a sinewy serpentine form with feathered wings and burning eyes. The impression was so instantaneous that he flinched backward even as he realized Edwin still stood in front of him with a quizzical look.

"What?" Edwin studied his face. "Did you see something?"

"Just… no. Nothing. It was nothing," Grenidor stammered and clamped his mouth shut.

Edwin stared at him in silence for long, tense heartbeats. Then he said, "You asked me about seeing the future. I told you how we can see probabilities, but cannot say with certainty what choices humans will make. I want to give you a warning."

He waited while Grenidor composed himself, then continued, "I see a time that may come when you will have to act decisively. You will know it is the time of which I speak if you bring the chained vampire to see Owen in a parley, and Aria Forsyth and a man you know named Bartok are also present. There may also be others.

"The captive vampire Feichin will be set free by Owen. It will be given the opportunity to kill you, if it wishes. You will have a gun with getlaril bullets concealed under your jacket. The others will be unarmed. You will have an opportunity to shoot the vampire if you act quickly, without hesitation. Aim for the head, and you will succeed. Hesitate, let the vampire get close, and it will kill you."

Edwin appeared to ponder this, then offered, "Perhaps it would be best to avoid the possibility by ordering the vampire killed now."

Grenidor rubbed his hands over his face to avoid Edwin's eyes.

Edwin's hand snaked forward to pick up Grenidor's notebook. Grenidor jerked it out of his hand and glared across his desk. "That's mine."

Edwin froze, eyes on Grenidor's face, and then he smiled. "Pardon me. I didn't know it was so personal." He withdrew his hand, and glanced at the Bible now visible on the desk. "You have a Bible." His tone grew frosty.

"It was seized from one of the Christians." Grenidor picked it up and tossed it into a drawer with the notebook, trying to look nonchalant. "It will be burned."

Edwin's eyes gleamed. "Good." He watched as Grenidor straightened and glared at him across the desk. "You have not made a decision about the ceremonies."

Grenidor hesitated, and said finally, "Not yet."

Edwin stared at him a moment, then inclined his head. "Choose wisely, then. Consider the power you could have." He rose and stepped out the door.

Grenidor waited several minutes, his heart still pounding, before he rose. He needed to hit the restroom, splash some water on his face. He opened the door to see Lt Crawford tapping away diligently at his keyboard.

"Sorry about the noise," Grenidor muttered as he hurried past.

"What noise?" Crawford looked up.

"Um... the shouting."

Crawford frowned, his face a mask of innocent confusion. "I didn't hear anything."

"Were you here?" Grenidor frowned himself.

"Yes, sir. For the past two hours. I'm working on that meeting report for General Harrison."

"You didn't hear anything?"

"No, sir. Not a peep."

"Never mind, then." Grenidor tried to smile as he turned away. In the restroom, he stared at himself in the mirror, rearranging his face into a less-panicked expression. Strong. In control. That was better. The young lieutenant had been out of the office off and on, so it wasn't entirely surprising he hadn't seen Edwin until now. But this made it clear that Edwin *could* prevent resistance if Grenidor served him. Edwin's shout would have been audible down the hall, and clearly discernible, if not ear-splitting, at Crawford's desk four feet from Grenidor's office door.

Why did I think 'serve him'? And why, now that I think about it, does it sound so accurate?

CHAPTER 11

MOST OF THE Fae were already gathered, but Aria saw no sign of other humans. Owen lay on a folded blanket near where she'd landed. They must have been there for a while, because someone had helped Owen put on a new shirt. His sword belt was around his hips again, though she she doubted he was strong enough to use the weapons. She looked back at the wall through which she'd hurtled. It shimmered, and she blinked. Was it really transparent, or was she imagining that she could see the balcony through the solid wall? She glanced back at Owen and saw his eyes sparkling with amusement.

She moved closer and knelt beside him. "What is it? Is it just an illusion?"

"No. It's solid. It's an *indohni*. A portal, you could say. It is opened and closed with megdhonia." He paused for a breath and winced.

"We are safe here for a while. We must discuss... matters of concern."

"What matters?"

He met her eyes for a long moment and then looked back toward the indohni. "Do not ask at this time."

She scowled at him. "Is anyone else coming?"

He sighed softly. "I hope so."

He said nothing else, and finally she stood. Bartok stood with his back to a wall, arms crossed in front of his chest, eyes alert.

Aria stepped closer. "What's wrong?"

"Nothing." His eyes moved around the room.

"You don't look like nothing's wrong." She turned toward the room herself. Most of the Fae were standing or sitting in several clusters near the far end of the room. They had the air of waiting for a decision. Cillian, Niamh, Ardghall, and Conri, the white-haired Fae who was the eldest of the group, had moved closer to kneel beside Owen. Niall stood just behind Cillian's shoulder, listening with his customary intensity as they spoke in an almost inaudible murmur.

"How many of them are there?" he said finally.

She gave him a curious look, but his face was serious and she counted. "Twenty-four, including Niall and Owen." She blinked again. "So, we're missing someone. Twenty-three got out of East-born, which makes twenty-five with Owen and Niall."

"Can you see them all?" Bartok glanced down at her and then around the room.

"Yes. Why?"

His eyes ranged over the room again. "It's disconcerting to be in a room full of people and not

193

see them. Gabriel and I thought there were perhaps eighteen at the most, but we never saw that many at once. Sometimes the room feels empty, and sometimes I can tell they're present, but I can't tell where they are, and I can't see them."

Aria stared at him and then back out at the gathered Fae. "Can you see Lord Owen?"

He stared across the room. "Is he there? I think I saw him for a split second, once."

Aria nodded. "What about Niall? Can you see him?"

Bartok shook his head. "Not now."

Niall stood and made his way toward them. He wrote in his notebook. Bartok jumped as Niall turned it toward them.

It is an unconscious habit of many years for us to remain hidden. Please do not take it as a personal insult or expression of distrust. We are present, and we appreciate your assistance. The flickers that you see are our true form in this physical realm. We become visible to human eyes when we are very relaxed, exhausted, or injured severely enough that we cannot maintain the concealment, or when we consciously choose to be noticed. We are not exactly invisible; we are just easily unnoticed and quickly forgotten by human eyes and minds.

Aria frowned. "But I've always been able to see you! I don't understand. I thought…"

Yes. We do not understand why. Perhaps it is a result of your Fae blood; but even that is a departure from history as we understand it. The last Fae-human child of whom we are aware was born a little over one thousand years ago. She was human, for all practical purposes. She never mastered megdhonia and lived a normal human lifespan. Her mother was Fae, her father human.

194

She saw her mother without difficulty but saw no other Fae unless they revealed themselves. We do not understand why you are different.

"Couldn't you see Owen back at the train station?" Aria asked Bartok.

"Not all the time. Immediately after the rescue, I could. When I went to offer to help, I could see him as I got close, but not from a distance."

He was too badly hurt to conceal himself. Cillian and Niamh extended their protection to him, and they chose to let you see him out of courtesy. The concealment is effective even during sleep, but not when a Fae is as close to death as Lord Owen was.

"What are they talking about?" Aria asked.

It is for Lord Owen to decide if you should know. He wrote the words quickly and turned away, avoiding her eyes as he hurried back.

A few moments later, another body hurtled through the indohni and landed in a graceful roll. Another Fae. He rose and stared at Aria and Bartok for a moment before heading toward the little group gathered around Owen. They conferred inaudibly for several moments before Niamh nodded and rose. She headed toward Aria and Bartok.

"We will rest here. Lord Owen is in pain and should not be moved again. Gabriel and the other humans are hidden."

Aria could feel Bartok's tension. She wondered what he saw.

Niamh continued, "Ardghal, Lorcan, and Aideen will purchase food. If you wish, you may go as well. There is some danger, but they will protect you if they can. Lord Owen says you have not seen sunlight in days." There was sympathy in her gaze.

195

"I would like to go. Thank you." Aria glanced at Bartok, and he nodded.

Ardghal led them through the indohni again, catapulting them across the alley and over the railing. He soothed the pain from her awkward landing with a sympathetic smile and a cool hand on her shoulder. The others followed. Lorcan appeared to be about eighteen, with a slim build and green eyes beneath a mop of dark hair. Aideen was a little older, a dark-haired beauty who resembled Niamh, though her features were softer. Their clothes were ragged and years out of style; both were barefoot.

Ardghal took the lead as they descended a long-disused stairwell and slipped down a hallway.

"Is this building abandoned too?" Aria asked.

"Yes. This section of the city has many buildings no longer in use. It is fortunate for us." Aideen's voice was low but clear.

Ardghal stopped before a battered metal door. "Stay close. We can keep you from being noticed, but it becomes more difficult with distance."

Aria nodded. Bartok glanced at her, and she slipped her hand into his. If he couldn't see the Fae, he'd have to stay close to her. He gave her a quick, surprised smile and she tried not to blush.

They slipped out into a deserted street and Lorcan closed the door behind them. The ground was littered with broken glass that glinted in the cold sunlight.

Ardghal hesitated again before entering the wider street. There were pedestrians walking on both sides of the wide sidewalks, as well as a steady stream of electric cars passing on the asphalt. Ardghal and Aideen led while Lorcan slipped behind them with sinuous grace. They walked some eight blocks before turning left, and then another three blocks before turning into a small ethnic butcher shop.

Aria couldn't read the writing on the sign and wondered what language it was. Something with curls. She should have paid more attention in school. Lorcan slipped inside after Bartok and let the door close behind him with a click.

Ardghal tapped a bell on the counter and waited. Lorcan and Aideen stationed themselves on either side of their door, their stances relaxed but alert as they watched the street.

A dark-skinned man emerged from a door to the back. "Yes?" he asked cautiously. He took in the ragged clothes of the Fae, glanced at Aria and Bartok, then focused on Ardghal again.

"We require meat. What is available?"

"You're… not human?" The man glanced out the windows, then back to them. "You are of Owen's people?"

Ardghal nodded. "Yes."

"Identification is now required for all purchases. Sales are recorded electronically, and purchases of over five pounds of meat by any single customer are flagged for review."

"Is that information offered in an attempt to be helpful?"

The man smiled faintly. "I believe you're closer to our side than the government is. I'd rather you not be captured."

Ardghal tilted his head as if considering his words. Bartok stepped forward. "I'm human. Why do you think the Empire isn't on your side? What side do you mean?"

Another cautious look. "Who are you?"

"Toby Bartok." He stuck his hand across the glass counter and the man shook it with a bemused expression. "We were under the impression that everyone had forgotten what happened in the war. Do you remember?"

"I'm Liviu. I never knew what happened. They didn't bother with telling us, much less making us forget." He glanced at the door again. "I'll make up an order for you. Do any of you have identification?"

At their head shakes, he rubbed a hand over his face. "I'll do my best. How many need to eat?"

"Twenty-seven."

The butcher let out a long breath, then disappeared into the back. They waited. Aria felt herself shifting from one foot to the other, alternately glancing from the windows to the back.

She realized Bartok was smiling at her and flushed. "Sorry."

Liviu reappeared at long last with several large bags in his arms. "Here. It's lamb. My friends and I can give up meat for a few days. I split up the purchase under our names. That should keep it from being flagged. But you'll want more. My cousin Artur owns a shop. Four blocks north, four blocks east, halfway down. It's small, but he should have what you want."

Ardghal took the bags. "Thank you. How much do we owe you?"

Liviu made a face as he thought, then shrugged. "Call it twenty dollars."

Ardghal pulled out several bills and handed them across the counter without comment.

Aria hesitated though. "That's generous. Is that enough?"

"You're welcome." Liviu smiled. "May God be with you."

They hurried on to the second shop, which felt to Aria much like the first. Artur was waiting behind the counter. Ardghal conferred with Lorcan and Aideen, and then asked for a smaller amount of meat. In a few moments they were back out onto the street. Ardghal led them a few doors further before entering a small grocery store. He picked out vegetables, fruit, and bread.

"What is this for?" Bartok asked. "This is too much for Aria and me."

Ardghal frowned. "An experiment."

They returned the way they had come, listening for sounds of pursuit that never came.

CHAPTER 12

GRENIDOR'S TABLET BLINKED. He pulled up the message.

Sir, the report on the vampire blood samples is attached, as well as a summary of all the blood analyses to date. Please respond with instructions.

Another tap and he read the report.

The first subject was Feichin, designated M19. The blood tests had all come back with astonishingly normal values, even after months of fasting. His values had been close to normal human values when he was captured, with obnoxiously healthy cholesterol levels and a slightly elevated red blood cell count. The blood was indistinguishable from human except by the Pyorski test, and tests of healthy vampires had resulted in values similar to those of extremely fit and healthy humans.

Feichin's latest round of tests had resulted in even lower cholesterol levels, both HDL and LDL, almost non-existent triglycerides, and lowered blood glucose. There was a note attached to the glucose levels, which Grenidor opened. *Lowered blood glucose, mean corpuscular volume, mean corpuscular hemoglobin, and iron levels, as well as lowered blood pressure, may indicate onset of anemia. Subject exhibits significant weakness and faintness not fully explained by blood levels; blood levels are consistent with a healthy but slightly anemic human, aside from the Pyorski results, which have not changed.*

Grenidor pulled up the live video of Feichin's cell. The vampire lay face up near one corner of the cell, right arm curled around his head. Grenidor zoomed in. The vampire's cheeks were sunken, dull eyes staring at the wall. Grenidor studied him. Without anger twisting his features, the vampire was wretched. Shirtless, his shirtless, emaciated frame should have provoked compassion. Grenidor pushed down the emotion, remembering Davis' grieving widow. The sharp lines of Feichin's ribs moved with each slow breath.

Feichin rolled to his side, curling one arm over his head. "Go away. I don't want to listen to you," he growled.

Grenidor zoomed out and panned around the cell. No one was there, and the microphone had picked up no sound.

The vampire lurched to his feet, staggering against the wall, and turned to snarl toward the camera. "You have already won! What more do you want from me?" His chest heaved, and he struggled to stay upright. "Get out." The growl was weaker, and he slumped down to sit against the wall. He let his head fall forward onto his bony knees and wrapped his arms around his head again.

Grenidor panned around the room again. Nothing. He read the rest of the report. Feichin, while vicious, had not thus far exhibited signs of the paranoia and hallucinations most of other vampires did. Perhaps this was the beginning. If so, why?

He compared Feichin's bloodwork to that of the vampire's daughter, Aithne, subject F11. She had been fed once a week but given access to water at will. She had lost about ten pounds in the last six months, indicating that the nutritional regimen was adequate for testing purposes. She'd been curvy but slim, and the curves had not quite disappeared. The most recent reading was 106.8, sixteen pounds heavier than her father, who stood three inches taller. Grenidor glanced back at Feichin's chart; how was it possible that a creature only five feet ten inches tall, weighing barely 90 pounds, could have killed Brent Davis? Feichin had been heavier at the time, but not more than 100 pounds, 105 at the most. Though he was older, Davis had been an exercise buff; he and Grenidor had spotted each other during weight training before. He'd been strong, especially for a stylus-wielding scientist. *It isn't natural.*

Aithne's blood revealed numbers virtually unchanged from her capture; cortisol was naturally higher, indicating a persistent level of stress, but it was lower than her father's. She had not yet spoken to any hallucinations.

Feichin and Aithne had been captured only a few months after the larger group that Owen had freed. Three other vampires had been captured

around the same time, though in separate incidents. Two had already been put down; they appeared to be completely insane.

Grenidor pulled up the video feed from M15's
cell. He'd given the name Meallan, which Grenidor
had not cared to learn how to pronounce. M15
paced in his cell; a sheen on the floor showed a
ring around the perimeter where his feet had worn
the concrete smooth in the past two years.

He growled as he walked, inarticulate rum-
blings that sounded like they came from a larger
body than he possessed. Occasionally he lapsed
into accented English. "I won't be told what to do!
I'm free!" The words were absurd, given the limited confines of his cell, but Grenidor didn't laugh.

Most of the test results had been compiled,
though the reports weren't yet written. None of the
blood from any of the vampires, even those that
called themselves Fae, had healed any wounds or
diseases in the human test subjects. Not cancer.
Not heart disease. Not damaged tissue or bone.
Not surface wounds. The scientists had been so
hopeful, and the constant failure was wearing on
them. They had, as yet, devised no way to use the
vampire blood for anything that benefited humans, despite numerous creative ideas and expensive tests. Injections did not give humans greater
physical strength or resistance to disease. It did not
cure anything. Perhaps the only thing that could be
said for it was that it never caused any rejection
symptoms; all vampires tested thus far could serve
as universal donors.

Vampires could not heal while bound with getlaril. M8, one of the young ones, had been hand-
cuffed with getlaril for three weeks after his tongue

was removed. The bleeding stopped and he had healed more or less as a human would have. Three weeks was therefore long enough to prevent magical healing, but the lower bound for the time required for getlaril to be effective was not known.

They could heal themselves and each other while unbound. Grenidor had hypothesized that physical contact and singing were required, but that had proven false. M8 had been able to heal himself of a cut although he could no longer sing. Others in his group had healed each other across the aisle between the cells when the getlaril bars were temporarily removed, leaving only the steel bars.

That test had been risky. Previous escape attempts, of varying degrees of success, had proven that the vampires could dramatically change the temperature of materials they touched, lending greater efficacy to their already formidable strength. Given five minutes, a vampire would either bend the steel by main strength, or freeze the bars and shatter the steel itself. That revelation, made some years before, had been the impetus behind the construction of the getlaril-lined cells, without which the entire experimental program would have failed.

Could a vampire heal a human?

Grenidor drummed his fingers on his desk as he thought. If an experiment were to be conducted... M15 and M19 would feed on a human if they could. That left F11, Aithne, or M6, Ailill.

He chose F11. She would have to be properly motivated. It presumably took some effort to heal; the others had been tired afterward.

Grenidor picked up his phone. "Rudovic, I need a test subject ...Possibly. Yes. As soon as possible."

An hour later an armored prisoner transport van arrived. The transport team hauled a man out of the back; his head was covered by a concealment hood and his hands were bound behind him. He didn't fight the team.

Grenidor directed the team to the experimental cells in the basement. The best room, perhaps the only one suitable for the experiment, was the room in which Feichin had been held. The prisoner's shackles were bolted to the metal chair. The transport team was dismissed; Grenidor didn't need them reporting his experiments.

Things have escalated. I need to understand what kind of creatures I'm dealing with.

The vampire transport team moved Aithne from her cell into the transport cage. Operated by remote control, it trundled through the hallway and into the experimental cell, with the team staying at a safe distance, weapons trained on the vampire. Grenidor dismissed the team once the transport cage was in position.

Aithne's wrists were bound above her head, and the position accentuated her already slim waist and delicate curves. He paused to admire, and she looked away with a flush spreading across her cheeks. *If she wasn't so dangerous...* the thought arrested him for a moment. A few weeks ago it would have been, if not repellent, at least embarrassing. Now he let his eyes linger, not caring that she saw.

Grenidor stepped forward and pulled the hood from the man's face. Wide, frightened eyes met his own. He hardened his heart.

He didn't look at Aithne as he spoke. "This is a test. If you heal him, you'll be fed tonight. If not, you'll have to wait two weeks." He pulled out his pistol and shot the man in the knee.

In the concrete cell, the sound was deafening; even Grenidor flinched at the noise. The man screamed, writhing in the handcuffs, unable even to clutch his wounded leg.

Grenidor stepped back, pushing down nausea.

"What was that for?" the man cried out, blood streaming down his leg. "I've done nothing!"

Grenidor raised the pistol toward the man's head, hand shaking, then let it drop. "Shut up. This isn't about you." He turned on his heel and left. He keyed in his security code on the outside of the door to lock it, then jogged to the viewing station at the desk nearby. He shoved the headphones over his ears and turned up the sound.

The man was twisting in pain, wrists and ankles bound, blood smearing over the seat and down the leg of his pants. His face was contorted, breath coming too fast. *Does it matter if he passes out? It shouldn't make a difference.*

The transport cage held Aithne with getlaril shackles, and Grenidor keyed in the release code. He also used the remote capability to unlock the door.

Would she kill him? What did that prove? Feichin had already proven Fae and vampires were the same thing. Perhaps… that would be a null result. No matter; the man was a Christian, condemned anyway. *What have I done? I've gone too far.*

Would she heal him? That would be proof of their ability to heal humans. Did it prove anything of their motivations?

I should not have motivated her with food. The results won't be valid. I should have said nothing and just watched what she did. Well, it will prove the capability. We don't know yet for sure that they can heal humans. It won't prove anything as far as motivation. Perhaps I should test that later.

The thought gave him pause. Perhaps it wasn't important whether they would heal humans without a reward. A captive vampire could be compelled to heal a human. But he'd thought first of compelling Aithne, rather than wondering whether she would do it willingly. *Would I heal someone for no reason? Probably not. But I would have... before. When did I change? Why did I change?*

He focused again on the screen. Aithne stumbled as her shackles released, and then darted to the man's side. He was shuddering, trying not to look at his knee, hands clenched into fists on the arms of the chair. She murmured softly, and he stopped twisting. Her head bent over the man's knee, and Grenidor growled in frustration. He switched to another camera at a different angle and brought the vampire's face into focus.

The bleeding stopped, and a moment later the man shifted and relaxed. "What did you do? It doesn't hurt anymore."

Aithne's head drooped, her forehead resting on his knee. Then she sat back on her heels, clasping her hands in her lap. "I healed it." She glanced at the camera Grenidor had used first, then turned to stare directly at him.

How does she know which camera I'm using? Grenidor scooted his chair back involuntarily.

"I didn't heal him for the food." Her words were quiet, but the microphone captured them clearly. "Shall I get back in my cage now?" She stood and stepped back into the cage. She raised her hands into position and waited.

Grenidor pushed the button to lock the shackles with a trembling finger. He closed the door to the holding cell and watched it latch.

He felt sick to his stomach.

He called the two transport teams. "Put F11 back in her cell." The prisoner was sent back. "Rudovic, don't let him talk to anyone. Solitary until... whatever you're planning on doing with him. ... No. It's none of your business!" he snarled and hung up the phone. Rudovic didn't need to know what he was working on.

Grenidor jogged back to his office. He locked the door and took off his jacket. He still felt sick. One hundred pushups. It didn't help the nausea, but it lessened the guilt a little. He started to rise, then stumbled when he saw Edwin sitting in his desk chair.

"How did you get in here?" he growled.

Edwin smiled at him. "I'm always here. You invited me."

"Not into my office!"

Edwin watched him standing there and deliberately put his shoes on the desk. "One invitation is sufficient." He smiled toothily at Grenidor's mounting irritation.

"Get out of my chair! I have work to do."

Edwin's smile widened, and Grenidor took a step backward involuntarily. Something flickered, an image of a snake's tongue darting out of Edwin's mouth. Grenidor blinked. *I'm going mad.* His heart thundered.

Edwin's smile softened, and he swung his feet to the floor. "Of course." He stepped around the desk and gestured for Grenidor to take the chair. "Have you decided who will perform the ceremonies I told you about?"

Grenidor took his place behind the desk but did not sit down. Somehow it seemed better to speak with Edwin from eye-level, a position of equality rather than a position of weakness. "No. I will not. I am concerned that... my government would not approve. Not of human sacrifice, definitely. Probably not of animal sacrifice either."

Edwin stepped forward, bringing them uncomfortably close. Grenidor tried not to step back. "You will face no human resistance. I have told you I can ensure this. Nor will the other side harm you."

"Yes, I know. I am uncomfortable with it myself. I... thank you for your offer." In the face of Edwin's unblinking stare, he floundered. Mind racing, he remembered the Bible he'd been reading. Perhaps it had information that could be useful. John's account had made him question some of Edwin's words. He cleared his throat, then said carefully, "How dangerous is the other side to us, really, if they won't harm us?"

Edwin sighed, a faint hissing sound that made a chill run down Grenidor's spine. He stepped back in an obvious attempt to seem less intimidating. "The Slavemaster is the most devious, most patient, and most dangerous opponent that has ever existed. Beyond human imagining. He uses even the most coincidental events for his purposes, and he manages to use even those sworn to our side for his own ends. Be wary of him."

"I understand that." He didn't. "But I want to know if they will attack us. You keep saying they are dangerous, but you said they won't attack by force. What do you mean, then?"

Edwin's lip curled and he turned away, pacing with his head down as he considered his words. "They will not attack by force, it is true. They do not wish to harm you, exactly... they wish to have you for their own. They would keep you as slaves. Willing slaves! It is a matter of freedom."

Grenidor nodded. "I see." But he didn't.

GRENIDOR WENT TO question the vampires again.

He went first to Aithne's cell. She sat on the edge of her cot with her head down, hands between her knees.

Grenidor spoke without preamble. "What do you know of a creature that calls itself Edwin?"

"I have not heard of such a creature." She looked up at him with disconcerting blue eyes. Cold as ice, blinking too slowly for a human, they made him want to step backward. She was better fed than the others; the experiments on her were mental rather than physical. Many kinds of music had been played at varying volumes. Long periods of darkness and absolute silence. Repeated experiments with sleeping and waking cycles.

"A creature of spirit." Grenidor was reluctant to say more. Edwin might know, and he might be angry. Also, Grenidor felt silly talking about it; his concerns felt foolish when put into words. *Something that might not exist at all seems to be threatening me. Or not. Offering friendship that I can't trust. Trying to… influence me. I think it's working.*

Aithne's gaze didn't leave his face. "I know there are such creatures. I have not spoken to any."

"Are they good or evil?" Grenidor didn't know where the question came from. The vampires were evil, of course. *Or are they? What is evil?* If not evil, they were at least dangerous. *A shark isn't evil; it doesn't seek to destroy good. It simply is a shark. A shark kills because killing is its nature. Perhaps they are like sharks. There is no use in being angry at a thing for its nature. But there is no need to feel guilty over killing it.*

Aithne, not privy to his thoughts, stared at him, trying to read the expressions that chased themselves across his face. "We are not permitted to judge good and evil. There is at least one that sometimes interacts with my kind. And at least one who interacts with the turned ones. They might be the same. They might not. We think they are different, but we cannot be sure. I have never spoken with either."

Grenidor stepped closer to the getlaril bars that separated them, though he was careful to stay out of her reach. She had not attempted violence toward any of the researchers yet.

But that's how Davis got killed. He trusted one of them. He trusted me. It was my fault.

He stared at her, wondering whether she would attack. Aside from his work on Owen, and the attack by Cillian, it was the closest he had been to a conscious vampire. She continued to watch him with guarded eyes until he turned away.

HE'S LYING TO ME.

The realization had come slowly. Edwin's words were smooth and convincing. Grenidor wanted to believe him; Edwin had answers, and he had power.

But he was lying.

He told me Owen let me live to test Cillian. But he also said he cannot see the servants of the other side and cannot guess their motivations. These cannot both be true.

Grenidor pondered the thought on the way to work at 6:30 in the morning, his expression set in stone. The other passengers on the bus were also silent at this early hour, bleary-eyed and morose.

He spoke to Feichin. If Feichin is on the other side… that does not make sense.

I think his statement about not seeing the other side is true, or at least partly true. He was angry when I read the Bible. His concern was not genuine, but the anger was. Which means the Bible holds power. Perhaps it repels him in some way, or can control him. Wait… he didn't come in when I put the Bible away. He came in when I stopped thinking about it. When I was finished with it.

This could be useful.

Perhaps it would be a good idea to study the Bible. Not because he wanted to become a Christian, of course. But the book had power that affected Edwin somehow, and Grenidor had precious few tools against Edwin.

But if he's watching, how can I study it without alerting him? If even the act of reading the Bible with the intent of learning blocked Edwin's attention and flagged Grenidor's activities for notice, how could he proceed?

Perhaps Bartok could explain the Bible and the power it had, even how to use it against Edwin, should that become necessary. *Maybe I could get enough to information to use against Edwin somehow. I'd need to think about my questions, make sure I ask exactly the right thing. No, if Edwin can't see what's the Slavemaster's servants are doing, or even what's in their immediate vicinity, he would know we were talking but he wouldn't know what we were talking about. So as long as I have a reason to talk to Bartok that Edwin will believe, I should be fine. Assuming I believe what Edwin says.*

It's not a good bet, but it's the best one I have.

Besides, I might understand the whole picture better than Bartok does, since I have Edwin's side of the story. Whatever that is worth. He could always reject what Bartok said, of course. At least he could use what Bartok said and what Edwin said to get closer to the truth. Hearing Bartok's side could only be useful.

If Bartok was as Grenidor remembered, perhaps they could even come to some agreement on where humans should really stand. The Conflict frightened Grenidor, and he had the sense of standing at the edge of a cliff, the weight of humanity on his shoulders. He had to move, but was blindfolded, unable to see which direction was safe ground and which was a sharp drop toward disaster.

If Edwin spoke to Feichin, and he does not speak to those on the other side... whose side is Feichin on? The question gnawed at him. In the office, he pulled up the feed from Feichin's cell. The vampire sat crouched in a corner, staring somewhere to the left of the camera. His eyes were dull. Grenidor grimaced. The vampire's condition was appalling. *Should I feel guilty? Because I don't. I think I would have months ago.*

Feichin's gaze shifted to the camera and he raised his lips in a soundless snarl. His words were so soft the microphone barely caught them. "I will kill you, Grenidor."

Grenidor swallowed and stared back at him, unable to look away. The vampire's eyes burned with hate. *If he ever escapes...*

His heart thudding, he flicked off the video. He caught a flicker of movement behind his shoulder and whirled. Nothing. He turned back to his computer only to startle again. Edwin leaned against his closed door.

"What are you doing here?"

Something about Edwin's smile seemed reptilian, a cold flicker in his eyes. "I came to see you, of course, to offer my assistance. You seem to be concerned about your government's reaction to what you have called 'human sacrifices.'"

"Is that description not accurate?" Grenidor asked.

Edwin shrugged. "Call it what you will. You have a perfect rebuttal to your government's objections. The 'conditioning' you have done so far works only to a point. Some of the rebels, such as Aria Forsyth, have obviously thrown it off. For the general population it fades in effectiveness over time, and it will become more prone to break from accidental inconsistencies. This will cause problems for you." Edwin's smile widened a little. "I can provide supporting evidence of this as needed."

Edwin watched him until he nodded, then continued, "Those who participate in ceremonies like the one I suggested tend to be more loyal and easier to guide. Your conditioning dulls their intellects. The ceremony is superior for your purposes; the participants will become fanatically enthusiastic for the cause. If an inconsistency arises, they actively refuse to see it, or explain it away, even incorporate it into their view, sometimes as proof that they are right. They will follow *whoever* they believe to... well, forever. Literally. All at the cost of a few disloyal people you are better off without, anyway."

Grenidor frowned, caught by the notion. *A few people loyal to me, rather than swayed by whatever propaganda the Empire dreams up next.*

"You understand what I am offering you? Political safety. Followers." Edwin's eyes gleamed. "Worshippers, if you chose."

Grenidor drummed his fingers on the table. "Yes... it is appealing. But you suggested using the Christians as the source of the blood. The sacrifice. But animals would suffice?"

"Yes."

"Then wouldn't it be safer, from a political standpoint, to use animals for the sacrifice and conditioned Christians as the... um... worshippers?"

"NO!"

The shriek nearly split his eardrums, and Grenidor flung himself backward, falling from his chair.

Edwin immediately calmed himself. "No. That would be a very bad idea. I have told you the Slavemaster would not attack you directly. He won't interfere if I enlighten you, even inspire you to eliminate his followers. If I instigated an attempt to subvert his followers with brainwashing, things are different. I doubt he would attack you directly, but he might attack me."

Grenidor righted his chair and lowered himself back into it. Raw terror made his hands shake, and he balled them into fists beneath the desk.

Edwin smiled, teeth gleaming. "At this point, I assure you that would be disastrous for you also. If you consider your actions, you have recently made many choices based on knowledge which you have, but others do not. Of course, these are wise decisions that you made to benefit mankind. However, considered by a less well-informed government or judiciary, they might seem less prudent, perhaps even immoral or criminal. I've shielded you from any problems or opposition while you make your choice whether to commit to our side. I understand there is a learning curve. Long-held attitudes that are counterproductive must be unlearned. Restraints must be discarded. Without me, you would quickly be unjustly judged by... well, the standards you would have used on yourself a year or so ago. I don't promise to protect you forever, but I want to give you the opportunity to join us.

"I'll be blunt. You have a choice: Go the rest of the way. Gain power beyond what any human has dreamed of for centuries… power you can use to benefit mankind. And, incidentally, rule the empire, above any laws or judgements by lesser men. Or turn it down. Your crimes will be found out.

"Can you imagine how those recordings of the Fae girl, the pretty one, being tortured would be received on the news? By a jury? Or even just the revelation that your creations, the vertril, roam the streets to do your bidding?"

Grenidor could not look away from that soft, smiling face. Edwin's red tongue flicked out and licked his lips, as if relishing the thought of Grenidor's public trial and execution.

"But I never tortured her." He knew the protest was futile.

"Did you not? There are recordings. You personally used hot needles. Again. And again. Brent Davis was present. He objected, and you killed him in a fit of anger." Edwin laced his fingers together and cocked his head. "It's all on the videos."

For an instant, Grenidor remembered doing it. A scalpel in his hand. Blood. The image was gone, but the memory remained.

I never did that. He made me remember it, but I never did it. He can change memories.

Grenidor tasted bile.

"You need me. More than I need you. You'd best come to terms with it. I don't demand that you like it. I demand only obedience, and I pay well for services rendered. I don't require that you serve me out of adoration, as the Slavemaster does. I don't care if… no, I *encourage* you to use our partnership for your own benefit."

Grenidor clenched his shaking hands, fingernails digging into his palms.

Edwin disappeared. Vanished, like he had that first time. Present, then NotPresent. *If only he would leave forever.*

But then, he's not really gone, is he? He's made it clear enough that he's always watching, always here. It's just that sometimes he lets me see a body. He wants me to think that's what he really looks like. Sometimes I see flashes of something else, another appearance. I don't think he means for me to see them. They don't seem to fit his agenda. Are they slips on his part? Am I seeing through his illusion to the truth, or at least another way of seeing him?

Here's a terrifying thought: Edwin says the Slavemaster is subtle and won't directly attack me. But might he momentarily interrupt Edwin's deception? If so, am I seeing more of the truth, or just another false vision, this one from the Slavemaster?

It comes down this: Is the Slavemaster interrupting Edwin's control of my perception, or is the Slavemaster merely imposing his own control?

Edwin himself says the Slavemaster wants my willing service. Does that mean he won't trick me? I know Edwin lies. How do I know that what he tells me about the Slavemaster has any truth in it?

Another thing: Edwin seemed genuinely terrified of the Slavemaster when I suggested using the Christians as worshippers. Edwin isn't similarly concerned about people not on the Slavemaster's side, even though he says that everyone not on the Slavemaster's side is more or less on his side by default. No true neutrality is possible. That means...

Stomach churning, Grenidor rose and paced, trying to control his racing thoughts. Passing behind his desk, he noticed the video archives were opened on his monitor, focusing on Aithne's cell.

He had not been using the archives, and he frowned. As he clicked the video closed, it started to play.

The image flashed up before he was ready, before he realized what he was going to see, and he almost vomited. He bent over with his head in his hands, listening to the quiet sounds from his speakers. Aithne's desperate pleading, tears and terror in her voice. Blood smeared on his hands. His own cold voice, demanding that she tell him where the others were, and Davis muttering his protests quietly.

He stopped the video, unwilling to watch the rest. *I never did that. Not with her. Not with needles or scalpels.*

I knew he was a liar. But I thought…

What? That I would be safe? That I could use him and somehow come out on top?

He jumped when his phone rang. "Grenidor."

"You promised results by now."

Grenidor flinched at the angry words from General Harrison, who had authorized the research project. A four-star, he'd kept the project, and Grenidor, under his personal authority despite changes of assignment and political turmoil.

"You said there would be something useful. I have a report in front of me that says, in a few more words, that the last fifteen years and thirty-eight billion dollars have been wasted. What have you been *doing*, Colonel?"

"Sir, the vampire blood has not proved as beneficial to humans as we hoped. But we have learned much. We are still investigating options for how to exploit their capabilities. The project has not been unsuccessful."

"Such as?"

Grenidor jiggled his foot and tried to sound confident. "Well, sir, we've discovered that they don't actually need to breathe. They want to, of course, but they can survive indefinitely underwater without access to air. That could prove useful."

"We have highly trained underwater teams already."

Grenidor spoke quickly. "Also they can heal humans. We weren't sure they could, but when sufficiently motivated, they can heal humans in a matter of minutes, without scarring."

A pause. "From what injuries?" The tone was neutral.

Grenidor hesitated. He was not authorized to conduct human experiments. But General Harrison had intentionally overlooked some irregularities before in the interests of getting results. How much detail should he provide? *Is anyone else listening? This line is not secure.* "Injuries that medical staff would have found challenging to treat," he said at last.

"I see."

The phone clicked, and General Harrison was replaced by the dial tone. Why did he call just then? Grenidor wanted to believe it was chance, but he couldn't squash the thought that it was Edwin's doing. General Harrison had read regular reports on the research. He knew the objectives: to determine if any of the vampires' physical capabilities could benefit humans, and to determine what methods were effective at eliminating vampires. He had reviewed the reports, budget and staffing requirements, and every other piece of important documentation for the last decade and a half. He had always been supportive, even when useful results had been less forthcoming than they had all hoped.

Was Edwin demonstrating his power? He'd promised no opposition, even almost unlimited power, if Grenidor served him. Was he now promising that there would be opposition, or destruction, if Grenidor did not serve him?

It is about serving him, after all.

GRENIDOR LOCKED HIS door and paced. He replayed the conversation with Edwin in his mind, turning it around and examining it from different angles. Grenidor had suggested using Christians as the worshippers on the spur of the moment. The idea of keeping them alive, sacrificing animals instead, seemed somehow more humane. *As if that is truly a concern.*

His ears were still ringing from Edwin's shriek. *That was not a human sound. He's clearly terrified of the Slavemaster. He says the Slavemaster will not attack humans directly. I think he would lie about that if he could, to frighten me. So he must be constrained in some way. Or... maybe the Slavemaster does not want to harm humans?*

The Slavemaster has some power over him, and even if the Slavemaster will not attack humans directly, he might attack Edwin. ... And would that be bad?

Perhaps the Christians can offer another perspective. Not that I believe them, or their stupid myths of a man who rose from the dead. I'm not that naive. Yet... the Bible has some power over Edwin, to control him or repel him. I need that.

221

Wait. Why *is what the Christians believe is so absurd? After all I've seen, I could believe almost anything.*

The speed of his pacing slowed as he considered the repercussions of that logic.

Edwin calls him the "Slavemaster." Is this the one the Christians call God? There are some parallels, now that I think about it. I don't know enough to judge. The Bible, if I believe it, says that God wants willing servants. If I even believe God exists. One of the writers even referred to himself as a slave, bought for a price. Wait, at one point Jesus said they were no longer slaves or servants, but friends. Didn't he? I haven't heard anything about it in years; I'm probably getting it all wrong.

I need to speak with Bartok.

Bartok could be trusted as much as anyone. If he could explain the Bible, there might yet be some hope, however tenuous. But how could he be contacted?

Directly contacting the political resistance was far too risky; any deliberate contact would be flagged by IPF intelligence, not to mention Edwin's reaction. Besides, even if Bartok was aligned with the resistance, many Christians were not. It was not even clear that Bartok was in Colonel Peterson's group. The fingerprint analysis proved they had both been at the Mayfair Hotel, but it did not prove they had been there at the same time, or that they had been in agreement while they were there.

If Bartok *was* with Peterson's group, Owen might still be with them, or might at least know where to find them. Peterson's group had cooperated with Cillian and Aria Forsyth to extract Owen from Forestgate. Owen was unlikely to have healed enough to have gone far, given the getlaril still in his body.

Perhaps… the thought knotted his stomach even as he thought it. *Perhaps… Aithne could find them.* He turned the idea over in his mind. That the thought occurred to him at all was interesting. It meant that on some level, he believed the Fae must, or at least did, speak truthfully, at least while they called themselves Fae. Vampires could lie. Vampires and Fae were the same… but not always. Perhaps Fae matured into vampires, or changed through some other process.

Feichin seemed to think it was a distinct event that caused him to change.

Grenidor pulled up the reports from the first year and a half of Feichin's captivity.

Feichin had fought when he was captured and had killed three soldiers. Grenidor found the report. "Subject was restrained by getlaril choke-strap. CPT Stone, 1LT Abramson, PFC Smith, PFC Hardwick, and PFC Palmer attempted to load the subject into the transport vehicle. Subject resisted ferociously, attempting to climb out the back of the vehicle. PFC Hardwick drew his service weapon, loaded with getlaril bullets. Subject dodged and grabbed the weapon, which discharged into PFC Smith, causing fatal injury. PFC Palmer drew his weapon almost simultaneously and shot. Subject was hit in the shoulder. Subject immediately grabbed the gun and spun PFC Palmer into the frame of the transport vehicle. PFC Palmer suffered several fractured vertebrae. CPT Stone retained hold of the choke-strap, and PFC Hardwick attempted to secure the subject using the transport vehicle shackles by remote control. Subject thrashed against the strap and managed to partially disconnect the choke-strap from the vehicle, giving it more freedom of movement. 1LT Abramson moved closer to attempt to reconnect the strap as CPT Stone and PFC Hardwick manned the choke-strap and shackles controls. 1LT Abramson was successful, but failed to get out of the subject's reach in time. Subject grabbed him and drew him close in an apparent attempt to bite him. CPT Stone dropped the choke-strap and shot them both. 1LT Abramson died immediately. Subject was incapacitated long enough to secure him in the shackles for transport. PFC Palmer died during reconstructive surgery the following morning."

Grenidor frowned. He must not have read the whole report before; he didn't remember that Feichin had not killed the men directly and deliberately. Feichin was, if not a sympathetic character then, at least not the monster he now appeared to be. The report was not unbiased, of course. The soldiers were convinced of the rightness of their cause. *I sent them on their mission.*

He refused to consider that he might have been wrong. Feichin was and always had been a monster. But perhaps… perhaps he might have considered the evidence differently, had he read the report with a different view. Perhaps vampires had to mature into their violence. Perhaps they were not always evil.

Am I willing to release one?

Feichin had not, apparently, killed all the soldiers deliberately. One had been killed by accidental friendly fire. One had been killed by crashing into the metal truck; that might have been deliberate or accidental. And the third had been deliberately shot by his superior.

Can they make more vampires? The legends said so. CPT Stone obviously believed it. Grenidor pulled up CPT Stone's record and clicked through to the confidential information. He'd been specially authorized to view certain information after the problems with PVT Thomson during Owen's interrogation. Certain personality issues were counterproductive to effective questioning.

CPT Stone had entered psychological counseling after the incident, citing grief, recurring nightmares, and overwhelming guilt. So he had been sincerely terrified that Abramson would be turned into a vampire.

But Grenidor had never seen convincing evidence that humans could be turned into vampires. Instead, he was beginning to consider that Fae turned into vampires. Always, or only sometimes?

Considering Feichin's record, Grenidor had to conclude that Feichin had changed when he killed Davis. For a year and a half after his capture, he had offered no violence toward the scientists. He had been angry. He had pleaded with them. He had called their actions evil and immoral. But... Grenidor was startled when he realized it... he had never even called the scientists themselves evil. He had not called them names, had not tried to hurt them, had not directly called them liars. Even when it was obvious they caused him pain, and even when it was obvious they lied to him. He knew, and yet he did not throw it in their faces.

Until the day he broke.

It was the beginning of his end. He had been markedly different since that day. Hostile, violent, foul-mouthed, and always, *always* angry.

When Meallan had been captured, he was further in his descent than Feichin was now. Foul-tempered, self-destructive, violent, and furious. Had he once been different?

The others that had been captured and terminated earlier in the research program had been like Meallan. He'd assumed that all vampires were the same. The difference between Fae and vampires was only terminology; mentally, and in his official reports, he referred to them all as vampires.

Yet Ailill had never offered violence after the initial fight in which he had defended the children in his care. He had been a problem for the scientists, difficult to control. That was before they learned how to secure the vampires with getlaril consistently, before they learned how strong they were. He had escaped twice, caused havoc in the lab as he tried to free the others. He'd been shot, burned, and shocked, but he'd never tried to injure his captors.

Aithne had not either, despite several opportunities.

Had they ever lied? Grenidor couldn't be sure. But the initial claims that they were not vampires, that they were different, might have some validity. Biologically, Fae and vampires were the same. Behaviorally, they were different.

It had taken Grenidor years to admit it; he'd been so focused on proving their biological commonality that the behavioral differences had escaped him. If they were vampires, they were to be feared and destroyed. They were vampires, ergo they must be destroyed.

But... he'd missed that critical difference, refused to see it. The meaning of it escaped him even still. It must be more than cultural, because Feichin had been Fae until he'd changed. After his change, he was a vampire, but he'd had no contact with other vampires. The change was intrinsic, internal, caused by something besides culture.

Perhaps...

Fae were allied with the Slavemaster. Vampires, Grenidor now believed, were not on the side of the Slavemaster. They might or might not be on Edwin's side, but Edwin himself said he didn't care, so long as one didn't serve the Slavemaster. Could changing sides be the difference? Or did they change sides as a consequence of their changed nature?

He found a phone number, then hesitated before lifting the phone. The psychologist would be able to give an opinion on the state of mind of the vampires, whether they were safe to release or safe to house with each other.

But Grenidor had a feeling he knew what the psychologist would say. Feichin was dangerous. Meallan was dangerous. Ailill, judging only from the video, would have been safe. Aithne was probably safe.

Besides, Edwin would know if he contacted the psychologist, and he would not be pleased.

DREAD CURLED IN Grenidor's stomach, so strong his mouth tasted sour. It was a dangerous plan, a gamble for a man who hated gambling. But he had few other options.

He opened his door only to step into Edwin and bounce back, off-balance and startled.

"Why, hello. I was just coming to see you," Edwin's voice had the sound of a pleased purr.

"Yes?" Grenidor swallowed.

"I have something for you. A gift." Edwin motioned that he should go back into his office, and Grenidor reluctantly complied. Edwin produced a gun and held it out on the palm of his hand.

"I have a gun already." Grenidor glanced at it and then back up to Edwin.

"Yes. But this one has getlaril bullets. Sometimes you only load yours with lead. Such as now." Edwin's toothy smile widened. "I just want you to be prepared for every contingency. Especially when I can't always protect you. Not that I do. You should be wary."

Grenidor's heart thudded raggedly. *He knows. He knows I'm going to see Aithne. Does he know why?*

"I am." Grenidor picked up the gun and checked the chamber, sighted it, unloaded it, and clicked the trigger. He loaded it again. "Thank you."

Edwin's smile faded and he gave Grenidor a look of concern. "You look tired."

"That's none of your business." Grenidor glared at him.

"I am concerned about you. Your reflexes must be flawless if you are to survive the meeting I fear is coming." Edwin frowned. "The vampire Feichin is weakened, but his hate is stronger than ever. He will kill you if he is freed."

Grenidor rubbed his thumb across the safety of the pistol. "Yes. I am aware of that. He will not be freed."

Edwin gave him a sideways glance. "It would be safest to kill him now. Eliminate the risk. You can still attend the meeting, if you must. Feichin is the greatest danger to you."

He does know what I'm trying to do. At least, he knows I intend to arrange a meeting. How much more does he know? Wouldn't he move to stop me if he knew it all? Or does he know that the meeting will result in my deciding in his favor? I don't understand enough.

"I'll take that under advisement." Grenidor used the voice he used with junior officers and uppity NCOs, the verbal pat-on-the-head.

Edwin smiled again and stepped backward. "Of course, you have work to do. I won't keep you from it." He stepped out into the hallway and waved his hand in an ostentatious flourish. "Carry on."

Grenidor walked out too, but turned toward the front door. He took a side corridor and walked to Osborne's office, a cramped space he shared with two others. Edwin's steps disappeared, and Grenidor risked a peek over his shoulder. Edwin was gone. *But is he watching?* Fear tightened his shoulders.

Osborne wasn't in, and Grenidor shook his head when his officemates asked if he wanted to leave a message. He had nothing to say to Osborne; it was only a reason to head away from the experimental cells in the basement. *But whenever I go, he'll know. Maybe I should have gone directly. Maybe now I look like I'm hiding something.*

He avoided Feichin's cell and went directly to Aithne's. She stood up when he entered, getlaril chains clanking softly. Tears streaked her face.

How close to her does he lose sight of me? "Come closer to the bars."

She moved closer. Closer. He was within reach now, and his heart thundered in his own ears. *She could kill me from here.*

She did not reach for him or touch the bars. "My father turned, didn't he?"

"What?" He wasn't expecting that question.

"He turned. I felt it before, but I tried to believe it wasn't him. But it is, isn't it? It's my father." Her head dropped, and she closed her eyes. Tears slid down her pale cheeks.

If she wasn't a monster... His heart twisted with some forgotten emotion, pity or guilt or something equally weak.

The getlaril shackles had burned livid circles around her wrists and ankles. Up close like this, he could see how the skin was blistered and raw.

"What did you do to him? He's always been so strong!" She stared at him, blue eyes pleading, and he felt himself slipping.

No! Be strong. "That's none of your concern." His voice came out as a snarl. "I have a bargain for you."

She stepped backward. "I don't wish to bargain with you." Her voice was still soft, but he could hear her anger and sorrow.

On impulse he reached through the bars and grabbed at a chain. She might have yanked his arm from its socket. She was strong enough. Instead she let him strain, watching him grit his teeth and try to pull her closer while she stood unmoving, resisting him without effort.

He threw the chain down in frustration and glared at her. "I wish to speak with a man named Bartok. Dr. Tobias Bartok. I think he's with Owen."

"I can do nothing. I am a prisoner." She held up her shackled wrists and raised her eyebrows.

He glanced over his shoulder at the empty hallway before speaking. "I can release you," he whispered.

She stepped closer. "Humans lie," she said. "Why should I believe you?"

"Could you find Owen, if you were free?"

"Yes." She held his eyes. "But I will not lead you to him. He is my king, and I'll not betray him."

"I won't track you." The idea was appealing, but if he wanted to speak with Bartok, there could be no record, electronic or otherwise, of Aithne's release. No one else from the IPF could know what he was doing.

"Humans lie," she repeated. "I have no reason to trust you."

"I don't care whether you trust me," he hissed. He glanced over his shoulder again. "I have... there is a creature that has been speaking with me about a... Conflict. It offers me help, and I've bene-fited, but I'm... growing wary. It manipulates me and I don't like it. The Bible has some power over it, repels it somehow. Bartok is a Christian and I think he might be able to explain some things. If you tell him, and we come to some agreement, it might benefit your kind." He felt his chest con-stricting with fear. "Come back and report to me if you can find him and what he says. Deliver the message directly to Bartok."

231

Her eyes were wide. "You have…" She raised one hand to her mouth and stared at him, her breath coming fast.

"Give me your word." He held her eyes. "Tell Bartok and come back to tell me what he says."

She closed her eyes for a moment and pressed her fist to her mouth, then nodded. "I will."

He stepped away from the gate. The control panel was eight feet away, and he hoped that was still close enough to Aithne that Edwin couldn't see what he was doing. He punched in the code.

The getlaril gate opened.

Aithne was still chained. He tasted bile in his throat and realized distantly it was because he was terrified. *This could be suicide.* He punched in the code to release the shackles. He heard only a soft clink. She must have caught them before they hit the ground and set them down gently.

She appeared at his shoulder, and he jumped. He stepped back, raised the pistol toward her face.

"I'm not going to hurt you," she said. The tear tracks on her face glistened in the harsh light. She nodded toward the control panel. "If you close it, my escape will be less obvious."

He nodded, heartbeat pounding in his ears. *She could kill me before I could get off a shot.* But she didn't. He punched in the code again, keeping one eye on her. She watched him, and he realized belatedly that she could see his fingers. Could see the code.

"I'm going to see my father." Her words were so quiet he almost missed them. "Then I'll take your message." She took a few steps away from him and vanished.

He cursed and took a step forward, pistol raised, then lowered it again. Where was she? *A vampire, or what could be a vampire, is loose in the halls. What have I done?*

Nothing attacked him on the way back to his office. He didn't see Edwin, much to his surprise and relief. *Perhaps he's busy tormenting someone else.*

He pulled up the video feed and methodically removed all traces of his tampering. Most of his conversation wasn't on camera; the camera was angled to capture the cell rather than the door. But he removed that section of video anyway, duplicated a segment of the cell sitting empty, and spliced it together. He removed all records of his code being punched in. *If I were more technical, I could do this better. This is my career down the toilet. But maybe I'll live through it. Maybe.*

He wasn't hopeful.

"YOU SHOULD BE there for it. Oliver Highchurch. Friday morning." Fletcher spoke with no preamble.

"Why?"

"You're the one who started the whole investigation. We weren't paying attention until you dropped us that hint. Where'd you get the info, anyway?"

Grenidor's eyes flicked to his closed door. He hadn't seen Edwin since yesterday, but he felt the familiar tingle on the back of his neck, like he was being watched. *Maybe I'm just paranoid.* "I can't reveal the source, Fletcher. It's private. I don't really want to be there."

Fletcher's voice hardened imperceptibly. "Sometimes we all have to do things we don't enjoy, Grenidor. Seems like the least you could do, to show your appreciation for the boys. They did a magnificent job on the interrogations. Got confessions of some sort from almost every one of them. Even a few leads on other Christians."

"Fine. Fine. I'll be there." Grenidor hung up on Fletcher's reply. He got up and paced, irritated and uneasy. He didn't want to see the execution. Reading the dispassionate summaries of the interrogations on his computer screen provided more than enough detail. *Christians are human, Pauly. Look what you've started. The interrogators have gone psycho on them. The confessions are worthless. Most of them are fabricated and the few that aren't... well, what do they prove? That Christians disagree with the Revolution's politics. How is that news? Confessions under torture can't be fully trusted anyway.*

Why would Fletcher care whether I'm there? I don't think he would, normally. Edwin would want me involved, but Fletcher would be just as happy to have it seem like his group's idea, now that there's some success to report. Is his insistence on my presence proof of Edwin's manipulation? How would I know?

With his eyes on the worn carpet of his office, he didn't notice Edwin until he ran into him. He stumbled backward. "Why can't you ever walk in like a normal person!"

Edwin purred, "I am far from human. Do you require a reminder?" He smiled, showing his teeth.

"No." Grenidor swallowed, feeling a sudden tightness in his throat.

"Sit. I have a warning for you." Edwin's eyes gleamed, and Grenidor retreated behind his desk.

Edwin sat first and gestured toward Grenidor's chair with a disarming smile. *He's toying with me. Playing good cop and bad cop in the same breath.*

Edwin waited for a moment before he began. "I have told you that the vampire Feichin is dangerous. You have ignored my warnings. Perhaps you have been distracted by your fear of being arrested and charged with your appalling crimes against that beautiful Fae girl." He smiled again. "That is a very real danger. But the danger of having your throat ripped out by Feichin's teeth should not be forgotten either. I don't take you for a stupid man, Grenidor. But you're acting like one. Kill him now, while you have the chance. Or die with your gun still in your hand, unfired, bleeding out in some forgotten concrete tunnel. I've given you enough warnings. Take them and live to see the benefits of cooperating with us. Or die."

Grenidor had the impression of a flashing forked tongue between razor-sharp teeth. He tried to keep his voice steady. "Thank you for your warning." He forced a smile.

Edwin hissed, a deep yet sibilant sound that reverberated in the small office, and then he stood. Without thought, Grenidor pressed his knee against the drawer that held the Bible. Edwin's eyes bored into him, and then he disappeared.

Grenidor let out a slow breath, and then blinked. For a split second, he saw an afterimage of something... else. A scaly figure, sinuous, coiled around itself, a forked tongue in a mouth full of fangs. A face both human and reptilian. Feathered wings. Short, muscular legs. A human figure. The image would not resolve into something his mind could comprehend, both human and dragon, beautiful beyond words yet viscerally repulsive. The memory of the image stayed with him, though the image was gone in a moment.

He pulled the Bible from the drawer and stared at it. The book didn't move, or glow, or do anything to indicate that it was more than a book. *Whatever power it has isn't obvious.* He flipped it open at random to somewhere in the middle. *Those who guide this people and mislead them, and those who are guided are led astray. Therefore the LORD will take no pleasure in the young men, nor will he pity the fatherless and the widows, for everyone is ungodly and wicked, every mouth speaks vileness. Yet for all this, his anger is not turned away, his hand is still upraised.* He blinked. Where were the encouraging words of John, the compassion and relentless love of Christ? On the next page, he read, *Woe to those who make unjust laws, to those who issue oppressive decrees, to deprive the poor of their rights and withhold justice from the oppressed of my people, making widows their prey and robbing the fatherless. What will you do on the day of reckoning, when disaster comes from afar? To whom will you run for help? Where will you leave your riches? Nothing will remain but to cringe among the captives or fall among the slain.*

Grenidor slammed the book closed, heart pounding. He opened it again, thinking he was on the same page. *I will not accuse forever, nor will I always be angry, for then the spirit of man would grow faint before me—the breath of man that I have created. I was enraged by his sinful greed; I punished him, and hid my face in anger, yet he kept on in his willful ways. I have seen his ways, but I will heal him; I will guide him and restore comfort to him, creating praise on the lips of the mourners in Israel. "Peace, peace to those far and near," says the LORD. "And I will heal them." But the wicked are like the tossing sea, which cannot rest, whose waves cast up mire and mud. "There is no peace," says my God, "for the wicked."*

He groaned and let his head drop to the desk. *I am the wicked. Even if I didn't torture Aithne, I did torture others. I'm guilty. There is blood on my hands.* He raised his head at a sudden thought. *Edwin keeps pushing me to kill Feichin. Yet... Feichin is under control. He's adequately restrained; we won't make that mistake again. The threat of physical danger from him doesn't make sense. Edwin wants him dead, and I don't think it's because he's concerned about me. Whose side is Feichin on? If he's on the Slavemaster's side... that doesn't make sense, because Edwin spoke to him before he spoke to me, and Edwin said he can't even see the Slavemaster's minions. So Feichin is not on the Slavemaster's side. Edwin wants him killed, and he also wants the Christians killed.*

Something does not add up.

He rubbed his eyes and leaned back in his chair. *Why do I get the feeling the flashes of a different appearance are more trustworthy than the face Edwin shows me?* He blinked at the sudden thought. Did the first of those flashes come after he'd read the Bible for the first time? *Why would I be more suspicious of Edwin after reading the Bible?*

Edwin himself said the words had some power to drive him away, or interfere with his surveillance, or control, or something. Is the Slavemaster that subtle? Is the Slavemaster deceiving me, or is Edwin? Or both?

A tingle between his shoulder blades made him feel like he was being watched. He leaned forward to place his elbows on the Bible and his chin in his hands. The feeling disappeared, and his thoughts continued almost unbroken. *Edwin wants something from me. Therefore he offers me things. He knows well what I want; this is unnerving. He wants nothing from Feichin, therefore he wishes to have him killed in order to... what? Prevent him from interfering with something that will happen at that meeting.*

Christians are his enemies. This makes sense, then, because Edwin does not hesitate to kill if it serves his purpose, and perhaps even because it simplifies things.

Why doesn't Edwin kill Feichin himself? Can he? I would think Edwin has the power to kill him. Is Edwin in charge of his own actions, or does he answer to higher authorities on his own side? Or maybe... he just wants me to do it. Maybe Feichin's death isn't worth anything if Edwin does it himself. Or maybe the Slavemaster won't let him interfere so directly.

Aithne healed a Christian. I didn't expect that. What does that tell me?

Did she know he was a Christian? Edwin would have, and if vampires are on the same side as Edwin, perhaps they can detect it too. I would have expected a captive vampire to kill any human when given the opportunity. Owen being the exception, for reasons I don't understand. That she healed a human invalidates the idea that vampires and Fae are the same; the distinction is more important than I had realized.

It also makes the Fae seem better than Edwin.

We have wondered whether, and feared that, humans could become vampires. That idea now seems implausible, if not foolish. Fae are pre-change vampires. Change is not inevitable, nor is it based on age; Ailill never did, and the older ones that escaped had not changed either.

Is it then a decision that a Fae makes? Out of anger? If so, Owen has been given every reason to, and has not.

However... if that fear had been true, would pre-change humans have been considered evil? No; the fact that they could become monsters would not mean that they were monsters. Pre-change Fae appear at least as good as humans.

Realistically, they treat us better than we treat them.

I have been WRONG.

I have tortured innocents, and killed them when they reacted in anger or fear. Even when they ceased to be useful.

Since I met Edwin, I have become much worse.

GRENIDOR GOT OFF the bus four stops early on the way home, not yet ready to face the cold loneliness of his apartment. There was laundry to be done, and he still didn't have any bagels, and he didn't feel like buying any. He walked a few blocks off the main bus route and found himself in one of the little ethnic enclaves that still made the city interesting. *As interesting as it can be.*

Even in his own childhood, Chinatown had been a tourist attraction, not a bastion of traditional, or even modern, Chinese culture. Now, what little remnants of Chinese culture remained were limited to copious amounts of red and gold paint, a few calligraphy characters on the store signs, and endless noodle and rice restaurants. The other ethnic areas were much the same, with a few signs of some cultural heritage but little to set them apart from generic Imperial culture. He wasn't even sure which group might claim this area. Were those Korean characters or Ethiopian letters? They jumbled together on the same sign, as if the owner himself was unsure what heritage to claim.

He peered in windows, unsure what he was looking for. He bought some pre-made sesame buns to microwave for breakfast, then continued on, the paper bag crinkling in his hand. The cold humidity turned into a misting rain, and he stepped into the nearest trinket shop.

Grenidor nodded at the shopkeeper as he entered, noting with only a twinge of amusement that the man's skin was as light as his own. *He's no more exotic than I am.* Souvenirs of places most Imperial citizens had never and would never visit were scattered in haphazard organization over tables and across shelves, a thousand colors gleaming in the harsh light. A table near the front was crammed with Imperial propaganda pieces, the cheap bits manufactured near the shipping district for the tourists who were not yet allowed into the new Empire.

He looked through the jumble and found a figurine of a bull among the eagles and the boxed collectable coins. It was about as long as his hand, carved of some dark wood and polished smooth. The legs were unnaturally thick, perhaps to keep them from breaking. The horns were of lighter wood, and they weren't glued in; one fell out as Grenidor picked it up. He shoved the horn back in the hole.

He stared at it a moment, wondering why it seemed familiar, or why he felt a sense of possession when he held it. He rubbed the pad of his thumb over the bull's back.

"I want to buy this." He placed it on the counter, half-expecting some curiosity from the shopkeeper. He'd made the decision on the spur of the moment, not really thinking about why he wanted it; now that the decision was made, he was ready to argue about it.

The man made change without comment, and Grenidor dropped the figure in his pocket.

In his dress uniform it would have been obvious, but in his BDUs, the outline of the bull disappeared into the folds of the thick camouflage fabric. As he walked home, the sharp wooden hooves scraped against his leg through the cloth. It felt comforting, like the heft of his pistol in its holster. Safety.

He did his evening pushups and then showered. While the water rained down, he thought about Aithne. How pretty she was. How she'd healed the Christian. *Should it have bothered me to shoot him? I think it should have.*

The bull sat on his nightstand beside his phone. He turned off the lamp and felt its sightless gaze on him in the dark. He turned his shoulder to it. But that simply made him more aware of it, an uncomfortable tension in his shoulders.

He told himself it was nothing, but sleep wouldn't come. Finally he rolled over again, grabbed it, and tossed it across the room. It hit the wall and clattered to the floor.

Eyes closed resolutely, he ignored it until he went to sleep.

Fletcher, who had been so insistent that he attend the execution, did not show up. Maybe it *had* been Edwin who wanted him there after all.

The condemned man sat in a chair bolted to the floor near one wall. The room was reminiscent of those used to hold the vampires, although steel was sufficient to control a human. However, the vampire interrogations had always been carried out privately, while executions required an audience.

Folding chairs lined the other side of the room, leaving some eight feet of space between the condemned and the first row of attendees. The prisoner wore a black hood cinched lightly around his neck. His clothes were stained with splotches of dried blood, and the short sleeves of his shirt showed dark bruises around his wrists and up his arms. He hunched forward, shoulders bowed and head drooping.

The executioner was a hard-faced man in his mid-thirties wearing a nametag that said *Virgil*. He stood by the prisoner, back ramrod straight. When Grenidor entered, Virgil gave him a respectful nod, and then stood at attention facing the other attendees.

The silence drew out, long and increasingly awkward. Virgil glanced at Grenidor once, and then again. Finally he said, "Sir? It's your command."

"Me?"

"I was informed that you were to give the command."

"Oh." Grenidor felt his pulse pounding in his ears. "I was not informed of that."

Virgil gave him a long, unsympathetic look. "Shall I confirm it for you, sir?"

Everyone was looking at him. The attendees were the interrogation and investigation teams, of course, men who knew the man's crimes and the sentence. A Christian, convicted of entering the Empire illegally, proselytizing against the laws of the Empire, conspiring to introduce prohibited materials into the Empire, and who knew what else.

It's not like he didn't break the law. He's a traitor.

"No. That won't be necessary. Do it."

"Yes, sir." Virgil saluted. He pulled a gun from the holster at his hip, placed the muzzle against the cloth over the man's head, and fired.

The figure slumped forward, arms slack. Blood and bone splattered the far wall, which Grenidor belatedly realized was padded with thick foam baffling. *Like a short range target practice room.*

His throat tight, he asked, "That's it, then?"

"Yep. Thanks." Virgil holstered the gun and saluted.

Grenidor raised a hand to his mouth, feeling nausea rise, and then shoved both hands in his pockets. *The bull and bullets.*

Hands still in his pockets, he walked to the wall. Facing away from Virgil and slightly turned away from the chairs, no one could see his hands. He hesitated, then pulled the wooden figure and a handful of bullets from his pocket. He swiped his hand across the blood, smearing it between his fingers, over the figure, and all over the bullets. He hid everything before he turned back around.

He gave Virgil a curt nod and fled back to the hallway. His hands were shaking, clenched tightly around the handful of bullets, the bull's wooden horns poking into his leg. The sound of his foot-steps echoed in the empty halls as he hurried away, louder than the pop of the silenced gunshot.

Back in his office, he finally pulled the bullets from his pocket and examined them. Dried blood darkened the metal and the creases in the skin of his fingers. The smooth wooden surface of the bull showed little of the blood, which had rubbed onto the fabric inside his pocket.

What was I thinking? This was a stupid idea. He considered throwing the bullets into the trash. *But what if Edwin's right?* He pulled out his pistol and unloaded it, reloaded it with the bloodied bullets, then shoved it back in the holster.

Grenidor pulled up the video feed from Feichin's cell. The vampire was crouched in the corner again with his bony legs pulled up and arms wrapped around them. His forehead rested on his knees, face hidden behind his bedraggled hair. He didn't look up.

It would be kinder to shoot him. Not to mention safer. But… if Edwin wanted Feichin dead, perhaps there was a good reason not to kill Feichin. Yet.

Feichin slowly raised his head, gaze unfocused until his eyes locked on the camera. *How does he know which camera feed I'm looking at?* He didn't use words; he didn't need to. He only hissed, lips pulled back from long, white teeth.

Grenidor clicked the video off. *It's only the light that makes his teeth look like that.* The thought didn't reassure him.

CHAPTER 13

"HELP ME UP."

Aria jolted awake at the words. She sat up in time to see Owen grimacing as Cillian slipped an arm beneath his shoulders. In a moment she was at his other side, and together they lifted him as gently as they could. Despite their care, she heard his soft hiss of pain, and the quickness of his breath told her that the pain did not abate much once he was upright.

Cillian sat back and studied him. "Why now, Lord Owen?"

Owen slanted him a sideways look, and Cillian smiled.

"My brother," he amended his words. "Why now? In another day or two, the pain will be less. We are safe here, at least for a while."

"Lachtnal. He is away again?"

Cillian's eyes dropped. "Yes."

"He is angry. He believes I was wrong to let Grenidor live, and you were wrong to obey me." Owen stopped, fighting pain again. "If he sees I am healing, perhaps he will not turn. But he is close, and growing closer."

Cillian sighed heavily. "Yes."

Owen studied Aria's face for a long moment, but said nothing.

"Can I do anything?" she asked finally.

A quick smile flashed across his face. "I doubt it. But thank you." His eyes flicked toward the indonhi before he looked across the room. "Bartok, will you speak with me?"

His voice was low, but Bartok must have heard, because he rose and came closer. He dropped to sit in front of Owen.

"Yes?"

"You were speaking to me of El's grace toward humans. If humans can be forgiven, do you think Fae can be as well?" His gaze was locked on Bartok's face.

Bartok sighed. "I don't know how it works for you. But God does not set anyone up to fail. If you were human, I would say yes. God wishes us all to be saved. But I don't even know if you have souls. Animals have no souls, and they can't be saved. They don't need to be. They can't sin, they merely do what they do. Humans are unique. We have free will."

Niamh had knelt behind Owen without a sound, and her nostrils flared at Bartok's words. "You think we have no souls? That we're animals?" Her quiet voice held a razor-sharp edge.

"I don't know. The Bible says nothing about Fae." Bartok's voice remained soft.

Owen sighed and leaned forward to rest his elbows on his knees. His head drooped, dark curls falling over his face. "We don't know either, Niamh. We think we understand these English words, but how do we know we understand correctly?"

Niamh did not respond, but her gaze rested on the back of Owen's head for a long moment. Finally she reached out and ran her white hand across his shoulders, her fingers lingering over one dark bruise at his shirt sleeve. She said something softly in the Fae language.

"No. It does not matter." Owen did not look up.

Bartok rose and walked away, only to return a moment later with the Bible in his hand. "Read this. Start in John. Whether you are human or not, God will give you grace if you ask him. I don't know what that will look like. But Jesus said he was the way to God, the only true way. If you call on him, you call on God's mercy."

Owen reached for the Bible. Cillian stiffened beside him, trembling, and Owen hesitated, his hand just above the book. "What troubles you, Cillian?"

Cillian's voice was nearly inaudible. "You hope in a love that is not offered to us. It is better to remain as we are." His voice cracked, and he shifted to kneel, bent down so his face pressed against Owen's knee. "We may not be loved, but we are not cast out either. I accept that as what is given to us. Do not hope for more."

Owen closed his eyes for a long moment, then took the Bible with his left hand while he rested his right on his brother's dark head. His words were so soft Aria barely caught them. "Beloved brother, I cannot let this go. This is an opportunity unlike any we have ever known. No one has ever offered us hope like this. Who are we to assume we know the limits of El?"

Cillian did not raise his head, and Owen's shoulders slumped even more. He put the Bible on the floor in front of his crossed ankles, and his left hand shook as he thumbed through the pages. 1 Samuel. Psalms. Isaiah. Jonah. Luke. Romans. James. Revelation. He blinked and flipped back to the beginning, looking for a table of contents. Bartok reached forward and turned to the beginning of John.

"Thank you."

Bartok watched him begin to read. After a moment, Owen shook his head slightly and rubbed at his eyes, leaned down farther.

"Do you want me to read it to you?" Bartok offered.

Owen glanced up. His lips twisted in a faint smile. "Is it that obvious?"

"That you can barely stay upright?"

"And my eyes don't focus yet."

Cillian raised his head long enough to help Aria and Niamh support Owen as he lay back down. Bartok began to read.

Cillian and Niamh remained beside Owen, listening, their gazes locked on the floor. Owen's eyes closed, and Aria couldn't tell if he was awake or asleep.

Aria, though, was filled with questions, and she kept biting her tongue. Who was the John who wrote the book? Was he the same John that cried in the wilderness? Bartok answered that unspoken question without prompting.

"This is the famous verse. You've probably heard it, even if you've heard of nothing else. John 3:16 *For God so loved the world that he gave his one and only Son, that whoever believes in him shall not perish but have eternal life. For God did not send his Son into the world to condemn the world, but to save the world through him.*"

"I have not heard that before," Owen whispered.

Niamh shook her head silently.

"*Whoever believes in him is not condemned, but whoever does not believe stands condemned already because he has not believed in the name of God's one and only Son.* Jesus is the only way to God, the only way to be forgiven."

"What of humans who never hear of him?" Niamh asked.

"That is for God to judge. But humans are sinful, and we are condemned because of our very nature. Listen: *This is the verdict: Light has come into the world, but men loved darkness instead of light because their deeds were evil. Everyone who does evil hates the light, and will not come into the light for fear that his deeds will be exposed. But whoever lives by the truth comes into the light, so that it may be seen plainly that what he has done has been done through God.*"

Bartok waited for more questions, but then continued. In chapter 5, he read "*For just as the Father raises the dead and gives them life, even so the Son gives life to whom he is pleased to give it. Moreover, the Father judges no one, but has entrusted all judgment to the Son, that all may honor the Son just as they honor the Father. He who does not honor the Son does not honor the Father, who sent him."* Bartok stopped and ran one hand over his face thoughtfully. "Even if you are not human, I think this sounds like you can be saved. It says *whoever* believes in the Son. It was written to humans, but God must have known your kind existed. He would have known you would read this. If it did not apply to you, I think he would have made that clear."

Three pairs of blue eyes rested on Bartok's face, but no one said anything. No, four pairs, because Niall was again crouched beside Owen, a silent shadow. Bartok began reading again.

Aria closed her eyes as she listened. The words seemed to flow around her, and she imagined Jesus doing the miracles Bartok described. John's words gave little detail, and she knew almost nothing about the Israelites among whom Jesus had lived. Israel was a desert land, she knew that, and the people spoke a language she'd never heard.

Niall hesitated, then pushed his notebook forward. *What does "everlasting life" mean?*

"When we die, our souls spend eternity with God, worshipping forever in perfect communion. In this life, we are always distracted by physical things, pain, responsibilities, trivial idols that take up our time. In heaven, nothing will come between us and God."

Owen frowned faintly at the ceiling, but said nothing. Niall poised his pen over the paper again, but then shook his head and motioned that Bartok should continue.

Aria realized that the Fae had gathered around them, listening in rapt silence as Bartok read. No one asked questions except Owen, Cillian, Niamh, and Niall, but they listened.

THE DRAGON'S TONGUE

"To the Jews who had believed him, Jesus said, 'If you hold to my teaching, you are really my disciples. Then you will know the truth, and the truth will set you free." He stopped and looked up, as if caught by a thought, then studied Owen's bruised face for a long moment. "I think you need only to recognize the one you have already been following, Owen."

Owen held his gaze. "Read. Please."

The debates among the Jews about whether Jesus was really sent from God caused a few murmurs among the Fae, but Aria couldn't catch any of their words. They questioned, and they listened. She had the feeling that they understood more than she did, and she felt herself catching at Bartok's words in desperation. *I should know this. I should understand it. Why did they hate Jesus so much? He didn't do anything to them.*

But he did. He challenged their power and their authority, and then said it didn't matter, because human power and authority are meaningless anyway. Can I accept that? Does it matter that the Empire controls us? Does it matter that the Empire is built on lies?

Bartok touched her knee to get her attention for the next part. *"I am the good shepherd. The good shepherd lays down his life for the sheep. ... I have other sheep that are not of this sheep pen. I must bring them also. They too will listen to my voice, and there shall be one flock and one shepherd."* He looked up. "We have always assumed that was a reference to Gentiles. Jews are Jews, and everyone who is not a Jew is a Gentile. But perhaps it could also include you."

Owen's eyes did not open, and Cillian bent forward to place his head near his brother's, listening to his breath. "He is asleep. Read again when he is awake."

Bartok nodded. He hesitated, and then said, "Thank you for listening, Cillian. I know it isn't easy for you."

Cillian glanced up, blue eyes bright in the dim light. "It is not. But if it is truth, I have not the right to deny it."

BARTOK READ AGAIN when Owen woke.

"*If anyone loves me, he will obey my teaching. My father will love him, and we will come to him and make our home with him.*" Bartok stopped again and stared at Owen.

"What?" said Cillian after a moment. "You are thinking something about us."

"I think you obey but you don't know why. Humans, at least some of us, know why we should obey, but we don't. We're both wrong."

Cillian's lips tightened, but he did not argue.

Bartok looked down again and continued. "*... As the Father has loved me, so have I loved you. Now remain in my love. If you obey my commands, you will remain in my love, just as I have obeyed my Father's commands and remain in his love... My command is this: Love each other as I have loved you. Greater love has no one than this, that he lay down his life for his friends. You are my friends if you do what I command. .... This is my command: Love each other.*"

Niamh murmured, "Aria says she loves my brother. Yet she knows nothing of obedience. Her disobedience was the cause of his capture and torture."

"Who are you to tell me whether I love him or not?" Aria's voice broke. "You didn't even offer to wash the blood off his face! What kind of love is that?"

Cillian snapped, "Your human love is worthless! You say love when you mean lust, or affection, or appreciation for a good cup of coffee! Your love is weak. You know nothing of obedience or trust. You sacrifice nothing. Love *is* obedience."

"You love out of obligation! Your heart isn't in it. What is love if it's defined by laws and regulations? Nothing!" Aria was shaking with rage.

"Love is more than a feeling! Feelings are worthless and fleeting. Obedience is what matters. I obey! You do whatever you wish and call it love."

Aria shot back, "But love is a choice! You have to choose to love and choose to obey, not just act like a… a… tree or a rock or something! Maybe the struggle is part of what makes obedience and love so important!"

Owen raised a hand and they both stopped, breathing heavily as they glared at each other. "She is right, Cillian. We have remembered obedience but forgotten love. We remembered the word, but lost the concept. We obey, not because we choose to, or because we love El, but because we fear the cost of rebellion. But perhaps…" he stopped, jaw tight.

Petro stood at the edge of their circle.

The other Fae shifted away from him in one fluid movement, their eyes wide. He strode toward them and knelt beside Aria, peering at Owen with his head cocked. Cillian remained frozen across from her, one hand still clenched as he watched Petro.

Bartok glanced around. "What's going on? Why did everyone move away?"

"I begin to understand. You have both forgotten something I never knew." Petro moved around, no, *through* Bartok to study Owen from the other side. "He is more human, but he has not lost any of what makes him Fae. This is unprecedented." He glanced up to catch Aria's eye. "I thank you. You have revealed something new to me."

"What are you talking about?" Aria asked, her voice still shaky.

Petro did not wish to answer her questions; that was clear. He meant to say what he meant to say, but no more. But she'd realized that he had difficulty refusing a direct demand from her, though she didn't understand why, and she asked again, "What are you talking about? What did I reveal?"

His mouth twitched, and he hesitated as he chose his words. "I thought love was a meaningless human emotion, sometimes a part of human decision-making but ultimately inconsequential. It is not. It is both more significant and more mysterious than I realized."

Bartok looked at Aria with his eyebrows raised questioningly.

Petro stood, as if he had made a decision.

Aria stopped him. "Wait! Why can I see you and Bartok can't?"

Petro again chose his words carefully. "Because he is human. I have not revealed myself to him, in accordance with the instructions I have been given in dealing with humans."

"Then why can I see you?"

"Because I have revealed myself to you."

"But why?" She knew she sounded petulant. "I'm human! What's the difference?"

Petro's eyes locked on hers. "It is not for me to say." He disappeared.

Aria dropped her head into her hands and bit back a scream of frustration.

Bartok hadn't heard or seen Petro, and Aria repeated his words for Bartok's opinion. She pushed her hands through her messy hair and stretched her tense shoulders. "My childhood was completely normal. I don't know what he was talking about." She scowled.

"What about before you were adopted? Maybe something happened then." Bartok put a hand on her wrist. "Relax. Can you remember anything from before?"

"I was a baby. I don't remember anything."

Owen's blue eyes were on her face. "You were adopted?"

She shrugged and then hunched her shoulders. "That's what the records said. No one ever told me." She motioned for Bartok to explain for her. *I should act like a grown up and explain it myself. But it's too much to take in right now. It doesn't even feel real. Mom and Dad were Mom and Dad. I even looked like them. A little. Well, not much.*

Bartok's voice faded and Aria looked up. Everyone was staring at him. Cillian said, his voice low and furious, "We have *never* stolen human children. Never!"

Owen put a restraining hand on Cillian's clenched fist. "He makes no accusation, Cillian." His eyes turned toward Aria. "You can remember nothing?"

Aria shook her head. "I was a baby."

Niamh shifted, hesitated, and finally said, "I am afraid of what I think." Her eyes on Aria, she spoke softly in Fae, her words only for Owen and Cillian at first. At length, Cillian raised his head and motioned to Conri, the eldest of the Fae at the other end of the room. He knelt beside them, his head bent low to hear Niamh's whispered words.

They all turned to look at Aria.

"We wish to taste your blood again."

"All right."

Cillian drew Owen's knife and drew it across her finger. She hissed at the stinging pain and bit her lip. Cillian licked the blood from the blade of the knife. Conri tilted his head back and squeezed her finger over his mouth until a few drops of blood fell in, then squeezed her finger again over Owen's mouth. Niamh, as before, licked the blood directly from Aria's finger. It was just as awkward and surprising as it had been the previous time; Bartok's shocked look did nothing to lessen the shiver that coursed down her spine.

Conri nodded thoughtfully. "I agree," he said.

Cillian frowned, but nodded reluctantly. Niamh licked her lips and watched Owen's face.

After a long silence, he said, "It is the best explanation I can see."

"What?" Aria's impatience burst out.

Niamh took Aria's hand and ran her finger over the cut. The wound disappeared, as did the pain. She licked her lips, seeming to consider her words. "In the past, humans have managed to surprise and kill Fae. It is rare, because we are wary, but it has happened. Twice, the Fae victims of such an attack included children. We assumed that our children were captured and experimented upon, or were killed as soon as they were undefended. We know of two Fae children who were stolen twenty-four years ago from a family that was killed in a forest some distance west of here. The elder brother of the girl survived; he was unable to rescue them, but he reported that the two infants were taken back with the humans. We believed the infants murdered. Now, we think you are one of those Fae children."

"What?" Aria blinked. "How can I be Fae? I'm not... I can't do magic or anything. I'm not like you," she finished, the words trailing away. "Sorry. I don't mean that as a bad thing. I'm just... I don't understand."

Niamh glanced at Owen, in case he wanted to speak, but he said nothing. His blue eyes rested on Aria's face, and she read weariness in them. Pain. Compassion.

Tears stood in Niamh's eyes, and she said softly, "I tasted the Fae blood in you, but it was faint. I assumed that meant your Fae ancestor was distant, and you were mostly human. Now, we think instead that you were born Fae. You never touched megdhonia, and you live as a human. But you were, and are, Fae."

"They did tests. They tested extensively. They were afraid I was Fae, or vampire, and wanted to be sure I was human before they did anything." Aria felt herself babbling. "I saw the records! How could they not know?"

"Humans have no knowledge of megdhonia. They test for external signs of what exists in our... hearts, or souls, or... the piece of us that is not contained in the physical world. We learn to access it as children. Fae parents sing over their infants, bringing them from helpless dependence into power. We learn to control megdhonia, and we learn to commune with El. These are inseparable. A Fae infant has no power over megdhonia. It is a skill; we are born with aptitude, but no ability. It is learned."

Aria frowned in confusion. "But then... you think I'm Fae?" she asked again. The thought seemed too impossible.

"We cannot know. I doubt we could confirm through long-buried memories in your mind, even if you invited us to look. But it explains why you can see us even when we wish to remain hidden. You were raised as human and never taught how to access megdhonia, yet your mother and father would have sung over you. You would have received a little of their power."

Niall had been scribbling in his notebook and pushed it toward her. *Perhaps this is also why Petro is interested in you. He said he was interested in decisions. Humans are free to choose from many choices. Our choices are tightly constrained. You would be a data point somewhere in the middle - born Fae, but raised human. Your decisions might illuminate something he is considering.*

Bartok read over her shoulder. He sat back with a thoughtful frown.

"What do you think?" Aria asked him.

He rubbed his hands over his face. "It is as plausible as any other explanation."

She stared at him, then scooted back. "I need some air."

She fled to the other side of the room, where she paced. The Fae were polite enough not to stare at her, but she barely noticed that simple courtesy.

I could be Fae. I could have been Fae! I could have learned magic like Owen. Is it too late? Do I want what they have? Does their magic come with narrowed choices? It doesn't seem to benefit them much. I mean, maybe they'd all be dead if not for magic, but they're not even allowed to fight back against Grenidor and the Empire. They're always on the run. But then, so are Gabriel and everyone else.

This is too much.

ARIA HUDDLED IN the corner with her knees pulled up to her chest. She didn't want to talk to anyone.

Who am I?

A thousand memories of her parents flooded her mind. Her father teaching her to ride a bike, careening around the too-small courtyard behind their apartments, shrieking with terrified laughter. Her mother had taken a few pictures, but they'd been lost in the intervening years. Singing with her mother and father in the car, going someplace she couldn't remember. Arguments over bedtimes and boys and her math grades.

They weren't perfect people, but they'd loved her. They'd loved her more than she'd understood. *They chose me. They didn't just end up with me by accident.*

Niamh rose and strode to her, eyes downcast. She knelt by Aria's side. "I know not what to say to you, except that I feel such sorrow words cannot begin to express it."

"I'm fine." Aria knew it was a lie, but she didn't realize there were tears on her cheeks until she spoke, her voice even more unsteady than she'd expected.

Niamh let out a breath like a sob. "No, child. I wept for what my son Niall lost. His voice, the song of his tongue rising like the song of his heart. His children, my grandchildren, who now will never be. A great crime was committed against him and against all our kind, who will now miss knowing the Fae who would have come from him. But your loss is perhaps even greater."

Soundless tears slipped down Aria's cheeks. "I don't even know what I've missed."

"May I sing for you? A song of loss, and sorrow, and comfort." Niamh's eyes were filled with tears, the compassion so warm and gentle that Aria almost felt her mother's arms hugging her again.

She nodded.

Niamh's voice remained quiet, her song for Aria alone. Her voice was clear as water, pure as the finest gold, and the warmth of it wrapped around Aria's heart. Gossamer-fine, holding depths and layers of emotion, her song acknowledged the loss and grief, embracing the anguish and sorrow, refining them, and pulling Aria into acceptance, even joy in the faithfulness of the one who listened to their song.

El's faithfulness? If he is faithful, why did this happen? Aria's question lingered, but the song removed the sting.

Niamh sang, and Aria listened, eyes closed, tears ceasing. Time didn't matter; the song was comfort and understanding, love and loss and forgiveness.

Niamh's voice faded, and Aria took a shaky breath. She looked up to see Niamh's eyes on her face.

"My brother Lord Owen would sing for you also, but I begged him not to use his last strength now. He has many responsibilities, and he must save his strength for what is coming. But he wishes you to know that his compassion is no less because he cannot sing this time. Next time, he will sing for you. His voice is beautiful."

Aria swallowed. "Thank you." She forced a smile, then found that it wasn't forced after all. *There is joy left in the world after all, however difficult to find. There is kindness.* "Thank you, Niamh."

Niamh hesitated, then reached forward. She pushed Aria's hair back from her face and behind her ear, her cool fingers barely grazing Aria's cheek. "When the sorrow strikes you, do not hesitate to ask for comfort. We cannot give you back what has been lost, but we can grieve with you so you are not alone in your sorrow."

A FIGURE FLIPPED through the indohni and landed with effortless grace. Aria watched her glance around the room, her eyes resting on Aria and Bartok for a heartbeat before she went to Owen. A Fae girl, too slim, but not as gaunt as Cillian or Niamh. Beautiful, with features that seemed somehow familiar. *But they're all beautiful. It doesn't mean there's a family resemblance.*

She spoke with Owen a moment, then looked over her shoulder at Aria again. Aria rose and crossed the room again, pushing her still-reeling emotions down. The young woman stopped speaking as she approached, her eyes wary.

"She is a friend, Aithne. Speak freely," Owen said.

261

Aria watched her as she ducked her head at Owen's command. Red welts ringed her slender wrists. Her voice was soft as she began to speak.

"I did not escape. I was released by Colonel Grenidor. He sends a message to you. He wishes to speak with a man named Dr. Tobias Bartok. He believes Bartok is with you. He has been speaking with something... dangerous."

Owen's eyes widened almost imperceptibly. "Bartok?"

Cillian looked across the room to catch Bartok's eye and wave him over again. A moment later, Bartok knelt beside Cillian, dark eyes on Aithne.

"You are Dr. Tobias Bartok?" Aithne studied him across their small circle.

"I am."

"Colonel Grenidor wishes to meet with you. He has been speaking with something I have not seen. Perhaps it is a dark one. He says it told him there is a conflict. It has helped him, but he believes it is manipulating him. He does not like to be manipulated. He believes you are a Christian, and he hopes you might be able to explain why the Bible seems to have some power over it. He hopes to come to some agreement with you. He hopes to save himself." Aithne's eyes were almost the same blue as Owen's, bright and intense as she watched Bartok. After a moment, she bowed her head. "I have my own theory, but I await Lord Owen's wisdom. I agreed to bring Grenidor your response to his request to talk."

Bartok looked at Owen.

"There is something else," Owen prompted.

"My father has turned." Her words came out in an anguished whisper, and she leaned forward to press her head to the floor beside Owen's shoulder. "I saw him, Lord Owen! He is no longer one of us."

Owen closed his eyes, then whispered, "Help me up." Again Aria and Cillian supported his shoulders as he sat up. He put one hand on Aithne's head, closed his eyes, and began to sing.

His face was white as marble, at least where the bruises had faded. The faint lines of pain around his eyes and lips made Aria want to reach out and cup his face in her hands, but she didn't. The gesture would be too intimate, and he would look at her with those clear, cold eyes that understood her love, and yet did not return it. It was better to squash the feeling.

Another image was superimposed over what she saw, more vibrant than Owen's bruised features before her eyes. *Which one is real?* Their positions in the vision were nearly identical, Owen sitting with one hand on Aithne's head, but they were upon a moss-covered rock, surrounded by trees. Owen stood, the song swelling around them as he raised his hands to the sky. His eyes were closed, voice rising higher, weaving around and between them in a golden thread.

Cillian and Niamh began to sing, and after a few moments the others joined the song. Every song was different, every voice raised in intricate harmony. Their voices made the air shiver and shimmer like water. Aria blinked, then closed her eyes as she listened. She couldn't identify all the voices, and the one she knew was Cillian's sounded deeper, richer than she remembered.

Owen's voice faded, but the music wrapped around Aria like a cloak, warm and gentle. With some effort, she opened her eyes to see Owen leaning forward, head hanging down between his shoulders.

She reached forward to put one hand on his arm. His bare skin was cold beneath her fingers, the muscles slack. He didn't react immediately, but after a moment he turned his head slightly to look at her, eyebrows slightly raised. She pulled her hand back, her face flushing.

He reached out to catch her hand, ran his finger across her knuckles, then bowed his head slightly. He let her go.

What does that mean? It was like an apology, but... for what?

The song died away. Aria felt Aithne's eyes on her, and blushed again. "Sorry," she murmured.

"You have no reason to apologize." Owen's eyes on her were gentle, and his lips held a faint, wry smile. "I should apologize to you. Perhaps some other time."

He knows I love him, and he feels bad he doesn't feel the same way about me, but he's too kind to embarrass me in front of another spectator. I feel like such an idiot.

But is it wrong to love him? That's no reason to be ashamed, is it?

She realized Bartok had watched it all, and she felt her flush deepen further.

Bartok said only, "I'm willing to meet Colonel Grenidor, but I'd like to talk to Gabriel first. It's dangerous, and I'd rather not drag everyone else into it." He studied his hands. "Anyway, I should return to them. If you don't wish to join us, I understand. You're probably safer away from the Resistance anyway."

Owen nodded. "Aideen is scouting. When she returns, she will tell us where they are. We will join them tomorrow. After we speak with Gabriel, Aithne will take your answer to Colonel Grenidor."

THEY HAD NO lights with them; all the lanterns and flashlights had been left with Gabriel and the other resistance fighters. The indonhi let in dim light while the sun was high, but as twilight fell, the shadows in the corners of the room deepened and spread until Aria could barely make out the pale skin of her hand in front of her face.

"We will eat now, while Lord Owen sits upright." Niamh spoke in Aria's ear, and she jumped. "Can you see?"

"Not really," Aria said.

Niamh raised her hand, and sphere of air shimmered to brightness above her palm. "Sit and eat."

"You can make light?" Aria gaped.

"No. It is…" Niamh groped for words. "I don't know how to explain in English. Cillian?"

Cillian, barely visible at the edge of the light, shrugged. "I don't know."

Owen's voice came from out of the darkness. "Your science explains energy as waves or particles. Both, actually. Light is energy. Niamh is transforming some form of energy into another form visible to you."

Niamh nodded. "Yes." She knelt in front of Owen, her fingers moving quickly as she sliced a piece of meat for him. "Eat, my brother." She watched him until he nodded, then turned to her own place.

Ardghal had set out the bread, apples, tomatoes, zucchini, and cheese. The Fae watched him, but no one said anything until Niamh reached forward to cut an apple in half. She sliced it twice more, then picked up one of the pieces and examined it. She frowned, bit it, and chewed.

She didn't cut out the core. She probably doesn't know you're supposed to do that.

Niamh's thoughtful frown deepened to a slightly disgusted expression, but she continued to chew. "It is edible," she said. "I make no claims to its nutritional value."

Ardghal humphed. "This is called 'cheese.'"

One of the other Fae leaned forward to examine it. "What is it made of?" he asked.

"I don't know."

Cillian grimaced. "I heard it was made of cow's milk. Why did you buy that, Ardghal?"

"I heard a human say once that she was fat because she liked cheesecake so much. I assumed that meant cheese was a rich, dense food." He glanced at Aria, as if for verification.

Bartok sat beside her, still silent, and she found herself saying, "Yes. It's high in calories. Much more so than apples and zucchini. Although I don't know if your bodies even work on calories..." she frowned. "Well, I guess they must, since I'm... I was... Fae."

Ardghal cut into the package, then abruptly put the knife down. "That is vile. I apologize, Lord Owen."

Bartok reached forward and picked it up. "Taleggio. This is good. You could have picked something milder for your first taste, though."

Aria retreated to a corner with Bartok. They ate apple alternating with bites of bread, cheese, zucchini, and carrots while they listened to the Fae puzzle over the food. The light faded when she finished eating. *Niamh was always aware of what I was doing. That's considerate. Or creepy.* She and Bartok slept back to back. The warmth of his body was welcome in the winter chill. The building was out of the wind and warmer than the underground train station, but that wasn't saying much.

She awoke because she was cold, Bartok's strong back gone from hers. He was sitting in front of Owen, head bent forward as they murmured to each other. She joined them. Pale light filtered through the indohni, painting the room in soft shades of grey and blue.

"The pain is tolerable. I am healing."

Cillian's words were almost inaudible, meant for her and Bartok and not the other Fae. "The getlaril is being removed from his body. He will heal more quickly now. Not quickly, but more quickly than before."

Owen closed his eyes in acknowledgment. "It is tolerable," he repeated.

Aria hesitated, then asked, "*How* is the getlaril being removed? Can we help with that?"

Owen gave her a quick, amused glance. "You cannot help. But I thank you for your offer."

Cillian held a cloth in one hand and dipped it in a cup of water. He raised the edge of Owen's shirt and wiped carefully just above Owen's hip. He showed them a smear of grey across the white cloth. "Some of the powder will come through his skin. The rest, as well as the bullets, will pass into his waste."

Bartok leaned forward and looked at it more closely, then touched the grey with one cautious finger. "What exactly is it?"

"I do not know the words in English," Cillian said.

Owen licked his lips. "It tastes of iron and silver, but there is something else too, something not of human science. Older, and colder than anything man possesses."

Cillian glanced at his face. "You think it is of the dark ones?"

"It is possible." Owen let out a soft breath. "We must rejoin Gabriel. You knew about Feichin?" He turned his blue eyes on Cillian.

Cillian bowed his head. "Yes, my lord. I did."

"How?"

"One of the hard drives you took from an Imperial facility had a series of videos on it. Among the videos was a sequence that showed how..." Cillian's hands tightened into fists. "He was starved, my lord. He was afraid for Aithne, and angry. They pushed him beyond what he could endure, and he judged them evil." His voice shook. "He murdered one of the scientists, but I felt him turn before that."

Owen did not answer for several long minutes. Cillian shifted beside him, but said nothing, his hands clenching and unclenching.

Finally Owen said, "We must join with Gabriel and the others. I must think. Bartok, I have need of your wisdom."

Bartok nodded. "I have no wisdom of my own. But I will do my best."

AIDEEN LED THEM to another train station a little farther east, close to the Anacostia River. The station was partially aboveground, but Gabriel and the others had stayed in the lowest floor, so any lights and movement would remain unnoticed. Niamh and Cillian carried Owen between them, his arms draped over their shoulders. Their progress was slow, but at last, with the Fae spread out around them, they stopped in front of the sentry.

"I wish to speak with Gabriel." Owen's voice had a weight of command that was undiminished by his obvious fatigue and pain.

"Yes. Go on." He waved them through. Aria didn't remember his name; she'd never spoken to him, but he nodded in recognition as she passed.

Gabriel met them as they approached the camp under one of the unmoving escalators. Cillian and Niamh helped Owen sit with his back against the concrete wall. Gabriel dropped to sit across from him.

"You had no casualties?" Owen asked first.

"No. I believe we have some of your people to thank for that." Gabriel inclined his head. "Please convey my appreciation."

"I will." Owen studied him. "You have a video of my cousin Feichin. He turned. I wish to watch it."

Gabriel pressed his fingers together in his lap, avoiding Owen's gaze. "It isn't pretty. Perhaps I could give you the short version verbally."

"I wish to watch it, Gabriel. I wish to understand why he turned." Owen leaned his head back against the concrete.

"I'd rather not show you."

"Why?" Owen's eyes were sharp on Gabriel's face.

Gabriel licked his lips and said reluctantly, "There is enough trouble between our people."

"Will hiding one man's cruelties make us trust you more?"

Gabriel sighed. "Fine. Give us a few minutes."

"Agreed." Owen closed his eyes as Gabriel stood, motioning Bartok and Aria to follow him.

Once he'd asked Jonah to get the computer up, Gabriel pulled them behind a concrete pillar. He asked quietly, "You have any trouble?"

Bartok said, "Not exactly. Feichin's daughter found us though. She says Grenidor wants to meet with me."

Gabriel rubbed one hand over his jaw. "Why?"

"He's searching. It sounds like he's in over his head and finally realizes it. Something's been manipulating him. I'll talk with him, but I don't want to endanger everyone. It could be demonic, for all I know."

Gabriel's frown deepened. "I don't want to endanger *you*. We have some issues of our own. We got a request for help."

"From whom?"

"Leo. One of his people is missing." Gabriel let out a breath. "Dandra."

"What?" Aria was confused. "Who's Leo? And what you mean about Dandra?"

"Leo used to be a covert ops guy. For the CIA, I think, or maybe it was military intel. He doesn't talk about it. At some point he got... disillusioned, you could say. Not that everything they did was bad, but the orders he got weren't making him proud anymore. So he quit. Found God. He was working for a contractor doing some high-tech stuff out at the far edge of the East Quadrant when the Revolution got hot.

"We've been in touch a couple times. He has a few people here. He didn't tell me what they were doing, exactly, but he's been kind of apolitical. God took over his life and he deliberately kept out of what was going on. Said he didn't want to know because it just made him angry. The important thing was souls. But then things 'got weird'—those are his words, not mine—and he started wondering what was really going on here. So he's trained a few people and they've been here doing recon for... whatever he's planning. Dandra was one of them."

"And now she's missing," Aria finished.

"Actually, no. Well, we knew that already. We just didn't know she was one of his folks."

"Where is she?"

"We don't know. Some of his people are missing, and she's one of them."

"And he wants us to find her?" Bartok asked.

Gabriel's answer was cut short as the Fae began to sing. One voice, then three, then two dozen Fae voices rose around Owen, clear and bright as crystal.

Owen walked along a rocky shore, salt water swirling around his ankles. He stooped to pick up a pebble and threw it out over the water, then continued walking. He threw another pebble, then dipped both hands in the water and splashed it on his face. He rubbed hard,

271

then threw his dripping head back and shook out his shoulders, as if removing a great weight. A gull crowed above him, and he watched it fly past, the corners of his eyes crinkling as he smiled. He stopped, then raised one hand to shade his eyes. Gaze fixed on some distant point, he stood without moving for several minutes.

The music died away, voices fading one by one. Aria, Bartok, and Gabriel stepped back around the corner to see Cillian and Niamh sitting on their heels in front of Owen.

Owen grasped Cillian's hand in his right hand and Niamh's in his left. He bowed his head. "I am grateful, my brother and my sister. You have given me much." He looked up to smile at them, eyes warm.

Niamh smiled, a sharp, pale beauty that made Aria catch her breath with sudden jealousy. "At last. You have suffered enough."

Cillian huffed. "There is a limit? I was not aware of such." But even he smiled.

"You're healing!" Aria could keep silent no longer.

Owen's clear blue eyes turned on her. "Yes. The getlaril is being removed more quickly." Then his eyes locked on Gabriel's. "I need to see the video of Feichin. I think... I hope... there may be a way back for him."

"Back from being a vampire?" Gabriel's voice hardened. "He's a monster, Owen. He's off the deep end."

Owen held his eyes as the seconds dragged out.

Finally Gabriel relented. "Can you walk? We can't move the computer."

Cillian helped Owen to his feet. Owen leaned on him, but moved under his own power across the platform and dropped with a sigh in front of the monitor Jonah had prepared.

"Where do you want to start?" Jonah asked.

"At the beginning."

Owen sat with his elbows on his knees, eyes shuttered and difficult to read as he watched Feichin speak with Davis. Aria's stomach churned at the thought of what came later, and she glanced surreptitiously at Owen's face again. *What is he thinking?* The skin around his right eye was no longer black and swollen; only an uneven purple-green tinge remained. She wanted to stay, wanted to offer some kind of comfort. *He probably doesn't need it. Not from me.* But she couldn't watch the videos again, couldn't even listen to them.

She fled to the far side of the room.

CHAPTER 14

HOURS PASSED. OWEN finished watching the videos and thanked Jonah for his assistance with the computer. Jonah nodded and chewed his lip thoughtfully as he watched Owen cross the platform. He lost sight of Owen quickly, his gaze scanning the platform uneasily.

"What did he say?" Levi spoke from beside Jonah.

"Nothing much. He's ready to kill someone though. He's furious." Jonah rubbed his hand over the handle of his pistol. "You trust them?"

Levi grunted. "Hard to trust someone who keeps disappearing."

Owen hesitated and glanced over his shoulder, then continued, apparently deciding not to correct them. Cillian darted to his brother's side, and Owen leaned on him the rest of the way. Aria thought his expression looked more like tightly controlled anger and soul-crushing grief. Once he reached his place among the other Fae, he closed his eyes and let his head rest in his hands for long minutes.

Across the platform, Gabriel spoke in the center of a small group, waving one hand at intervals. Aria couldn't quite hear his words, but she could tell the Fae were listening. Bartok said something, and Gabriel frowned fiercely. Bartok repeated it. Gabriel nodded.

The two of them walked some distance from the others, glanced back, and then continued around the bend in one of the tunnels. Owen caught Lorcan's eye and gave him a slight nod, and the young Fae slipped after them unseen.

"Why did you send him?" Aria asked. "Are you spying on them?"

Owen gave her a wry smile. "I can hear what they're saying from here. I sent him to protect them. There are turned Fae in these tunnels."

She swallowed. "Like Feichin?"

His voice lost its hint of amusement. "Worse. Feichin remembers what he was."

She tried not to shiver, but his eyes showed his sympathy. "Don't be afraid. They avoid us. We remind them of the light of El, and it burns them."

"Is that why the legends of vampires say they avoid sunlight? Turned Fae are vampires, aren't they?"

He gave a faint, sad nod. "They are what inspired the legends, yes."

"Can they make more vampires?"

He blinked at her. "What?"

"Could they bite a human and turn the human into a vampire?"

275

"Of course not. Only a Fae can become a vampire. It is the result of choosing rebellion." He looked down, spreading his hands out and inspecting his empty palms as if answers would be found there. "Inevitable, or so we thought. We are made to be one thing, shaped and defined by the power and rules that El gives. Disobedience twists that one thing into an abomination; power without control, desire without fellowship, judgment without justice or mercy. A vampire is a Fae who has turned away from El. They are miserable, locked in pain and isolation. They cannot fellowship with each other; they have neither the capacity nor the desire. They desire El, yet hate Him. He cannot abide them, because they chose to disobey. However..."

He tilted his head, his expression sharpening as he listened.

"What are they saying?" she finally ventured.

Owen's eyes flicked to her, then to Niamh in a silent command. Niamh moved to speak into Aria's ear.

"Gabriel received word earlier from one of the men that Christians are being arrested and tortured. He was planning a rescue operation." She paused, listening, then continued, "Dr. Bartok argues that the chances of success..." She frowned and glanced at Aria, then raised one hand to cup it behind Aria's ear.

Bartok's voice came to her, distant but clear. He was speaking emphatically, as if repeating a point he'd already made. "You know we'll lose people. I'm not saying it's not worth it, but it would be wrong to demand it of them. Doomed rescue missions aren't what they signed up for.

These are political rebels. For a mission like that, they need to be volunteers. They need to be Christians, or at least they need to know exactly what Christians believe."

"They're good men, Bartok. They'll want to do it."

"They'll follow you, maybe. But is it right to ask someone unsaved to die for someone who is saved? They need to know, Gabriel."

"Fine," Gabriel growled. "You know we don't have many Christians. Not enough for a mission."

Bartok didn't back down. "You know I'll go, if we have a team. Christians have been martyred since the beginning. It's not nice, but it's a fact. That won't end until Christ comes back."

Gabriel spat, "You've chosen an inconvenient time to remember God! Where was this morality when we went into Forestgate?"

"You're right." Bartok's voice lowered. Aria imagined him looking down, deliberately softening his expression. "I haven't been much of a witness. And I haven't bolstered your faith much, have I?" He paused, then said, "I've sinned against you, as well as the others. Will you forgive me, Gabriel?"

Gabriel made a choking sound. "Shut up, Bartok. I don't want your apologies."

She could hear rustling, and quick, irritated footsteps. *Gabriel wants to rescue some Christians. I would never have thought Bartok would object to that.*

Bartok said again. "If you assemble a team, I'll be on it."

There was silence for a few moments, then Niamh murmured, "They're coming back now."

Aria glanced at Owen. His eyes were locked on the tunnel entrance. A few moments later, bobbing flashlights showed Gabriel and Bartok approaching.

Owen pushed himself to his feet, leaning heavily on Cillian's shoulder as he rose. He strode quickly to meet them a short distance from the other humans, Aria following without thought. The moment he became visible to them was obvious; both Gabriel and Bartok twitched in surprise, hands going to pistols before they recognized him.

Owen's eyes were locked on Gabriel. He spoke in a low, tense whisper. "You knew? You're a Christian?"

Gabriel nodded.

"And you didn't tell me?" Owen's nostrils flared. "I didn't realize you hated me that much."

"I don't—" Gabriel began.

"You *knew*! You knew our people lived without hope, and you said *nothing* of grace!" His voice cracked. He took a deep, shuddering breath, as if he wanted to sob but restrained himself. When he spoke again, his voice was softer. Sadder. "I did not even know you were a Christian. I have known Dr. Bartok for scarcely two weeks, and he has told me more of grace than you ever have."

Lachtnal stood off to the side, and he stepped forward now. Gabriel twitched, and Aria guessed Lachtnal must have made himself visible.

"I am not sure he was wrong, Lord Owen. Even if we Fae can be saved, perhaps we should not be. Perhaps grace is not meant to be offered to everyone. Or perhaps his hatred of us is characteristic of Christianity. Why presume that Bartok is the representative and Gabriel is the hypocrite?

Perhaps Gabriel is the true representative of Christ."

Gabriel made a little sound as if he had been punched hard in the stomach.

"Salvation does not make them good. Perhaps the one who offers it is not good. Or perhaps salvation as they conceive of it does not even exist. If it does exist, I question the holiness of any God who offers salvation to fallen men."

Owen stood preternaturally still, the dangerous, electric stillness of the air before lightning; one hand rested on the hilt of the sword slung on his hip. "Have a care, Lachtnal." His words were so soft Aria felt them more than heard them. *Careful. You tread on the knife's edge, Lachtnal.*

Lachtnal stared at Gabriel a moment longer, then turned to look at Owen with cold, unreadable eyes. "I obey, Owen." He bowed, the movement so slight that it rang of insolence rather than respect.

Owen watched him go, his hand not leaving the hilt of his sword for minutes after Lachtnal had disappeared from Aria's sight.

He murmured something, and a moment later three Fae, whose names Aria could not remember, were at his side. He said something to them, his voice inaudible, and they nodded, then disappeared again in the shadows.

Then he turned back to the men. "I must be alone with my thoughts." He bowed, then walked into the darkness, his steps a little unsteady.

Gabriel stared after him, mouth open, before clenching his jaw. He dropped his head into his hands.

Bartok started to say something, but then stopped. The silence was too oppressive, the weight of guilt too heavy.

Niall stared at Gabriel, his eyes bright and hard, before slipping silently away.

Gabriel didn't look up for long minutes.

I should go after Owen. But what right do I have to tell him anything? To even ask him to come back?

When Gabriel raised his head, his eyes were red.

Aria whispered, "I didn't know either. If you believe it, why didn't you say anything?"

He didn't look at her. "Because I'm a coward. Because I'm ashamed. Because I wasn't living the way I should. Does it matter? God let me down. I trusted him, and he let those bastards kill my son! Without Michael… what difference does it make? I lost the only thing I cared about." His hands clenched. "I wanted to stop believing. But I couldn't… I was too angry. If God didn't exist, then it was just chance that Michael died. Chance that Jennifer died in the wreck instead of me. Chance that I avoided the brainwashing. Chance that any of it happened!" He ran shaking hands over his thinning hair. "If it's only chance, there's no point in fighting. I'd have blown my brains out already. I thought of it. Wanted to. But… I lived to spite God, to tell him that he couldn't destroy me. Stupid, isn't it? It's not like I was really living."

"But if it's true, it doesn't matter whether you're angry, does it? Truth doesn't change because of what we feel!"

He let out a long breath. "No. But I didn't want anything to do with God, and I certainly wasn't going to be singing his praises to anyone. Much less Owen. They're not human anyway; who knows whether they can really be saved?"

Bartok spoke for the first time, his voice quiet and clear. "If we don't speak, the rocks themselves will cry out. Who are we to decide who deserves to hear God's truth?"

Gabriel glared at him.

"What do you really believe, Gabriel? Is God sovereign, or is he not? You think God doesn't know how much it hurts to watch a son die?"

Gabriel spun, slamming his fist into Bartok's face. Bartok stumbled backward, hands coming up, palms out. Gabriel snarled something inarticulate, breath quick and unsteady, fists clenched at his sides.

Bartok spit blood and cupped his left hand over his mouth, exploring the damage with careful fingers. "I'm not going to fight you, Gabriel. Your fight isn't with me."

Gabriel choked out, "I know."

"I'm sorry I couldn't save him." Bartok shook blood from his hand and pressed his fingers against his lips again, watching Gabriel. Finally he turned away.

Aria glared at Gabriel before she fled too. She had to get away. Gabriel's expression was set in stone, his mouth tight and eyes shuttered. *How could he not have told us?*

She followed where she thought Owen had gone, a tunnel obscured in darkness. At the entrance she hesitated, then went back for her flashlight, avoiding the eyes that followed her movements. The Fae were hidden, dispersed around the camp and tunnels, but she didn't want to see them either.

She flicked the light on as she entered the tunnel, but it showed no traces of Owen's passage. That didn't prove anything, though. She followed the tunnel until she came to an intersection, and debated a moment before choosing the left side.

The cool air was still as death, but she continued. The faint noises of the camp faded behind her into silence. *There are vampires in these tunnels. Like Feichin, but worse.* Fear slithered down her spine, and her breath felt like a silent sob. *I should have brought a gun. I should have stayed back. Where did he go?*

She continued to a cross tunnel and flicked the light to each side. Even so, she almost didn't notice him and started to continue across the intersection.

"You should go back." His voice was low and a little hoarse.

She whipped around and flicked the light into his face. He flinched, turning away from the blinding light. He was slumped against the wall of the tunnel, legs stretched out in front of him and hands loose in his lap.

"Sorry." She stepped closer and sat down beside him. Beside him, she could hear the rough edge in his breathing.

"You should go back," he repeated. He didn't look at her.

"I wanted to see if I could do anything."

He shook his head. "No. I… this is new." The naked pain in his voice made her catch her breath. "I trusted Gabriel. I thought I understood him. But this…" He stopped and took a deep, shuddering breath. "Grenidor's efforts hurt less than this."

She slipped her hand into his and leaned her head against the wall beside his shoulder. He let his head fall backward, staring across the tunnel at the far wall.

"You trusted him after he shot you?"

He gave a soft, mirthless chuckle. "That was petulance, nothing more. This…" His voice caught, and he stopped.

"I don't understand," she finally whispered. "Why does it hurt you so? He wasn't living his faith. Even I understand that."

"If you knew someone was dying of thirst, isn't it hatred to not tell them of water only just around the corner?"

She had no answer to that. Of all the things to upset him, this wouldn't be the one she'd expected. *But maybe that's because I haven't ached for hope the way he has. Maybe I should.*

Silence wrapped around them. His hand warmed in hers, and she watched the soft rise and fall of the cloth of his shirt as he breathed. Beneath the faint metallic tang of the blood from his wounds, she caught an almost imperceptible hint of his body's scent. *He smells like moonlight and frost.* Her leg cramped, and she shifted, stiff and uncomfortable on the concrete floor. In the thick, cold stillness, she grew drowsy, and her head drooped. She felt herself sliding slowly down the wall, but her mind was foggy with sleep. Curled up on the floor, she dozed off still holding his hand.

She dreamed of everything and nothing, confusing images and feelings that slid past each other into obscurity. An image of Amara, months ago when they studied for a test together. The expression on Dandra's face when she refused to answer Aria's questions about Owen. A glimpse of the grey room, the needle in her vein as she'd received the first injection. Her fear.

She woke to a movement beside her. Disoriented, she sat up only to blink at the darkness. "Are you there?"

"Yes."

"How long did I sleep?"

"A few hours."

She winced as she straightened. "They'll be worried. We should go back."

He sighed. "Yes." But he didn't move.

She groped for his hand again. "Are you all right? Can I do anything?" *Way to be comforting, Aria. Come find him and then fall asleep.*

"There is nothing you can do." After a long moment, he said softly, "You might pray for me."

"I… all right." She wanted to say *I'm not sure I'm even a Christian. I'm not sure I like this God. You and Bartok think grace is everything, but I think God asks too much. How can I trust a god who lets you suffer so much? How can I trust a god who lets my family die? Both families.* But she didn't. She stuffed the words and the anger down. *God, if you listen at all, heal Owen. All the way, not just barely enough for him to walk. Prove you exist, and I'll believe. Prove that you're good, and I'll believe. Prove there's a reason to worship you, and I'll believe. Wait, I guess I'm supposed to be praying for Owen. Heal him. Make all this worthwhile.* She thought about the Empire and the brainwashing. What could they do? Was there any hope?

She woke again to Owen's hand on her shoulder.

"Aria. We must return now." His voice was barely audible.

"I'm sorry. I didn't mean to fall asleep. Again."

He gave a soft huff that she imagined went with a wry, sad smile. "Neither did Peter."

Peter? Oh. Christ's friend. He'd been talking to Bartok too much. The twinge of jealousy surprised her, and she considered it a moment before she stood.

"Do you need help up?"

"Please." He found her hand, but leaned most of his weight on the wall as he stood, stifling a grunt of pain. "I need to speak with Gabriel."

His steps steadied as they drew closer to the camp. *He's pretending. Faking it. Not for me, but for... whom?* He stopped at the entrance and looked back into the darkened tunnel.

"Come out, Lachtnal."

A moment later, Lachtnal stood in front of them, his face hard and unreadable. "Yes, Lord Owen?"

Owen's hand tightened on hers almost imperceptibly. "You have spent much time in the tunnels alone."

"Yes, Lord Owen."

"Is there a reason you have chosen not to swear your allegiance to me yet?"

Aria glanced up at Owen's face. He'd never demanded allegiance, never made much of his obvious status. *Why now?*

Lachtnal's lips narrowed, then he dropped his eyes. "No, my lord Owen. I will do it now, if you wish."

"If it is freely given." Owen's voice remained mild.

Lachtnal wavered a moment, as if reconsidering, then dropped to one knee. He took Owen's

285

hand and placed it on top of his dark hair. Head bowed, he took several deep breaths, then stood again. "I will return to scouting, with your consent."

"As you wish."

Lachtnal brushed by Aria on his way back into the tunnel. Owen turned to watch him go. Aria couldn't read his expression, but she didn't think it looked triumphant. More... tired. And sad.

THE FAE SANG over Owen again before they talked with Gabriel and the others. Aria was lost in the music, the clear voices wrapping around her as light dappling through leaves.

When the music faded, Owen let out a breath, as if he had been holding it for hours. He said something in Fae, and the others smiled. Cillian ducked his head and grinned, his white cheeks flushing.

Owen rose and walked to Gabriel, his steps steady, though not as quick as they might have been a few weeks earlier. Gabriel and Bartok were focused on the papers spread out between them. Bartok's lip and jaw were swollen and faintly purple in the harsh electric lamplight. He absently licked the split in his lip as he bent forward to look at a schematic.

"Gabriel." Owen knelt in front of him, cool blue eyes holding Gabriel's gaze.

Gabriel withdrew almost imperceptibly. Fear flickered across his face, quickly hidden.

Owen said softly, "I forgive you, Gabriel."

Gabriel swallowed. "I don't ask you to."

"I know. I do it anyway."

Gabriel let out a short, sharp breath. "Right. Because that's how you are. You and Bartok."

Owen sighed, a quiet, weary sound. "It's how I want to be." He met Gabriel's startled look with a faint smile. "I spent time with El, and that is the answer I received. I obey."

"Thank you." Gabriel's voice was choked, and he scrubbed his hands across his face, hiding his emotion for a moment.

Owen looked down, then back at Gabriel's face. "I had before, you know. But in my time with El, I came to understand that it was important that you know I forgive you. It was important for you to hear it. And it was important for me to say it."

Gabriel looked down, rubbing at his eyes.

"Aithne will carry the answer to Colonel Grenidor tonight. I wish to meet Feichin. Dr. Bartok, will you speak with Grenidor?"

Bartok answered, "Yes. Not here, though. What about the courthouse basement?"

"Acceptable. Feichin must come."

Gabriel shook his head, but Aria thought it was more in disbelief than in refusal. "He's dangerous, Owen. You've warned me about fallen Fae before."

Owen held his gaze. "Do you trust me, Gabriel?"

Gabriel sucked in his breath. There was a long silence, and Owen waited without speaking. Finally, Gabriel murmured, "I do."

"I must speak with Feichin."

CHAPTER 15

AITHNE HAD NOT RETURNED.

Perhaps she won't.

No, it was too soon to expect her. She had no way of knowing where Owen was, and what if Bartok was not with Owen? She had agreed to give the message to Owen.

Can I trust her?

Of course not.

Why not?

Grenidor's doubts whirled. He rubbed one finger over the smooth wooden back of the bull figurine in his pocket. Edwin had not been back, but Grenidor felt the tingle between his shoulder blades at times. *Does that mean he's here, or just that I'm getting paranoid?* One of the first things Feichin had said, after he'd turned, was that Edwin claimed he was always watching.

He went down to the interrogation cells in the basement, hand on the grip of his still-holstered pistol. Aithne's cell was empty. Ailill's was in another corridor, also still empty. The only two left were Meallan and Feichin. *When did I start thinking of them by name, rather than by number?* He went to Meallan's cell first.

The vampire was in one of his quiet moods, standing in the middle of the room staring at a point on the wall. He didn't move for minutes at a time. He was no longer being interrogated, but Grenidor had not yet decided whether to terminate him, and if so, how. Beheading was sure, as was being shot with getlaril bullets, provided that the bullets stayed in the body.

Meallan looked toward Grenidor, but his gaze focused at something off to the side. "Why are you here, beautiful one?" he hissed. "You know I am lost already." Teeth bared, he stalked forward, and Grenidor brought the pistol up. But Meallan wasn't looking at him, and Grenidor watched him warily, staying far back from the getlaril bars separating them.

Meallan hissed again, an inarticulate sound that set Grenidor's teeth on edge. Then what sounded like cursing, though it wasn't in English. He paced away, then flung himself at the bars. Grenidor barely held his fire. The bars were thick, strong getlaril, and they didn't even rattle as Meallan's lanky body crashed into them and bounced backward. He tripped on the getlaril chains that bound his ankles, then recovered only to crouch, arms raised protectively over his head.

"You would be more confident in the bullets if you tested them before the confrontation," Edwin said from behind Grenidor's shoulder.

Grenidor jumped at his voice. "He's contained."

"And the other one? Feichin?" Edwin raised an eyebrow. "It would be wise to eliminate the threat he poses."

Grenidor forced a smile. "Yes. I'll consider it."

"There is one other protection I can offer you. The bull, the one with blood on it, in your pocket. You neglected the gold, but it will be still be of some use. Your pistol would be of no use against the power that aided the Slavemaster's minions in their infiltration. You wouldn't even be able to see it; you didn't when it helped Cillian and Aria. The bull will symbolize my power, synthesize it into a protective force, if you will. The vampire Owen, Bartok, and Aria will be at the meeting, but there will also be other vampires. You will be greatly outnumbered, and there is no chance you will be able to shoot them all.

"When it is time, shoot Feichin and Owen, if you can. Even if your shots fail to kill them, pull the bull from your pocket. Shout "By the power of Edwin, I drive back the supernatural forces of the Slavemaster!" This will leave the room to you, Bartok, and Aria. You are more than capable of defending yourself against them, but without this, you will be immediately killed by the vampires or the power that aids them."

Grenidor swallowed. "And that would work?"

Edwin smiled, the picture of reassurance. "Yes. If you trust me, it will. My power to protect you relies partly on your trust in me. If you doubt me, it's more difficult to focus my power to aid you. You know I don't care for you personally, but it would set back my own plans if you were to die. I have every reason to want you to live through this confrontation. So, when the times comes, trust me to aid you, and use the bull to call on my power."

That seems... fraught with danger. But then what isn't?

Edwin put a hand on his shoulder and began walking, his grip firm. "Come. You are hesitant because you are a merciful man. But this is war. Consider the costs of your actions."

He drew Grenidor down the hall to Feichin's cell and stopped. Feichin crouched in the far right corner, knees pulled up to his chest again, face hidden.

Grenidor tapped the pistol barrel against a bar. "You alive in there?"

Silence.

"Wake up. I have a question." Grenidor didn't know where the words came from.

Feichin raised his head and looked across the room. Grenidor stifled a gasp and stepped back, farther from the bars. The camera hadn't caught the full horror of the vampire's emaciation; cold blue eyes burned with hatred in a face that looked like a skull. He bared his teeth and growled, the sound deeper than Grenidor had expected. *It's not natural.* His teeth looked long and white, caught by the harsh light.

Edwin's voice whispered beside him, "Do it now. While he's captive."

Feichin pushed himself up, one hand braced against the wall. He'd punched a new hole in the belt that held up his trousers, but they still barely hung on him, sharp hipbones protruding. Even across the cell, Grenidor could see the vampire's pulse below his sternum, the bones moving with each shallow breath. Eyes locked on Grenidor's, he crossed the room in a split second, faster than Grenidor would have imagined possible.

"You're still dangerous," he murmured. The pistol grip in his hand was comforting.

"Yes." Feichin smiled slowly. "I am." He raised his hands, palms upward. "Speak, Grenidor. What else have I to break the monotony of captivity, except to imagine my teeth in your throat?"

"What do you fear?"

Emotion flashed across Feichin's face too quickly for Grenidor to interpret it. Surprise, perhaps. "Not you."

"Just answer the question." Grenidor tried to ignore Edwin beside him. "What do you fear?"

Feichin glanced to the side, his expression distant. His mouth twitched, and the words seemed to be dragged out of him. "Justice."

Grenidor rubbed his thumb over the familiar grip of the pistol again. "Don't we all?" The question came out of its own accord, and he stopped, surprised by his own honesty. *Don't I fear justice? Because what I have done cannot be met with anything other than condemnation.* He glanced at Edwin again, who was smiling at the vampire.

"What do you fear, Edwin?" he asked, without thinking.

Edwin said softly, "Do it now. You see how he wishes to kill you." Edwin's eyes did not leave Feichin.

"Thanks for your advice." Grenidor twitched his shoulder free of Edwin's grasp. "I'll consider it."

Edwin walked away without looking back.

Feichin glanced after him, but made no comment.

"Did you see him?" Grenidor asked.

"Not as you did. He speaks to me of other things." Feichin smiled again, teeth glinting. "The taste of your blood."

"You lie!"

"Sometimes." Feichin's smile broadened. "But that was true."

Grenidor backed away. *Shoot him. Shoot him now!* He considered it, his shoulders pressed against the opposite wall of the corridor. Feichin stood, a motionless statue on the other side of the bars, the smile still twisting his lips. *No. Not yet.* Grenidor keyed the code into the control panel to close the viewing door. As it slid closed, he heard the soft clank of the chains as Feichin stepped away.

Grenidor waited in his office for Aithne, jittery and nervous. *They'll kill me if they find out I released her.* Not immediately; there would be a trial, but the verdict and sentence were inevitable. Maybe he could claim she was a test case. It might be possible to train some vampires to work for the Empire, and she was the least violent of any currently in custody. If she carried out the assignment reliably, that could be useful. But even if Edwin couldn't see Aithne directly, he would see Grenidor's trial and his pathetic defense, and he was more terrifying than anything the Empire might threaten. No, better to say nothing and hope.

It would be difficult for her to infiltrate the facility again, though not impossible. Edwin did not return either, but Grenidor couldn't shake the feeling that he was being watched. Always watched. It was nearly eight o'clock when he left, the halls mostly deserted.

The bus was running on the night schedule already, and he began the long walk to the A7 line, which ran more frequently. This part of the city had not suffered many vampire attacks; they preferred the poorer areas, Anacostia and the denser side of Chinatown. All the same, he felt his shoulders high and tense as he walked, hand close on the pistol concealed beneath his jacket.

Aithne appeared beside him silently, her hand on his arm preventing him from drawing the gun. "Silence. I will not hurt you."

He grunted his assent, and she removed her hand.

"Dr. Bartok will meet with you, but there are conditions." She enunciated clearly, eyes on his face as she gauged his reaction. "Meet at the old courthouse in the basement in two hours. Bring no weapons. Come alone, except for my father. Bring Feichin."

He almost stopped in surprise. *It is just as Edwin said. A confrontation. Owen will release Feichin, and Feichin will kill me. If Owen doesn't first. Or one of the others.* "It's too dangerous. How can I trust you?"

She snorted softly. "If I meant to kill you, I would have already. You have what we want. Lord Owen wants Feichin, and he will have him. Bartok will meet you as you requested. You wish for help. Do not be too foolish to take it when it is offered."

Grenidor continued walking. A man on the sidewalk walked by them, head down against the chilly wind, and Aithne slipped out of his way without a sound, only to take her spot at Grenidor's shoulder again.

"If you have been speaking with one of the dark ones, you need help more desperately than you can possibly understand. Do not spurn it out of pride."

His heart caught in his throat. What if Edwin *could* hear her after all? No, it was impossible; he would have done something before now to betray the fact that he knew about her release. Wouldn't he

"I wait for your agreement," she said.

"Two hours is close to midnight." *It will be dangerous. I haven't driven one of the transport cages before. I assume it can be done by one person.*

"Are you afraid of the dark? I will escort you if you wish."

He glanced at her, but saw no trace of derision in her face. *Afraid of the dark! Well, perhaps a little. Not the dark, but the things that live in the dark. But daylight... some deeds can't bear the light of day.* "That won't be necessary. I'll be there."

"Can you come without alerting security?"

"Yes. I will be there." He didn't soften the irritation in his voice.

She nodded and disappeared from his side. He turned to look behind him, but she was nowhere to be seen.

HE CIRCLED THE block and walked back to the office. The card swipe as he entered would log his presence. *That may be a problem. It probably won't matter. I'll probably be dead anyway.* He tried to keep his thoughts resignedly pessimistic. Panic fluttered inside his chest, threatening to burst out at any moment.

Edwin appeared by his shoulder as he walked down the stairs to the basement holding cells again. "The time is near." His voice was deep, reverberating in the narrow hallway, and Grenidor couldn't help flinching. "You are playing a dangerous game. You toy with independence, as if you ever had any choices. Your role is set. You have chosen your path."

"I don't know what you're talking about." Grenidor tried to brush off Edwin's comradely arm around his shoulders, but the man, *no, he's not a man!* would not let go.

"You take risks." Edwin spun him around, his unimposing form proving stronger than it appeared. "This confrontation is more dangerous than you know. I have given you advice, but you have trusted in your own wisdom. But what do you truly understand of the vampires? What do you understand of the Slavemaster? You know nothing! You are a child playing with forces you cannot comprehend. Heed my advice, and you'll live, free to choose as you will. Toy with the other side, and they will destroy you."

Grenidor swallowed. "I understand." *I understand your threats. I'm not sure what to do about them. This is bigger than Bartok. If I were a good man, I'd leave him out of this. But it's too late, isn't it?*

He almost stopped at a sudden thought. Edwin *knew* what he was doing, knew his maneuvering with Aithne and that the meeting would be arranged. At least he mostly knew; after all, he'd described it in some detail, before Grenidor had any thought of the meeting himself. He *knew*, and he didn't care about Grenidor's secrets. Grenidor also knew with a chill certainty that Edwin didn't care whether Grenidor lived or died. He cared only about something that might happen at the meeting, something that he wanted to either prevent or make more likely. Edwin wanted him to kill Feichin, but he didn't care about Grenidor himself. So something about Feichin, or Grenidor, or both, might mess up his plans. But he wasn't allowed to directly interfere; if he could have, he would have.

Why did I think 'not allowed' rather than 'can't' or 'won't'? But somehow it seems accurate.

I know Edwin lies to me, but some things he tells me are true. He might even protect me from discovery, as he promised. If I do as he wants, he might give me the authority he talked about.

Why? If he doesn't care about me, it's because it gains him something.

He wants me as a puppet.

That doesn't mean I'm safe. Another puppet would do just as well.

Edwin watched him get the transport cell ready and test the controls. He drove it to the door of Feichin's cell, opened the transport cell door, and checked that the secondary containment safeguards were operational. The cell bolted temporarily to the walls on each side of the door, providing not even an inch of space through which a vampire could escape.

Edwin seemed jittery too, and spoke suddenly. "Be careful. Keep your gun ready. He'll move fast, and you won't have a second chance to shoot him."

He considered asking Edwin whether he had the power to stop one half-starved vampire, if he wanted to, or whether his ability to see possible futures didn't show him there was virtually no way Feichin could escape at this point. It seemed obvious that Edwin's constant warnings about Feichin were simply intended to put Grenidor even more on edge, ready to shoot without hesitation. Nevertheless, baiting Edwin seemed like a bad idea.

So Grenidor only nodded. He pulled up the viewing camera and found Feichin slumped in a corner, arms wrapped around his head.

Grenidor thumbed the button for the microphone. "I'm going to open the door. Get in the transport cage."

Feichin did not move.

Grenidor pushed the buttons and heard the door swish open. Feichin raised his head and stared across the room with unfocused eyes for several seconds before his face hardened. Grenidor spoke into the microphone again. "Get in the cage. I'll shoot you if you don't, and you'll end up in the cage anyway."

"Where are we going?" Feichin hissed, his eyes on the camera.

"Shut up and get in."

Grenidor doubted whether he would cooperate, but after a moment, Feichin pushed himself up and walked slowly across the cell. The camera caught the sharp ridges of his spine and ribs as he moved under the light to climb into the cage. Grenidor pushed the buttons to close the doors and checked the cameras again. *That was almost too easy.* But he knew Feichin complied only because the chances of killing Grenidor were greater if he changed locations. If he could have escaped from the holding cell, he would have already. The transport container offered more, or at least different, options for escape.

Back around the corner, he could see Feichin. The vampire crouched in the center of the cell, not touching any of the bars. His gaze stayed on Grenidor, but he said nothing as he watched his captor check the locks again before pushing the button that would unbolt the transport cell from the holding cell door.

Feichin's eyes flicked away for a moment and he seemed to be listening. His lips lifted in a faint, predatory smile, and he focused his gaze again on Grenidor. Grenidor drove the transport cage without speaking. Edwin stayed near his shoulder, twitchy and nervous, and said again, "Be careful." Then he disappeared.

Grenidor hesitated at the bank of elevators. How difficult would it be to get out undetected? He checked his watch and cursed. Time was running out. Almost an hour had already passed. The courthouse was not close, and the transport cage did not move quickly.

He chose a large utility elevator, but it was still barely large enough for him to press his back against the wall in order to stay out of Feichin's reach. The vampire watched him, cold eyes gleaming, but did not attempt to reach through the bars. *I should have gotten him in the cuffs. But it would have taken too long. He can't escape. He can't. Stay calm. Don't rush, and don't panic.* His heart raced.

He peeked out the door before driving the transport cage through the delivery bay and out into the cold night air. The guards were nowhere to be seen, which relieved and worried him equally. *Is that Edwin's doing? Aithne's? Can she do that? Or is our security just that bad?*

The closest vampire transport vehicle was at the loading dock for another building thirty yards away. He jogged across the courtyard, started the truck, and drove it back to where Feichin waited in the cage.

Halogen lamps lit the damp asphalt and cast ghoulish shadows across Feichin's face as he stood briefly, swaying in the center of the cage before dropping to crouch again.

"What's out there?" Grenidor murmured.

"Are you afraid of monsters? Like me?" Feichin's voice was equally low, his eyes leaving Grenidor as he glanced around the deserted courtyard. "You don't have to worry about them. You travel with a horror even they have the good sense to flee."

"You mean Edwin?" Grenidor asked.

"Is that what he calls himself?" Feichin's mouth twisted in a mockery of a smile.

Feichin crouched in the cenger of the cage and watched Grenidor lower the ramp. Grenidor drove the transport cage up the ramp and activated the automatic clamps, checking that the cage was tightly secured. Grenidor closed the back door with a bang, then slid into the driver's seat.

Grenidor glanced over his shoulder at Feichin as he drove out into the silent street. The vampire stared back at him, hard eyes gleaming in the dim light. Grenidor swallowed his terror and turned back around.

The colonel knew the way to the courthouse; at this hour, there would be little traffic, but if anyone saw him, he could be questioned. With his authority, he'd be allowed to continue, but it would be impossible to pretend it had never happened. No one noticed. The streets were empty. Edwin, or Aithne, or perhaps some other power, was keeping him hidden.

He reached the courthouse and circled it before choosing the lower utility entrance. The ramp down to the door was long and dark, and he hesitated before parking the transport vehicle. He opened the back and lowered the loading ramp again, then drove the cage down onto the sidewalk.

Grenidor paced behind the cage as he drove it down the ramp toward the courthouse. The door opened before he reached it, and he hesitated again.

This is suicide, Pauly. You've lost it. Turn back now. But he followed the cage in. *I can't handle Edwin on my own.*

The basement beyond was well lit, but he didn't see anyone immediately. He stopped the cage some ten feet inside the door and stood near it, eyes searching the empty room. Feichin rose slowly, eyes focused on something Grenidor didn't see.

"Owen," he hissed. "Why have you summoned us?"

Grenidor glanced at him, then gasped in surprise when he looked back at the room. Fae were ranged out around them, with Gabriel, Bartok, Aria, and several other humans among them.

Owen stood in the center, only ten feet from Grenidor. He looked almost completely healed, only a faint green bruise shading his right eye. Grenidor drew the gun without thought, his finger on the trigger as he aimed at Owen's chest.

Owen began to speak.

CHAPTER 16

ARIA LISTENED, SPELLBOUND.

"We Fae have believed for generations that we were different than humans. We thought we were stronger, more pure, because we so rarely chose rebellion. But this was grace to us, not our own strength. Yet we can reject this grace. We can choose rebellion.

"When we do, we believed we were lost. We believed there was no way back.

"We were wrong. Feichin, we can return to El. We can come back."

Feichin growled, and Aria flinched. Even from across the room, she could see the trembling fury in his skeletal frame, the hatred that twisted his face. "What do you know of rebellion, Lord Owen? You have never felt its shame."

Owen held his gaze. "I lied to Colonel Grenidor. He asked me something too terrible to answer honestly. Not only we, but humans, would suffer too greatly if I had given him the truth. I lied. Do you feel it on me, Feichin?"

Feichin froze, still as stone. "You lied?" he whispered.

"Yes. I was forgiven. I prayed for mercy, Feichin. El granted it! We can be forgiven. But we must ask for mercy. The humans have a book that speaks of Jesus, the Son of God. He is the one who judges, and the one who gives mercy. Ask him for forgiveness, and you can come back."

Feichin's voice deepened to a growl. "Do you know what has been done to me?" He raised his arms and gripped the getlaril bars, ignoring the pain. He screamed, "Do you know what I have done? I cannot be forgiven!"

Owen's voice rose too, clear and powerful. "El has pursued you. It is not chance that you've heard the truth. Mercy has hunted you until you cannot help but face it! Who are you to reject El's mercy?"

Feichin's arms dropped and he paced in the narrow confines of the cage before he stopped abruptly to face Owen again. "Free me."

Aria could see Grenidor trembling, the gun wavering between Owen and Feichin. He put a hand in his pocket and drew out something small and dark, half-hidden as he gripped the pistol with both hands again.

Grenidor said, "Don't. I'll shoot."

Owen took a step forward, slow and even. He looked toward Grenidor, authority thrumming in his voice. "Dr. Bartok will speak with you in a moment. Hold your fire."

Grenidor's finger tightened on the trigger, and Aria caught her breath, expecting a gunshot at any moment. But Owen stepped forward again, the movement smooth and calm. Another step, and another, until he was only a few feet from Grenidor. Then he was face to face with Feichin, only the getlaril bars separating their faces.

Feichin stared into his eyes. "Can I come back?"

"Ask for mercy, and you shall receive. As it has been given to you, give it." Owen held Feichin's gaze. "Not on your own strength, but with El's strength."

Feichin gave a minute nod. Beside Aria, Cillian sucked in his breath, his eyes widening. Owen placed his hand on the lock. It clicked, and Owen swung the cage door open.

Feichin jumped out, the movement so fast Aria saw him only as a blur. He stood in front of Grenidor for a long moment, sharp ribs heaving. When the words came, they were not loud, but they were clear and unmistakable.

"I forgive you, Grenidor."

He whirled and flung himself at Owen's feet, face pressed to the ground. "I want to go back! Ask El for mercy for me, my Lord Owen. I am not worthy to sing to him myself." He sobbed, face hidden in his hands.

Grenidor stared, eyes wide. With a sudden movement, he hurled the pistol and the dark thing in his hand at them, spun, and sprinted away up the ramp.

The gun and the little wooden figure clattered to the concrete, the sound fading as Feichin wept.

OWEN KNELT, HIS hands on Feichin's shoulders, his own head bent down. His tears fell onto Feichin's matted hair, but only Feichin's soft, agonized weeping could be heard. Minutes later, Aithne crept to Feichin's side, and she knelt beside him. Feichin flinched away from her, but she wrapped one strong, slim arm across his bony back and held him close.

Bartok put his hand on Aria's shoulder. "Pay attention. You need to understand too."

"Understand that they can be saved?" Aria asked, her eyes still locked on the drama playing out before her.

"Understand how *you* can be saved. It isn't enough to be good."

Aria found herself trembling. Cillian slipped from beside her and approached the gun. He studied it, then turned to the other object.

"It is a statue," he murmured. He peered at it cautiously, then picked it up, only to hiss in pain and drop it again. He glanced again at the gun, then began to unload it, spilling the bullets on the ground without touching them.

"It's..." He looked up, eyes wide. "Petro?"

Aria's heart lurched into her throat. He had been standing among them all along, but no one had paid him any attention. He'd somehow seemed like just another Fae, their attention sliding off him.

Now he wanted to be seen.

To Aria's eyes, he looked much like the last time she'd seen him, a form like a large, unnaturally beautiful human man, with white robes and skin of an indistinct metallic color. She blinked;

there was a moment's suggestion of great wings folded on his back, but she didn't see them anymore.

"Continue your statement," Petro commanded.

Cillian frowned. "This statue, and the bullets… something is wrong with them. They feel evil."

Petro knelt, his shoulders level with Cillian's, his form broad and imposing. *Is he larger than before?* "Yes. They are."

Feichin raised his head, tears streaking his white face. "Is this Conláed?" he murmured to Owen.

Petro turned his glowing green eyes on Feichin. "That name is sometimes used for me. You interest me, Feichin." He stood and circled Owen and Feichin, his clothes moving in an unseen wind. Owen kept one hand on Feichin's shoulder, the gesture protective and reassuring.

Bartok strode forward. "What's wrong with the bullets?"

Cillian said, "They burn. I don't want to touch them."

Petro said, "They are covered in the blood of a martyr. They would kill you if you were shot with them. Grenidor is playing with something more powerful than he realizes." He seemed to grow taller, and his eyes blazed. He looked at Feichin and said, "Tell me."

Feichin murmured, "The same thing that spoke to me has been speaking with him. In a different form. Promising him different things."

"What has been speaking with you?" Cillian asked.

"Something like Petro. But different." Feichin's thin body shuddered. "Beautiful beyond description. Seductive. Terrible. It promised me my darkest desires. I would imagine it promises Grenidor the same. What he thinks he wants. Power. A weapon against... pure Fae." His eyes lowered.

"This was not a weapon conjured for use against Fae." Petro's voice rang. "You are weak and easily injured. Getlaril is sufficient to kill your bodies. This was conjured against me."

"Would it hurt you?" Aria asked. *They probably wouldn't ask. They're too afraid of him.*

Petro's eyes blazed. "Injure? No. But the profanity of such an attempt..." He glanced to the side, his rage almost palpable. "I have also been tempted. In anger, I might have destroyed the one who used the weapon. I might have destroyed everyone present. In doing so, I would condemn myself."

Owen gave a thoughtful nod. "Grenidor's fate did not matter to the dark one. You were the real target."

"Yes." Petro looked toward Feichin and Owen again. "One of several." He tilted his head to the side, staring at Feichin. "You were lost. Now you are accepted again. It wished to prevent that. It will be angry."

Feichin swallowed and bowed his head, trembling. Owen tightened his hand on Feichin's shoulder.

"You love Feichin, do you not?" Petro circled them again, his eyes locked on Owen. "Why?"

Owen tilted his head. "Why do I love him?"

"Yes. What he has done is abhorrent. Vile. Yet you love him. I do not fully understand how this was important, but it was."

"Because he was *mine*. He was meant for more than depravity."

"Possession? You wished to possess him again?"

"I wished to free him!"

Petro reached forward to grasp Feichin's head between his hands and tilt his face upward. He looked into his eyes, then let go. Feichin skittered backward, his spine pressed into Owen's knee.

"I thank you, Owen. You have revealed a new data point that makes my options more clear." He disappeared.

FEICHIN SAT IN a corner, shoulders hunched, eating with steady determination. Owen and Aithne sat with him, their words inaudible to Aria but seeming to offer some comfort to Feichin. After a few more minutes, Owen rose, motioning for Cillian to take his place.

Owen said to Bartok, "I thank you. Feichin has been restored to us." He gave a courtly half-bow that made Bartok redden with embarrassment.

"I'm glad."

Niamh appeared at Owen's shoulder and murmured in his ear. Owen looked up sharply. "Lachtnal! Come here."

Lachtnal eased forward, brushing by Aria on his way. "Yes, my lord Owen?"

"What troubles you?" Owen's voice softened.

Lachtnal did not look at him. Instead, his eyes were drawn inexorably to Feichin, and his lip curled. "Feichin is different."

"Yes. El gave him mercy." Owen reached out to put a hand on Lachtnal's shoulder, but the Fae twitched away from him.

"Perhaps El isn't as holy as we imagined." He snarled, his expression twisting. "What kind of holiness could abide that?" He flung his arm toward Feichin, who looked up, eyes stricken. "You should have killed him, Owen. *And* Grenidor, for what he did." He growled, the sound reverberating from the walls as he turned and fled.

Owen dropped to his knees and buried his face in his hands. His shoulders shook as he wept.

ARIA INSERTED HERSELF among the Fae, although she knew it was really none of her business. Feichin glanced up at her with shadowed eyes, but said nothing. She tried not to show her fear, but her heart pounded in her chest. *He ripped out a man's throat with his teeth.*

Owen glanced across the little gathering, blue eyes searching. "Niall?" he asked.

No answer, but then Niall wouldn't have answered. He should have come forward, though. Owen glanced around again, then said more loudly, "Niall?"

Nothing.

Niamh reappeared from somewhere in the back and handed him a piece of paper, her pale face set. Owen read it quickly, his right hand raised to his lips. "May El help him," he murmured.

"What is it?" Cillian asked.

Owen handed him the paper, and Aria read over his shoulder.

Lord Owen, pray for me. I have gone after Col Grenidor. The shadow over him terrifies me, but it terrifies me more to understand what El wishes of me, and to not act because of my fear.

I thank you for showing me what love means. Dr. Bartok spoke of love manifested in grace. For far too long, we have failed to understand this. We separated obedience and love, as if they were not two songs sung in the same voice to the same El.

You, Lord Owen, have shown me both. Obedience is love. Love is obedience.

Pray that I am obedient.

AFTERWORD

Thank you for purchasing this book. If you enjoyed it, please leave a review at your favorite online retailer! This story is continued in A Long-Forgotten Song Book 3 (fall/winter 2015).

C. J. Brightley lives in Northern Virginia with her husband and young children. She holds degrees from Clemson University and Texas A&M. You can find more of C. J. Brightley's books at www.CJBrightley.com, including the epic fantasy series Erdemen Honor, which begins with *The King's Sword* and continues in *A Cold Wind* and *Honor's Heir*. You can also find C. J. Brightley on Facebook and Google+.

THE KING'S SWORD

ONE

I crossed his tracks not far outside of Stonehaven, and I followed them out of curiosity,
nothing more. They were uneven, as if he were
stumbling. It was bitterly cold, a stiff wind keeping
the hilltops mostly free of the snow that formed
deep drifts in every depression. By the irregularity
of his trail, I imagined he was some foolish city boy
caught out in the cold and that he might want
some help.

It was the winter of 368, a few weeks before
the new year. I was on my way to the garrison at
Kesterlin just north of the capital, but I was in no
hurry. I had a little money in my pack and I was
happy enough alone.

In less than a league, I found him lying face-
down in the snow. I nudged him with my toe be-

fore I knelt to turn him over, but he didn't respond. He was young, and something about him seemed oddly familiar. He wasn't hurt, at least not in a way I could see, but he was nearly frozen. He wore a thin shirt, well-made breeches, and expensive boots, but nothing else. He had no sword, no tunic over his shirt, no cloak, no horse. I had no horse because I didn't have the gold for one, but judging by his boots he could have bought one easily. There was a bag of coins inside his shirt, but I didn't investigate that further. His breathing was slow, his hands icy. It was death to be out in such weather so unprepared.

He was either a fool or he was running from something, but in either case I couldn't let him freeze. I strode to the top of the hill to look for pursuit. A group of riders was moving away to the south, but I couldn't identify them. Anyway, they wouldn't cross his path going that direction.

I wrapped him in my cloak and hoisted him over my shoulder. The forest wasn't too far away and it would provide shelter and firewood. I wore a shirt and a thick winter tunic over it, but even so, I was shivering badly by the time we made it to the trees. The wind was bitter cold, and I sweated enough carrying him to chill myself thoroughly. I built a fire in front of a rock face that would reflect the heat back upon us. I let myself warm a little before opening my pack and pulling out some carrots and a little dried venison to make a late lunch.

I rubbed the boy's hands so he wouldn't lose his fingers. His boots were wet, so I pulled them off and set them close to the fire. There was a knife in his right boot, and I slipped it out to examine it.

You can tell a lot about a man by the weapons he carries. His had a good blade, though it was a bit small. The hilt was finished with a green gemstone, smoothly polished and beautiful. Around it was a thin gold band, and ribbons of gold were inlaid in the polished bone hilt. It was a fine piece that hadn't seen much use, obviously made for a nobleman. I kept the knife well out of his reach while I warmed my cold feet. If he panicked when he woke, I wanted him unarmed.

I felt his eyes on me not long before the soup was ready. He'd be frightened of me, no doubt, so for several minutes I pretended I hadn't noticed he was awake to give him time to study me. I'm a Dari, and there are so few of us in Erdem that most people fear me at first.

"I believe that's mine." His voice had a distinct tremor, and he must have realized it because he lifted his chin a little defiantly, eyes wide.

I handed the knife back to him hilt-first. "It is. It's nicely made."

He took it cautiously, as if he wasn't sure I was really going to give it back to him. He shivered and pulled my cloak closer around his shoulders, keeping the knife in hand.

"Here. Can you eat this?"

He reached for the bowl with one hand, and seemed to debate a moment before resting the knife on the ground by his knee. "Thank you." He kept his eyes on me as he dug in.

I chewed on a bit of dried meat as I watched him. He looked better with some warm food in him and the heat of the fire on his face. "Do you want another bowl?"

"If there's enough." He smiled cautiously.

We studied each other while the soup cooked. He was maybe seventeen or so, much younger than I. Slim, pretty, with a pink mouth like a girl's. Typical Tuyet coloring; blond hair, blue eyes, pale skin. Slender hands like an artist or scribe.

"Thank you." He smiled again, nervous but gaining confidence. He did look familiar, especially in his nose and the line of his cheekbones. I tried to place him among the young nobles I'd seen last time I'd visited Stonehaven.

"What's your name?"

"Hak-" he stopped and his eyes widened. "Mikar. My name is Mikar."

Hakan.

Hakan Ithel. The prince!

He looked a bit like his father the king. It wasn't hard to guess why he was fleeing out into the winter snow. Rumors of Nekane Vidar's intent to seize power had been making their way through the army and the mercenary groups for some months.

"You're Hakan Ithel, aren't you?"

His shoulders slumped a little. He looked at the ground and nodded slightly.

He had no real reason to trust me. Vidar's men would be on his trail soon enough. No wonder he was frightened.

"My name is Kemen Sendoa. Call me Kemen." I stood to bow formally to him. "I'm honored to make your acquaintance. Is anyone following you?"

His eyes widened even more. "I don't know. Probably."

"Then we'd best cover your tracks. Are you going anywhere in particular?"

"No."

I stamped out the fire and kicked a bit of snow over it. Of course, anyone could find it easily enough, but I'd cover our trail better once we were on our way. A quick wipe with some snow cleaned the bowl and it went back in my pack.

He stood wrapped in my cloak, looking very young, and I felt a little sorry for him.

"Right then. Follow me." I slung my pack over my shoulder and started off. I set a pace quick enough to keep myself from freezing and he followed, stumbling sometimes in the thick snow. The wind wasn't quite as strong in the trees, though the air was quite cold.

I took him west to the Purling River as if we were heading for the Ralksin Ferry. The walk took a few hours; the boy was slow, partly because he was weak and pampered and partly because I don't think he understood the danger. At any moment I expected to hear hounds singing on our trail, but we reached the bank of the Purling with no sign of pursuit.

"Give me your knife."

He gave it to me without protest. He was pale and shivering, holding my cloak close to his chest. I waded into the water up to my ankles and walked downstream, then threw the knife a bit further downstream where it clattered onto the rockslining the bank. Whoever pursued him would know or guess it was his, and though the dogs would lose his trail in the water, they might continue downstream west toward the Ferry.

"Walk in the water. Keep the cloak dry and don't touch dry ground."

"Why?" His voice wavered a bit, almost a whine.

I felt my jaw tighten in irritation. "In case they use dogs." I wondered whether I was being absurdly cautious, whether they would bother to use dogs at all.

He still looked confused, dazed, and I pushed him into the water ahead of me. I kept one hand firm on his shoulder and steered him up the river. Ankle-deep, the water was painfully cold as it seeped through the seams in my boots. The boy stumbled several times and would have stopped, but I pushed him on.

We'd gone perhaps half a league upriver when I heard the first faint bay of hounds. They were behind us, already approaching the riverbank, and the baying rapidly grew louder. I took my hand from the boy's shoulder to curl my fingers around the hilt of my sword. As if my sword would do much. If they wanted him dead, they'd have archers. I was turning our few options over in my mind and trying to determine whether the hounds had turned upriver or were merely spreading out along the bank, when the boy stopped abruptly.

"Dogs."

"Keep walking."

He shook his head. "They're my dogs. They won't hurt me."

I grabbed the collar of his shirt and shoved him forward, hissing into his ear, "Fear the hunters, not the dogs! You're the fox. Don't forget that."

30260569R00179

Made in the USA
Middletown, DE
18 March 2016